WHEN I COME AROUND

A RETRO ROMANTIC COMEDY

CAROLINA CLASSICS
BOOK 4

KAREN GREY

Published by HOME COOKED BOOKS

A division of Jasper Productions, LLC

Cover artwork © 2024 by L.J. Anderson of Mayhem Cover Creations

First edition, February 2024

Content guidance for this book can be found at
www.karengrey.com/contentguidance

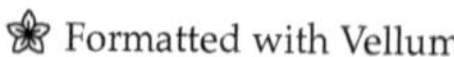 Formatted with Vellum

PRAISE CAROLINA CLASSICS

★★★★★ "Dust off your old Nokia phones and brush up on your snake game because we're going back to the 90s!" - *Jojo Reads Romance*

★★★★★ "After finishing this story, I want to load up the 5 CD changer and take a road trip to the beach. A fun, sweet and a zigazig-ahmazing 90's retro story that brings all the feels in the best possible ways." - *Bookbub review*

★★★★★ "With perfectly placed pop-culture references, expressions, and music, Karen Grey has a magical way of making her stories a visceral experience and transporting readers back to the nineties." - *Bookbub review*

★★★★★ "So heartfelt and relatable - I was drawn in and hooked from the first page." - *Goodreads review*

★★★★★ "Made me laugh, tugged at my heartstrings, and threw in some steam for the triple crown win." - *Bookbub review*

★★★★★ "Bursting with nineties pop culture references, complex characters, and delightful storytelling!" – *Goodreads review*

★★★★★ "This romance has all the feels, it's romantic, and funny, and it's full of sizzling chemistry with wonderful characters you can't help loving." – *Bookbub review*

★★★★★ "Reading this is like immersing yourself in your favorite dramedy." - *Bookbub review*

CONTENT GUIDANCE

The content notes below are meant to give readers a generalized view of potentially triggering subjects within this novel.

- Use of expletives: frequent but not mean-spirited
- Sex/Nudity: several sex scenes on page
- Violence: pushing and shoving on page
- Alcohol use: multiple characters on page
- Emotional trauma: involving current and past familial relationships of main character
- Miscarriage: main character (described from past)

If you'd like a more detailed list of content warnings (which may include spoilers) they are available at:

https://www.karengrey.com/contentguidance

"I think sometimes... you have to lose somebody completely before you can figure out what they really mean to you."

—Dawson, *Dawson's Creek*

"I stepped up! She's my friend and she needed help. And if I have to, I'd pee on any one of you!"

—Joey, *Friends*

"Can you believe what's possible these days? Conversations through your computer?... It's like living in the future."

—America Online commercial, 1996

ONE

Subj: Wedding Schedule
Date: 9/24/1999 4:55:01 PM
From: makeupchick1200
To: VioletCastingCarolina

Dear Violet,
First off, my deepest apologies for missing
your bachelorette party. Hardy had a last-
minute work event that I couldn't get
out of.
But don't worry! I will be ready bright and
early tomorrow to do your hair and makeup
and my bridesmaid dress is ready to go.
I'm so excited to be included in your
wedding party!
XOXO,
Whitney

FORD

WEDDINGS SUCK.

Don't get me wrong. The simple ceremony on the beach in

front of the hotel where my friends and I worked through high school and college went off without a hitch—pun intended—the weather pleasantly warm for North Carolina in September.

It's awesome to see one of my best friends so deliriously happy. Violet's face lights up every time she looks at her new husband, Nate. Like he hung the moon *and* invented chocolate.

It's not like I'm jealous of them, either. I may have spent many a night on a couch or bed watching movies with Violet, but I never liked her romantically. She's always been like an intimidating older sister, even though we're the same age.

Nor am I envious of the other love matches forged by friends in the close-knit gang that's been together since preschool.

Not of Sully, who obviously adores Helen, a badass production manager who rescued his heart.

I'm stoked for Dani, who seems like she's falling for Luke, the famous actor I thought she hated when she worked as his driver a few years ago.

I've accepted that the true love thing ain't likely to happen for me. I've simply got too much going on career-wise to invest in a serious girlfriend, even if I was good at relationships.

Case in point: I wasted every single one of my chances with Whitney, the fifth member of our friend group. Always asking for too much too soon at the wrong time. Just generally leaping before looking, I drove her away so fast and so far, the girl I always dreamed I'd end up with is now married to a man I can't imagine anybody being happy with.

Hardy Fucking McRae.

Whitney and Dani are in Violet's wedding party, but the groomsmen are all Nate's friends who came in from California, so I've managed to avoid Whit all night. Haven't seen her jerk of a husband, either. If he's here, he's probably schmoozing with people who have more money and class than I do.

Not that I'm complaining. I'd just as soon punch the guy as talk to him.

The only thing weddings are good for is hooking up with women interested in a one-night stand. Tonight, even that lacks appeal. So, as soon as the cake's been cut and the bride and groom have left the building, I am packing it in.

I'm just on my way out the door, having said the obligatory thank you's and goodbyes, when a woman who looks only vaguely familiar grasps my arm. "Are you Ford?"

"That's me. What can I do for you?"

"There's a young woman asking for you in the ladies' lounge."

She practically pushes me inside the women's restroom, a fancy one with an outer room full of chaise lounges and mirrors, but I barely notice the décor once I locate Whitney.

I'm at her side before I take another breath. I don't know anything about medicine, but her pale skin, shallow breath, and hollow-eyed expression make it clear something is very wrong. I turn back to the guest who found me.

"Call nine-one-one, please. Now."

WHITNEY

Strong arms scoop me up, holding me close like I'm something precious. Shivering, I turn into the broad chest and allow myself a deep inhale of his scent. Beachy, briny, it takes me back to a time when I felt safe.

Now I'm somewhere else, blinded by harsh lighting. Cool air chills my heated skin. A familiar callused hand engulfs my tiny one, pressing something into my palm before brushing a kiss to my forehead.

Blinking my eyes open, struggling past the fog in my head, I open my hand, hoping that this nightmare has a bright spot. That I didn't imagine being carried like a damsel in distress by a prince who has always protected me.

Saved me.

Defended me.

But my palm is empty.

And it only takes a few moments to understand why.

Stupid girl. You're in a hospital. You're not wearing clothes. There's no way they'd let you hang onto a dirty old bracelet.

But then a memory surfaces. A nurse's soft words.

Rolling over and reaching for the drawer in the bedside table takes a ridiculous amount of effort, like I weigh a thousand pounds instead of ninety-five. But when I manage to open it, I'm rewarded by the silky softness of worn embroidery thread. Lifting the token of our friendship, I bring it to my nose, and then I know I didn't dream that rescue.

Because it smells like him.

The boy I've always loved.

But never deserved.

FORD

I swear I can still feel Whitney's limp body in my arms.

After the EMTs finally showed up, they whisked her away. Dani got to ride in the ambulance with Whit, while I followed in my car. The nurse in charge of the ER can't—or won't—tell me anything.

Fumbling through my suit jacket pockets for my cell phone, it takes me a few moments to remember that Wallington's service is still so bad that I left it at home. Thankfully, I've only paced the length of the waiting room a few times when Dani walks through the swinging doors leading back to the exam rooms.

After a quick scan of the waiting area, she heads for me. "Anybody else here yet?"

"I didn't tell Vi. Whit wouldn't want her wedding totally ruined."

Dani's eyes brighten when they flick over my shoulder. Seconds later, Lukas Keith slips past me to envelop her in a hug.

I just stare, my mouth gaping. I haven't had the bandwidth to keep track of the status of their relationship, but I swear I've never seen Dani look like she does right now. Like she's finally handing a burden over to someone else.

Well, good for her. A real relationship may not be in the cards for me, but I can still be glad for my friend.

But right now, I need info, so I clear my throat. "What happened? Is she okay?"

Dani turns out of Luke's embrace to face me, but I can't help but notice how she leans into him. "I only got, like, two seconds with her before they wheeled her away."

"To where?"

"The ICU. They were yelling something about her being septic and going into shock."

Sully appears from behind me. "What does that mean?"

"Pretty sure septic means a full body infection," his girlfriend Helen adds.

"Hey, guys." I step back to let the two of them into our circle. I wonder momentarily how often a bunch of people in formal attire end up in the ER waiting room. A wedding party minus the bride and groom. With a bridesmaid fighting for her life.

"They asked if she'd been pregnant," Dani says.

"Was she?" Helen asks.

Dani just shakes her head. "I wish I knew. We've barely

seen Whit since she got married. I could hardly believe she came to the wedding."

"*Been* pregnant?" Sully asks. "Like she was and isn't anymore?"

Dani winces as she nods. "It seemed like they really wanted to know if she'd miscarried. Or had an abortion."

"Same thing," Helen says. "An abortion and a miscarriage are the same as far as your body is concerned. If either of them isn't complete, you can get an infection."

"So, what now?" I ask Dani. "Can we see her?"

"They said once she's stable, we can go in one at a time. But that might be a while."

"Is it just me, or is something fucked up here?" Sully asks.

"You mean other than the fact that she's sick as a dog?" I shoot back.

"I know what you mean," Dani says. "It's kind of weird that she didn't want us to call her husband. Or her parents."

"Maybe she didn't want them to know that she was slumming it by going to Violet's wedding." I suggest.

"We've been friends since kindergarten," Dani counters.

"But her parents never approved of us. And Hardy's the same," I argue.

"We were never good enough for any of them, that's for sure," Sully says, shaking his head. "I never will understand why she said yes to that guy in the first place."

"You don't think we pushed her into his arms with our ultimatums?"

The awful confrontation stirred up in the wake of Hurricane Beverly roils my stomach even now. Not only did Sully and I ask Whit to choose between us, but when she refused to do so, I blamed her for ruining the friendships the five of us had maintained since childhood.

"I don't know. It's all water under the bridge as far as I'm concerned." Sully adjusts his tie pin with the *Lawson's Reach* logo, and I wonder for the umpteenth time if I should've given up booming on a regular gig with excellent union pay, to take one small job after another as a sound mixer.

And to get out of town so I wouldn't have to run into Whitney. Or her asshole husband.

"Looks like we might be here awhile," Helen says into the silence. "I'll get coffee."

"I'll go with you." Sully follows her. Since we all developed our coffee preferences side by side, the same way we grew up, he doesn't bother taking our orders.

Luke puts a comforting arm around Dani and leads her to a bank of chairs, where she collapses, resting her head on his shoulder like it belongs there. Also, something I've never seen her do.

Left to myself, memories from the past couple of hours return. Whitney's always been petite, the easiest to sling up on your shoulders for a game of Chicken in the ocean, but when I carried her down the hotel hallway tonight, she was feather-light, her bones practically poking through her skin.

As she clung to me, her scent filled my nostrils. The coconut sunscreen I always associate with Whit was gone, replaced by a perfume that didn't suit her, underlaid with something rotten. Like Hardy literally got under her skin and festered there.

As if my thoughts conjure him, the man himself blasts into the room. They grant *his* wish when he demands to see Whitney.

Which is just wrong.

Right, you idiot.

It may feel wrong, but he is her husband. I, on the other hand, am not even husband material. I'm a good time, a nice roll in the hay, a fun guy to have a girl's arm for a night, maybe two. But that's it.

Work takes me all over the country, often at the drop of a hat. Not too many women want a guy who's rarely around. I don't have a home because I don't need one, but people get judgy about it. It's one thing for a guy just out of college to crash in hotel rooms or at his parents' house, but it's another kettle of fish when he's rounding thirty.

The truth is, I've given up a lot to get where I am in the movie business. It doesn't make sense to risk what I've achieved for something I'm obviously not good at. I need to calm down, be happy for my coupled-up friends, ensure that the girl who got away is going to live, and then get out of town again.

Where I belong.

WHITNEY

The sounds and scents of the hospital are an oddly comforting cocoon. The bed cradles my fragile body. The chilled air and cloud of antiseptics preserve me while I heal. The monitor by my side is a sentry, its gentle but insistent beeping protecting me from intruders.

Until the creak of a chair breaks through the mechanical sounds, and a different smell invades my nostrils. The unmistakable combination of cedar and sandalwood tells me my husband is in the room. Hardy's choice of cologne, Platinum Égoïste by Chanel, suits him to a tee.

I will the muscles of my face to relax, even as I sense him moving closer to the bedside.

"What did you do, Whitney?" His voice is hushed. So soft I can barely hear the words, they still manage to convey his anger. "You were pregnant with my child, and you didn't even tell me?"

The bed sinks slightly in his direction, and I have to stifle a gasp. I learned early on to play possum as much as possible with this man, whether he wanted sex or to vent his anger. It doesn't work here. The heart monitor betrays me, the racing beats broadcasting my terror.

"I know you're pretending. You think you can fool me, you stupid bitch?"

"Excuse me sir," a woman calls sharply. "Visiting hours are over for the ICU."

"I'm her husband," he says, switching easily to that silky smooth tone of his.

"You could be the president of the United States," she says, with an authority I wish I could muster. "But you still aren't allowed in here right now."

Hardy takes my hand and presses it to the area where his heart would be if he had one. I want to wrench it away, but something churns through me. Not exactly pain. Or maybe it is pain. Suddenly, the sounds in the room dim too. Lights flash beyond my closed lids, people in scrubs rush in, but the air is hazy.

The wave of pain disappears. Is replaced by relief.

And then I'm above it all. Floating.

Just like in a movie. Is it a movie?

A movie set. With a body on the hospital bed below that looks like me.

Damn. I look terrible. Greasy hair and a face in serious need of concealer and blush. I am as pale as a ghost.

Or am I the ghost?

"She was perfectly healthy before this happened." Hardy's shout pierces the fog and wraps around my throat. "We are planning to have children. This is total bullshit."

Alarms from the machines get louder, freeing me to float further away. Maybe it would be better if I just died.

You can endure a thousand paper cuts.

Until suddenly you're hemorrhaging.

A slew of other medical folks rushes in, but Hardy just cranks up the volume. It's nice to be detached for once, to watch him spout off from a distance. To not be the one in his crosshairs.

When someone yells "Get him out of here!" it's actually fun to watch him turn purple with rage when it isn't directed at me.

But it doesn't last, floating up here, feeling nothing. My body wants me back. A current of blood pulling at me. I swim against its riptide, fighting. Not for my life. For release from this mess of a life.

Because I'm not afraid of dying.

I'm afraid of living.

But just like every other little thing, it's apparently not up to me.

I plummet back into my pitiful body, suddenly gasping for air, every single muscle rigid, every cell howling with pain.

Until whatever's in the mask over my face sends me away again.

TWO

```
Subj: Divorce Law
Date: 9/26/1999 9:10:09 AM
From: Hardy_McRae_Properties
To: W_Parsley_Assoc_PLLC
```

William,
Please fax the documents re: the matter we discussed to my downtown office ASAP.

WHITNEY

"GOOD LORD. She's looking like ten miles of bad road."

My mother's irritated tone reaches deep into my consciousness, yanking me awake. Bracing myself for the usual onslaught of criticism, I'm blindsided by pain slicing through my belly when I try to sit up.

"Honey are you all right?" my father asks. "Do you need me to call someone?"

"Yes, please," I say, my throat scratchy.

A flurry of activity and questions from medical professionals has both my parents stepping back. Before she leaves, a nurse tells them that visiting hours will end shortly. I can take whatever my mother's got to dish out for ten minutes, so I muster up a polite smile.

She starts right in, of course. "I don't know what you said or did to make Hardy mad, but you need to apologize, because without him, you don't have a pot to piss in or a window to throw it out of."

"But mama—"

"Mm-mm," she says, her head shake sharp. "No excuses. You made your bed; you lie in it."

"Now, honey—" my dad begins.

Hand in the air, my mother cuts him off. "Reg, you stay out of this. You spoiled this girl to the point she wouldn't know the truth if it slapped her upside the head."

I try to find his eyes, wishing I could let him know that it's okay, but his gaze is on the ground. Meanwhile, my mother sets an overnight bag by my bed.

"I understand you not wanting Hardy to see you like this." She waves a hand in the air, encompassing my entire body and the machines I'm hooked up to. "It's shameful when your body betrays you like this. So, I brought you a few things. Makeup and perfume, and a nice robe."

She wags a finger at me. "You need to make an effort. Just pull yourself together and remind him of what you bring to the table. Not being able to bear his children will be a big obstacle, but he'll forgive you, if you—"

"If it isn't the man himself," my father says loudly, cutting her off.

My mother's expression flips so fast from threat to appeasement it makes my head spin. "Isn't it wonderful that he's taken off work to visit?"

"I've just stopped by to deliver this," my husband says, slapping a manila envelope onto the bedside table. "But it's good you're both here. I'll be having Whitney's things delivered to your house tomorrow."

"Wh-Whitney's things?" My mother's voice falters, but she rallies quickly. "Oh, of course. We'll take care of her as long as you need us to. I'm sure you don't have time to be waiting on her hand and foot while she recovers."

Without a glance at me, Hardy points at the envelope. "This is a notarized statement indicating that your daughter and I have legally separated. Since I have to wait an entire year for a divorce, I need to get this started."

"D-divorce?" My mother's smile remains bright but she's obviously fighting for composure. "But y'all have barely been married a year."

Hardy crosses his arms. "When we agreed on this marriage, I was clear. My inheritance is predicated on siring heirs."

"It's hardly her fault that—" my father begins.

"This is entirely her fault," Hardy says. "I am done with her lies and her drama. She's all yours."

With that, Hardy turns on his heels and slams out of the room, almost knocking over a nurse on her way in. She tells my parents that visiting hours are over, saving me from a real argument. Not that I'd win it. I never do.

My mother stands and leans in like she's going to give me a kiss goodbye, but she murmurs threats in my ear instead. "I refuse to pay for the consequences of your actions, Whitney. Do what you need to do to get back in the good graces of your husband, you hear me?"

I'm too chickenshit to say anything but, "Yes, ma'am."

My father steps to my bedside to pat my hand. "When the doctors say you can leave, we'll take you back to Hardy and get everything straightened out. Don't you worry, honey."

I don't argue. Not because I hope he's right, but because I know he's wrong.

And I'm not even a tiny bit upset.

I haven't worked for a year.

I don't have a penny to my name.

Still, losing any chance at motherhood is a small price to pay to be free of that man.

FORD

Unfortunately, it's a long wait to find out if Whitney will be okay. When we get the news that she's having emergency surgery, we decide to split up and take shifts. Since I have a change of clothes in my car, I volunteer to take the first one.

Once I'm out of the suit that felt like it was suffocating me, I get comfortable on a couch in the ICU waiting room.

Maybe a little too comfortable, because the next thing I know, loud voices jolt me awake.

"Hardy," a woman says behind me, her voice plaintive. "Whitney is so much more than—"

"Plenty of women in this town can host a party and charm my guests," the asshole says, cutting her off. "Being the hostess with the mostest doesn't mean jack shit if she can't produce children."

I'm pretty sure they haven't noticed me slumped down in my chair, but I have to force myself to stay there. *Can't produce children?* I'm not sure which is more shocking: this news or the idea that he just sees her as some kind of broodmare.

"Now, Hardy. Let's not be rash." I now recognize the woman's voice. Whitney's snob of a mother. "I'm sure we can figure something out."

"Mrs. Moore, I'll ask you once," Hardy snaps. "Don't touch me."

"But Hardy—"

"And that development deal? You're out. There are plenty of realtors in this town I'd rather work with. People I can trust."

"You'll regret this Hardy McCrae," Whitney's mother's voice shifts to a warning hiss.

"Oh, believe you me. I already do."

The moment I hear the doors open and close, I'm on my feet and on his heels.

I'm not a guy who gets in fights. I was a skinny nerd as a kid and I'm still not a huge guy. But once I pass through the sliding doors and inhale the crisp evening air, I have only one thought in my mind. He's the reason she's fighting for her life, and I am going to punish him.

I race to catch up to him and then spin him to face me. Shoving him up against a pillar at the edge of the parking garage, I get in his face. "What the hell did you do to her?"

"What the fuck is your problem?" Hardy *is* a big guy, and he's always been a bully. I shouldn't be surprised when he doesn't flinch.

Before I can formulate an answer, his eyes narrow in recognition. "Oh, wait, I remember you. You're one of the Fischer brothers—the auto shop guys." He pushes me away and then dusts off his jacket with a sneer, like I'm covered in grease. "You want to service my fleet; you'd best watch your step."

He slithers into the garage, but I catch up and shove him from behind. "I don't give a shit about your cars. I want to know what you did to Whitney."

"My wife is none of your goddamn business," he spits over his shoulder.

I'm not letting him walk away without finding out what the fuck is going on, so I sprint ahead to get in his way. "You made it my business. Are you starving her? She's thin as a rail."

He sighs, like I'm the idiot here. "Haven't you heard of heroin chic?"

Swallowing past the lump of fear gripping my throat, it

takes everything in me to contain my anger in the fists at my sides. "I'll say it again. What did you do to her?"

"Oh, no. This is all on her." His lip actually curls. If he had a mustache, he'd probably twirl it. "She didn't take care of herself. And she lied to me. I didn't even know she was pregnant, let alone that she lost the baby."

"But is she going to be okay?"

"No, she's not going to be okay. She's a crazy, selfish bitch. They carved out her damn womb, all because she had to go to a damn party." With that, he spins on his heels and stalks away.

"You're just leaving?" I ask, following him.

"Again, it's none of your business," he calls over his shoulder. "But come to think of it, she ain't mine anymore, either."

His words have my steps faltering, but it doesn't stop me from adding, "If you did anything to put her life in danger, I'll kill you."

Before I can catch him, someone grabs my arm from behind. When I wheel to face the threat, Sully steps back, hands up. "Whoa man, it's me."

"Glad I've got a witness to you threatening my life," Hardy calls. "What's your name, son?"

"I'm not your son, asshole," Sully says. "Now get out of here before I decide to help him."

Hardy looks like he's about to argue, but then just shakes his head, points his key fob at a Jaguar to unlock it and slips inside. He revs the engine aggressively before driving away.

"That's a tiny dick car if I ever saw one," Sully mutters.

I can practically feel the adrenaline draining out of me, but it spikes again when I remember his words. *Carved out her womb. Not my business anymore, either.*

Sully places a hand on my shoulder and squeezes it briefly before dropping it again. "She'll be okay."

I have to clamp my back teeth together to keep the emotion at bay. The fear. The guilt. "We don't know that."

"She's tougher than she looks."

"Well, she looked pretty damn bad."

"I'm gonna tell her you said that. She'll be pissed."

"I just hope she gets a chance to be," I spit out, before heading back into the hospital.

THREE

```
Subj: Whitney
Date: 10/02/1999 12:45:30 PM
From: VioletCastingCarolina
To: Ford_soundguy
```

```
Ford, you need to come to Dani's house
before you leave town for the Savannah job.
We'll all be there at five tonight.
Vi
```

WHITNEY

I'M DISCHARGED from the hospital a week after being rushed to it. The doctors say I'm well enough to go home, but I still feel like death warmed over. Not to mention the fact that I no longer have a home.

Neither my parents nor my husband returned to see me, but at least one of my four childhood friends—minus the one whose wedding I disrupted—visits every day. Violet returned from her honeymoon the day I got out, but it's Dani who picks me up and takes me to her house.

I'm not sure if it's because they're worried about me or if

they still hang out together all the time, but my friends seem to spend an awful lot of time at Dani's place. So much so that it almost feels like the last year of college. Back when Violet and I rented rooms from Dani after she inherited the little bungalow from her aunt. When Sully and Ford spent more time here at Dani's than they did at their own crappy apartment at the beach.

Before I blew everything to pieces, that is.

I'm still sleeping way more than I'm awake. Between the full hysterectomy and getting pumped full of antibiotics, I beat the infection. But the surgical incision is still healing, and my body feels like a sack of lead weights I have to drag around.

Looking around the room that used to be mine, I try to figure out what time it is. What day it is, even. I picked this bedroom way back when because I like to sleep in, and it faces west. The sun peeking through the window shades tells me it's probably late afternoon.

When I roll over in the bed, using my arms to push up to sitting so as not to pull the stitches in my belly, Skye stretches from the floor with a whine and pads over to snuffle at me.

"Hello, pretty girl."

Dani, Vi, and I adopted the little Carolina Dog when she was a puppy, but I never really held up my end of that bargain. I can't be relied upon to take care of myself, let alone another creature, but Skye doesn't seem to hold it against me. In fact, she shadows me as I shuffle to the bathroom, waits for me by the door, and then presses against me and lets me hang onto her for balance when I get dizzy on my way back to the bedroom.

She's not big enough to take my full weight, so I put my other hand on the wall until my vision clears. When I try to move again, I'm still shaky, so I ease onto the seat in the old telephone nook to rest a moment.

While I'm catching my breath, a conversation wafts down the hall.

"I agree. She needs her friends right now," Dani says.

"It's probably a good thing that I have to leave town for work," Ford says, his tone sharp. "Is what you're saying."

"What I'm saying is, there's a lot of history. Complicated history."

"Yeah, hard to forget it here in this living room."

The anger in his voice literally hurts my heart, but I can't say I don't deserve it. I was an idiot about him and Sully. I can't blame him for still being mad at me.

"I can't help but notice that you went from dating every woman in town between the ages of twenty-one and forty-one," Violet says, "to not dating at all."

"You keeping tabs on me?" Ford shoots back.

"Of course, I am. I worry about you. I worry about all y'all." Even from here, I can tell Violet's not kidding.

"Good lord, Vi," Dani says. "You gotta relax. You're gonna make that poor kid nuts."

It's still hard to believe that Violet is having a baby. Almost as hard to believe as my own pregnancy. I thought the pill was nigh on foolproof, but I guess I was wrong. About that, and so many other things.

"Pfft, I worry about y'all because you're idiots," Violet says with characteristic snark. "My kid will be brilliant."

This gets a laugh out of Ford, but it ends in a sigh, and I can just picture him running a hand through his hair, which always falls back to frame his high cheekbones beautifully, even though he probably just uses shampoo from the grocery store and wouldn't know a blow-dryer from a curling iron.

I've always envied that hair as much as I longed to run my fingers through it. Right now, I run my fingers over the soft threads of the friendship bracelet I've worn since being released from the hospital. If I'm not careful, I'll wear it to death.

"Yeah, well, I quit all that," Ford says. "Work is my focus right now. I doubt if I'll ever be ready to settle down. I like being able to take off across the country without worrying about who I'm leaving behind."

"What about us?" Violet asks.

"I know y'all get it. Career is important."

"It's not like I'm going to quit working just because I'm married and having a kid," Violet argues.

"But your setup means you can have both," he says. "You've got an office in one place. You're your own boss."

"My husband's boss too, don't forget," she adds.

Ford laughs, but this time the laughter fades into something that sounds like frustration. "Building my resume as a mixer, not taking jobs as a boom guy even while I'm spending tons of money on new equipment, means I can't afford to date. Financially or mentally. Managing my crew, dealing with set politics, and fixing things when they break, means I don't have the bandwidth to deal with a girl who needs more from me than I can provide."

I'm not sure if they stop talking, or if his words echo so loudly in my ears they drown out the rest of the conversation. Either way, I get the message.

I'm a burden that Ford's not planning to take on.

It hurts. A lot. But I think that all in all, it's a good thing.

Because this girl has to figure out how to be someone who doesn't need anything from anybody.

As soon as she can walk down the hall by herself, that is.

FOUR

```
Subj: Week Two sound
Date: 10/17/1999 9:10:55 AM
From: LAproduction_Hellhound2
To: Ford_soundguy
```

```
Ford, attaching the list of questions from
the editing bay about last week's record-
ing. Can you give them a call to address?
```

FORD

I'VE BARELY HAD a moment to breathe since I arrived in Savannah a couple weeks ago. We had only one prep day and one scout day. Then we dove into a series of long-as-hell shooting days. Multiple location changes, scenes with tons of talking characters, and a lighting guy that isn't interested in flagging for the boom, all are keeping me and my crew on our toes.

When I wake up from a late afternoon nap on a Sunday, my gaze finds my computer. I could check emails. Make sure there isn't anything from production in LA.

I boot up the laptop, pushing the hope that there'll be an email from Whitney aside. As I switch out the cable connecting the room telephone to the jack for the one from the modem, open the AOL program and start the connection process, I wonder if I should email her. Just to make sure nothing's up with Gertie, the car I lent her after Hardy took away the keys of the car she'd been driving because "he'd paid for it."

Most people find the pinging and hissing of the modem seeking a match across the phone lines annoying, but I think it's pretty cool that simple tones can carry so much information.

When my emails finally populate the America Online dashboard, I'm rewarded for my persistence with the little guy announcing that "You've Got Mail." There are a few messages from the production office. From the subject lines, it looks like a question from the editing department, and new script pages. They can wait. Because the only one I'm opening right now is from an email address that's new to me, even if I can guess who it is.

Of course, Whitney would choose "makeupchick1200" as her moniker. I should talk. I snapped up "Ford_soundguy" for myself. After I open the email, however, I notice that it's not just addressed to me. Looks like she's sending a group email instead.

Others in the group have already replied, so I have to click again to get to her original email, heart pounding at the subject line. Does "Heading west" mean Whitney is going to LA? What the hell?

```
Subj: Heading West
Date: 10/17/1999 2:55:01 PM
From: makeupchick1200
```

To: VioletCastingCarolina, SullyCall-
away999, DanielleGoodwin856, Ford_soundguy

Hello friends!
Thanks to Helen, I've landed a job on a
made-for-TV movie working out of Charlotte
and I'll be heading there next week.
Sully - thanks for suggesting that we
communicate with the group email and thanks
to Helen for the connection.
Violet - you need to keep us posted on baby
news, please!
Dani - sorry I'm bugging out on helping
with Skye yet again, but at least I'll be
out of your honeymoon cottage.
Ford - I hope it's okay that I take Gertie
with me. I won't drive her too much once
I'm there, I promise. I'll let transpo take
me where I need to go!
I'm excited to get back to work but I'll
miss y'all!
Love,
Whitney

Subj: RE: Heading West
Date: 10/17/1999 3:02:54 PM
From: VioletCastingCarolina
(Reply All)

Good for you getting that job, Whit!
Baby seems to be growing on schedule
because I'm already as big as a house. I am
having a hard time finding a casting

assistant. Let me know if anyone has any
ideas.

Subj: RE: RE: Heading West
Date: 10/17/1999 3:34:12 PM
From: DanielleGoodwin856
(Reply All)

____

I've got a couple ideas for you, Vi.

Subj: RE: RE: RE: Heading West
Date: 10/17/1999 3:55:09 PM
From: SullyCallaway999
(Reply All)

____

Helen does too, Vi.

Subj: RE: RE: RE: RE: Heading West
Date: 10/17/1999 4:02:19 PM
From: VioletCastingCarolina
(Reply All)

____

I need to get the new person trained up
before I take maternity leave, so call me
with names ASAP, please!
Should we all get together for dinner
before Whit leaves?
Ford, could you come home next weekend?

Subj: RE: RE: RE: RE: RE: Heading West
Date: 10/17/1999 5:15:20 PM
From: makeupchick1200
(Reply All)

I'm actually leaving Saturday (as long as
Ford lets me take Gertie) so I won't be
here next weekend.
And no pressure, Ford. I can take the bus.
Once I'm there, I won't really need a car.

Subj: RE: RE: RE: RE: RE: RE: Heading West
Date: 10/17/1999 6:45:01 PM
From: Ford_soundguy
(Reply All)

Whitney, of course you can take Gertie. But
you should swing by the shop and get her
oil changed before you go. I'll call my
brother and let him know you're coming.
Vi, I don't think I can make it back weekends. They're kicking our butts with the
schedule. Mostly nights, but we still start
early Mondays, so my weekend is short.

AFTER I SEND THE EMAIL ABOUT GERTIE, I NOTICE ANOTHER
email chain from my Wallington friends. But this one doesn't
include Whitney.

Subj: What's up with Whitney
Date: 10/17/1999 10:55:09 AM

From: VioletCastingCarolina
To: SullyCallaway999, DanielleGoodwin856,
Ford_soundguy

Okay, gang.
Good news is, Helen helped Whitney get a
movie gig as a hair & makeup floater
outside Charlotte.
Bad news: she's still not herself and now
we can't keep an eye on her.

There's more from the group, stuff about Violet's baby shower and other random stuff, but it's the last one that has me scratching my head. Violet wants to set up something called a Buddy List.

I have no more emails, so I log off and disconnect from the modem, not wanting to waste the precious internet minutes. Just as I do, my hotel phone rings. Figuring it's one of the guys wanting to grab dinner, I answer right away. "This is Ford."

"Hey, Ford, it's Vi."

"Vi? How'd you get this number?"

"I'm fine, thanks, despite feeling like I'm bigger than Gertie. I've seen women who have this cute little baby bump with no other evidence that they are growing a human inside, but not me. I have extra padding everywhere."

"Uh, okay?" There's no way I'm touching that. Violet may be one of my closest friends, but even I won't say anything about her gaining weight. "Everything else good?"

"To answer your question, we cast your show, so I got the number for your hotel from the production list. Then I just asked for your room."

Also not going to point out that she's not answering my more recent question. Vi has always been what you'd call temperamental, and pregnancy seems to have escalated her flares. "How can I help you?"

"Since you haven't chimed in on the Buddy List chat, I'm assuming you don't know how."

I start to contradict her, but she's right. "What's wrong with email? Or calling, like this?"

"If we do the chat, we can all talk in real time. It'll be more efficient than email and, unlike the phone or the email, it's free. We just have to all agree to be online at the same time. If you download the AIM software, it doesn't even use up AOL internet minutes."

"Seriously? That's pretty cool."

"Your username is the same as your email name," she clarifies, before telling me where to find the program. "We're setting it for Monday nights at nine, figuring that's the time we're most likely to be off work with access to a computer. So please load up the AIM and be there tomorrow night, okay? We need to do some brainstorming about Whit."

"Is she invited to this chat?"

"Not this one, no. But I'm chatting with her when I can. You could too."

"Won't this be, like, gossiping?"

"I don't know what else to do. I'm worried about her. It's a gut feeling that I can't ignore."

"Okay. I'll be there. If I'm not, it's just because we ran late."

"Thanks, sweetie. See you on the little screen tomorrow."

She hangs up without saying goodbye, and I make the modem dial up again. After the usual static and clangs, I'm back online. It doesn't take long to find the program, but it'll likely take a while to download, so I grab a beer from the fridge and leaf through the stack of restaurant menus provided by the hotel.

I can't call for takeout while the computer's online. My stomach's complaints almost have me giving up and trying again later when someone pounds on the door. I open it to find my crew on the other side.

"Something wrong with your phone?" my boom guy Walt asks. "It's been busy forever."

I gesture at the computer. "Nah, I'm just trying to download something."

Ronnie, the third man on my crew, sticks his head in the doorway. "That could take all night."

"Tell me about it. You guys headed out for dinner?"

"Yeah, we're meeting a bunch of people at a seafood place one of the locals recommended. You wanna come?"

Working with this bunch of people all week, I hardly need to spend more time with them on the weekend. "Thanks, but I'll just grab some takeout."

"Okay Old Man." Walt and Ronnie are only a few years younger than me, but they like to tease me for being a stick in the mud. "See you bright and early tomorrow."

"Not as early as y'all." One perk of being the department lead is that my guys get there before me and leave after me. "Gonna be another full week, so get your beauty sleep."

The two guys leave, bantering over who is beyond help in the beauty department. Walt's tall and broad and Ronnie's on the slight side, and neither of them has any problem attracting women from what I've seen. I give them a head start and then head out myself. Hopefully, by the time I'm back, I can do as my friend ordered and be all set up to join the chat tomorrow.

Violet can be dramatic, but this time I'm afraid she's right. Whitney's relationship with her husband seems like it might've been very different from anything any of us could've imagined. And not in a good way.

I'm in no position to be her knight in shining armor, but I'm not going to sit back and watch her fail, either.

Monday, 10/19 9:02 PM
VioletCastingCarolina: Everybody here?

SullyCallaway999: I gotta say, this feels kind of like talking behind her back.

DanielleGoodwin856: Agreed.

VioletCastingCarolina: I am too worried to let this go y'all.

Ford_soundguy: How has she been since I left?

VioletCastingCarolina: Physically, she's mostly better. Still needs to gain weight, but the doctor gave her the okay to go back to work. Mentally, though, she seems…

DanielleGoodwin856: Broken.

SullyCallaway999: Definitely different than she used to be.

Ford_soundguy: Maybe that's a good thing.

VioletCastingCarolina: Don't be mean.

Ford_soundguy: I'm not. But sometimes you have to hit rock bottom to make a change.

VioletCastingCarolina: How long does your Savannah job run?

Ford_soundguy: Through October.
I do feel bad about leaving so
soon after she got out of the
hospital.

DanielleGoodwin856: Never known
you to put friends before work.

VioletCastingCarolina: That's
not fair. Connections Ford made
in college and then out in LA
have helped us all.

Ford_soundguy: It wasn't easy.
Especially the first time.
Leaving everything and everyone
I knew to go to LA where I knew
exactly one person?

DanielleGoodwin856: You dragged
Sully along, so you'd know two
people?

Ford_soundguy: It was his choice
to go, and I think in the long
run he'd agree it was good
for him.

SullyCallaway999: I'm right
here, guys. I just can't type as
fast as y'all do.

SullyCallaway999: Probably
would've been good for all
of us.

VioletCastingCarolina: Not me. LA was not for me. I am a small-town girl. Anyway, I wasn't accusing you of ditching your friends. I'm just saying that Whit's got a lot of healing to do. The infection, a hysterectomy, that's no joke. What she needs right now is friends, not someone who can't decide whether or not he wants to risk his heart.

DanielleGoodwin856: Geez. Don't hold back now, Vi.

VioletCastingCarolina: Nate and I might have had a rocky start, but one thing I learned is that you gotta get right in your head and your heart before you can meet someone even halfway. And with Whit, she'll need more than that. At least until she can stand on her own two feet again.

Ford_soundguy: Wait. Are you talking about me?

SullyCallaway999: I don't think she meant me.

Ford_soundguy: I told y'all, I'm focusing on work right now. Speaking of which, I got an early call. I'll check in later in the week.

FIVE

```
Subj: Crew Check in
Date: 10/23/1999 10:01:39 AM
From: LoveLost_production_office
To: makeupchick1200
```

```
Hello Love Lost crew:
The office will be open from 10a - 6p today
for you to pick up lodging info and sign
paperwork.
Looking forward to working with you all!
```

WHITNEY

AS I CROSS the bridge over the intracoastal on my way out of Wallington, it's like I'm literally taking the road to independence. Of course, I wouldn't be on this path if I didn't have my friends watching out for me, giving me the boost I needed to start over.

So, as the miles fly by outside my window, I whisper thanks to all of them.

To Helen, for hooking me up with a job shooting out of town. Which not only gets me out from underfoot of all the happy couples, it gets me away from my family. It also gives me a chance to save money, since I'll get per diem for my meals and have my housing covered for the next two months.

To Violet, who hooked me up with new-to-me work clothes from the costume vault at the Wallington studios. Most of the clothes I used to wear to work are gone. Hardly anything I bought during my marriage would survive a day in the makeup and hair trailer. Nor do I want or need any reminders from the past year.

To Sully, who gave me his old laptop so I can keep in touch with my pals via email while I'm gone, without having to pay for long-distance calls.

And to Dani, who not only nursed me back to health, but gifted me a pile of AOL CDs so I wouldn't even have to pay for the internet.

Last but never least, Ford who, even though he has no interest in me romantically, has loaned me his most cherished possession: Gertie.

She's no consolation prize for the man himself, but she's a hell of a lot more practical. I couldn't do this job without transportation. No matter how he feels about me, I'll be forever grateful that he at least trusts me. The moment he gave me the keys will be forever seared in my memory. I've never known him to let anyone else drive the beautiful Robin's Egg blue 1969 Ford LTD he refurbished in high school and has babied ever since, let alone take her hundreds of miles away.

Of course, I *had* a car. A cute little silver BMW Z3. But like everything else from my marriage, it wasn't really mine.

Anyway, I may have pared down my belongings, but that tiny convertible wouldn't even have held my makeup kits.

One enormous car fits everything nicely.

A win-win all around.

IT ONLY TAKES A COUPLE DAYS FOR OUR DEPARTMENT TO FIND ITS groove. Not that we have a choice. The cinematographer and director of this sentimental drama have worked together multiple times. The shorthand they've developed has them moving through setups faster than any team I've ever seen. No standing around twiddling our thumbs and gossiping in the makeup trailer on this show.

Which I'm thankful for, to be honest. Keeping busy is good for me. And not because I'm running away from the train wreck of my life, though I guess I literally have.

My dogs are barking by the end of a fourteen-hour shift, but I wouldn't want to be anywhere else right now. "I missed this," I say out loud after I dump a dustpan full of hair clippings and who knows what else into the trash.

Susan, the makeup key, snorts out a laugh before spritzing a mirror with glass cleaner. "Cleaning up after people?"

I grab the cleaning spray and wipe down the counters. "Working. On a show."

"Had you been working in a salon instead?"

"Oh, no."

"No license?"

"Oh, I have one." I went to cosmetology school a couple years after graduating college. It's not exactly required to do hair and makeup on a set, but my first mentor said it'd look good on my resume. Unfortunately, paying for that program was just another rung in my debt spiral, since there was no way my parents were going to pay for it. They didn't want me doing what my mom calls "trailer trash" work, even though top stylists make as much or more than she does in real estate.

"I get it. Sometimes you hit a dry spell and just can't get hired. I know how that is. Although, I have to say I'm surprised." Susan tips her head and studies me, her expression sympathetic rather than judgmental, thank goodness.

"You're good, and I thought there was a lot of work in Wallington."

She's from LA, like all the department heads. They've pulled the rest of the crew from locals in the surrounding states. Not too many from Wallington, though. Which means that I'm not only far away from my parents and Hardy, but I'm also out of the circle of people who know my history.

"I actually wasn't allowed to work."

"Health issues?" Susan asks.

"Husband issues," I say, even as I know that anything I confess is likely to be shared. This department is known as gossip central for a reason. But it feels good to own this, so I add, "He wouldn't let me."

Her jaw drops. "Does the guy know it's almost the twenty-first century?"

I drag the laundry bag full of dirty towels toward the door of the trailer. "It wasn't like he forbade it. He just had all kinds of arguments for why I shouldn't."

"So, what happened? I mean, you're here now." She grimaces, like she's not sure she wants to know. "Is he… dead?"

I can't help the laugh that escapes my mouth. "No. I didn't take a contract out on him or anything. My life isn't a thriller. More of a Lifetime movie. I just…" This is where I draw the line. No need to get into the whole sob story. "We're separated, to be divorced."

"Good for you. Who needs 'em, anyway?" She tosses a final wad of paper towels before pulling the bag from the can. "Most of the time, they're more trouble than they're worth. I mean, what're the odds of finding a guy who'll put up with this carny life?"

"Unless they're in it themselves," I say, my fingers ducking inside my sleeve to find the friendship bracelet. Even though it no longer smells like Ford, its softness comforts me.

Susan huffs, making her opinion of the male half of the

population even clearer. "That can get awful messy, awful fast. I've witnessed too many ugly on-set breakups. Lost too many good workers because they didn't want to leave a boyfriend. I say, keep the drama in front of the camera, if you know what I mean."

"You bet your britches I do." I kick the dirty laundry out the door and down the stairs and banish any romantic thoughts about a man who shares this lifestyle. Besides, the one person I sometimes let myself fantasize having it all with isn't interested in me. Even if he were, I can't risk the best chance I have at supporting myself, and as Susan so wisely counseled, the two definitely don't mix.

"Oh, hey," she says, just as we get to our cars in crew parking. "Speaking of drama, I heard our sound guy's quitting."

"Uh-oh. Why?"

"Something to do with an emergency at home. Anyway, they're looking for somebody who can replace him for the rest of the show."

Squelching the flicker of hope that Ford might be able to do it before it can catch, I just nod. He already has a job. And I just promised my boss I wouldn't create drama.

But then Susan says, "If they can't find somebody who'll do it for the budget they've got, we might get laid off until they do."

SIX

Subj: URGENT - we need a mixer
Date: 10/29/1999 8:35:55 PM
From: makeupchick1200
To: VioletCastingCarolina, SullyCall-
away999, DanielleGoodwin856, Ford_soundguy

Hey, y'all. I'm just putting the word out
in case anyone has any ideas. Our sound
mixer's wife had a terrible accident. He
left, but his boom guy isn't hacking it in
his place, so they're looking to replace
the crew ASAP.
How's everything back in WAL?
XOXO, Whitney

Subj: RE: URGENT - we need a mixer
Date: 10/29/1999 8:50:01 PM
From: VioletCastingCarolina
(Reply All)

I'm assuming Ford won't be done in Savannah
in time or you'd have just asked him,
right?
Pretty sure all the WAL mixers are booked,
but I'll shake the trees around here.

Subj: RE: RE: URGENT – we need a mixer
Date: 10/29/1999 9:10:12 PM
From: SullyCallaway999
(Reply All)

I'll call a guy I know who's based in the
DC area. I'm assuming the UPM's already
looking in Atlanta?

Subj: RE: RE: RE: URGENT – we need a mixer
Date: 10/29/1999 9:24:05 PM
From: makeupchick1200
(Reply All)

Yes, they started calling people in Atlanta
the minute the mixer left, but no luck
so far.

FORD

THIS TIME when my hotel phone rings, I'm more prepared.
For one, I just said goodnight to my crew. After the day we
just had, I doubt either of them wants to talk to me. For the
other, I know I've ignored the emails about Whitney's show
needing a new mixer for too long.

Thing is, I could do it. I'm just not sure I want to.

"Hey, this is Ford."

"Are you dead?" Dani asks without preamble.

"Not unless you're talking to my ghost. Which I guess is possible."

"Ha-ha." She grunts like she's dropping into a chair. "So how come you haven't replied to Whitney's call for help? Sully said you're wrapping this week."

Damn it, Sully.

"We are, but I've got a line on another thing starting in Florida after Thanksgiving."

"A possible job or an actual offer?"

"It'd be for a producer on this show. He basically said it's mine if I want it."

"But it wouldn't be till after Thanksgiving. So that's several weeks without work for you and your crew. Whereas Whitney's show would be a sure thing to take y'all through to Christmas. We talked and we really think you should take it."

"We?"

"Violet, Sully and me."

"Have you talked to *Whit* about this? Maybe she wouldn't want me to do it."

"Apparently, they might have to shut down. They're that desperate."

When I say nothing, she adds, "She needs the work. Financially and probably psychologically."

"I thought she was happy to be out of that marriage."

"I'm sure she is. But if you were there in person, we'd know for sure."

"What if I just went and visited? After my show closes?"

"She'll just put on the 'I'm fine and dandy' dog and pony show until you leave. She's not going to just up and tell you everything."

"You're probably right."

"So… you'll go? You'll take the job? And figure out what she's dealing with post-Hardy, so we know how to help her?"

The image of Whitney deathly pale in my arms—so different from the tiny but scrappy girl I've always known—pierces my stubborn heart.

"If the job's still open and they want me, I'll take it."

"And you'll keep your dick to yourself?"

"Jesus, Dan."

"I'm just saying—"

"I can control myself. I'm not that big of an asshole."

"Good. 'Cause I think she's had enough of those for a lifetime."

```
Subj: RE: RE: RE: RE: URGENT - we need a
mixer
Date: 10/30/1999 11:14:45 AM
From: Ford_soundguy
(Reply All)
```

```
Whitney, I called your UPM, and I'll be
there next Saturday.
```

```
Subj: RE: RE: RE: RE: RE: URGENT - we need
a mixer
Date: 10/30/1999 12:34:49 PM
From: makeupchick1200
(Reply All)
```

```
What????? Did you quit your show?
```

Subj: RE: RE: RE: RE: RE: RE: URGENT - we
need a mixer
Date: 10/30/1999 1:30:05 PM
From: Ford_soundguy
(Reply All)

Of course not. Tomorrow's our last shoot
day. We have two wrap days, but I only
really need one.
Did you not want me to come?

Subj: Love Lost job
Date: 10/30/1999 2:45:34 PM
From: Ford_soundguy
To: makeupchick1200

You included me in the group email. Did you
not think I'd want the job?

Subj: RE: Love Lost job
Date: 10/30/1999 3:15:36 PM
From: makeupchick1200
To: Ford_soundguy

I didn't think you were available.

Subj: RE: RE: Love Lost job
Date: 10/30/1999 3:29:02 PM
From: Ford_soundguy

To: makeupchick1200

If you don't want me there, I'll turn it
down.

Subj: RE: RE: RE: Love Lost job
Date: 10/30/1999 4:07:19 PM
From: makeupchick1200
To: Ford_soundguy

I want you to take it, okay? You'd do a
good job, and we need someone who knows
what they're doing. I guess I'll see you
this weekend!

SEVEN

The office will be open from 10a - 6p today for you and your crew to pick up lodging info and sign paperwork.
We appreciate you jumping in to help out!

FORD

IT'S a straight shot north from Savannah to Charlotte, so the uninterrupted five-hour drive gives me plenty of time to think. Which is a good thing and a bad thing.

Funnily enough, the conversation that keeps running through my head is one I had with Dani a couple months ago. When she was trying to convince herself that she hadn't fallen for Luke.

When did you get so smart? she asked me. I don't remember exactly what I said in return, but it was something about being a sound guy and listening.

Thing is, I don't feel so smart. Especially about relation-ships. People in general. I can observe and think I understand what I should do, but when it comes to carrying out the plan, I always seem to fuck things up. And if you're not good at something, why waste time on it?

At least I have work. It was a big risk to leave the steady booming gig on *Lawson's Reach* to take a mixing job on an indie movie. But I managed to turn that first one into several more. This last project proved that the risk is paying off. I've got a great crew, and my reputation is growing. I'm known as a guy who's on top of the latest technology, who's a good problem solver, who gets the job done with no drama.

Mixing suits me, so much better than booming, anyway. Rather than literally rubbing shoulders with people all day long, I can set up in a quiet corner where I'll be left alone. Headphones on, board lit up, I have a great excuse to avoid chatter. I need to listen.

I mean, it would be nice to have someone to come home to. Someone to take care of. But the only person I can even imagine taking that role in my life is in a mess of a marriage, because my selfish actions put her there.

I still can't believe how I overreacted a year ago. Just because Whitney and Sully got locked in the K-Mart overnight, I stupidly jumped to the conclusion that they'd hooked up. When she denied it but refused to move to Cali-fornia with me—a ridiculous ultimatum if there ever was one —it exploded into a blowup between the five of us.

That fight had to be at least a part of what drove her to marry Hardy. The thought of what he may have put her through has my hands gripping the steering wheel tightly. Just the way I'd like to wring his privileged little neck.

Which is exactly why you have to try to help her, you idiot.

Thankfully, the guys on my crew were fine with jumping onto another show without a break. Happy for a job to carry us through Christmas that'll still allow them to go home for

Thanksgiving. What they may not enjoy? A boss who's even grumpier than usual.

But then again, what's another six weeks compared to umpteen *years* wishing I were enough for her?

In high school, she was literally the Princess of the Azalea Belles who dated the captain of every team there was. I, on the other hand, was the skinny motorhead she counted on to help her with homework. In college, one pre-law or pre-med student after another courted her, while I spent every moment making student films. The summer we worked as PAs on the same movie, she flirted with every guy on the set but me.

Now, I'm not only wracked with guilt that my actions had her marrying that bully, Hardy, but I've got the prospect of watching her put another bunch of guys under her spell while I stand by, trying to figure out what's going on in that head of hers.

Our friends seem to have confidence that I'll be able to get Whitney to unburden her woes to me. I'm not sure how the hell that's going to happen when all she's ever done is push me away.

At the very least, I can, and I will, look out for her. Whether she thinks she needs me to or not.

Yeah, it's going to be torture.

"YOU GET WHAT YOU PAY FOR" IS USUALLY A GOOD ARGUMENT TO make when you're bidding a for a job. It's one my dad and uncle make all the time when a customer complains about a bill from their auto repair shop. You can pay less, sure, but you'll be coming back to me to pay even more to fix the problem created by the guy who charges less. Because that guy doesn't know what the hell he's doing.

In the movie business, that doesn't always go over well.

And I'm not one to trash another guy's work. But when I listen to the *Love Lost* dailies, it sure is on the tip of my tongue.

"He came out of retirement to do this job as a favor to the director," Tim, the UPM says. "But his equipment should've stayed in retirement."

"Let me guess," I say, doing my best to avoid criticizing the other mixer. "He was working with an old Nagra setup?"

"Unfortunately, yes."

Since pretty much everything has gone digital now, the old recording equipment just doesn't translate, and you end up paying a fortune in post.

"It frustrated him that it wasn't working as well as it used to," Tim adds. "So when his wife broke her arm, I think he was glad of an excuse to bail. We're lucky you were available."

"Timing worked out," I say. "My guys are happy to have something to fill the gap between now and Christmas."

We chat a bit more about expendables and the demands of the upcoming week's locations. Then he hands over keys to three motel rooms and an updated script.

"See y'all bright and early Monday morning."

"Any recommendations for where to eat?"

Catering provides meals during the work week, but per diem covers the weekend. Production is squatting for a couple weeks in a town near Lake Norman, north of Charlotte. Vacationers probably fill it up in the summer, but on the drive in, it looked like a lot of places had shut down for the season.

"People have been going to a place called Buddy's on the main drag about a mile up the road. Nothing special, but it's got cold beer and decent burgers."

"Sounds perfect. Maybe I'll see you there."

Before I can get out the door, he calls me back. "I almost forgot. One of the makeup girls left a note for you. The pretty one," he adds with a grin on his face that has me swallowing a growl. "You know her?"

I recognize Whitney's scrawl on the outside of the envelope. "She's a friend from home."

"Just a friend?"

"Yep. She's married," I add with a warning look. Not for long, but this guy doesn't need to know that.

"So am I," Tim says with a grin. "But you know how it is. While the cat's away, the mice can play."

I just nod and get myself out the door before I say anything that'll get me fired. It's pretty common for people to hook up when they're out of town, especially when working long hours in an isolated location. Hell, I've had more than a few showmances. The wrap date makes it easy to keep things simple, and that's the only kind of relationship I seem to be able to engage in.

I've only had a fling with a married woman once, and I'll always regret it. In my defense, I didn't know she was married until her husband showed up for a surprise visit. We didn't get caught, but when she showed up at my door an hour after he left, it literally turned my stomach.

Yet another reason to stay away from Whit, I remind myself after handing my equipment trailer over to the teamsters and getting my guys situated at the motel. I don't let myself read her note until I've unpacked my suitcase, gone for a run, and showered. By that time, I have only ten minutes before I promised to meet Walt and Ronnie so we can grab dinner.

It's just a regular business envelope, but when I open it, I swear she's somehow tucked a bit of her scent inside. Which I inhale like a total dork. I didn't see her much this past year, but the couple times I ran into Whitney in town, she smelled like someone had doused her in some cloying perfume.

The same stuff she was wearing the night of Violet's wedding.

She must've left that behind at Hardy's house because

what I smell now—a mixture of sun and sand and sweat that's all her—brings up memories of lying next to her on the beach, her head thrown back in laughter, her blond curls cascading towards the sand.

Blinking back to the present, I open the paper and, as usual, have to work to decipher her messy scrawl.

Welcome back to NC, sweetie!
I'm so excited to have you join us. Not sure when you're getting in, but most of the crew will be at Buddy's for karaoke tonight. You should come!
XOXO Whit

Even the thought of listening to off-key shout-singing broadcast over subpar sound equipment gives me heartburn, but it looks like I have no choice. Buddy's is the only game in town.

Also, I can't say no to this woman.

Two hours later, I'm wishing I had.

After a brief hug from Whit followed by a decent burger and fries, I need more than a beer to spend another minute watching the woman I once thought would be the love of my life flit and flirt her way through this bar. Add bad singing and worse acoustics, and I'd have to be drunk as a skunk to endure any more of this.

I don't even know why I came. Why I even took this job. I'm over her. I need to be over her. But that doesn't mean I want to sit here and watch other guys paw at her while she bats her eyes at them.

How am I going to get through nine weeks of this? Maybe I should just screw up. Quit.

Good plan, Ford. Sacrifice the reputation you've worked so hard to build for a woman who's never thought of you as more than a childhood friend.

I'll stick around, do the job I was hired to do. Make sure Whitney's not falling to pieces. But I don't have to deal with this. So, I pay the check for me and my guys, bid them goodnight and head for the door. Before I can escape, however, a delicate throat clearing over the mic has me stopped in my tracks.

Just get out of here, you idiot.

Do I listen to the voice of reason in my head? No, I turn around. My eyes zero in on the stage, where Whitney shields her gaze from the harsh spotlight as familiar notes picked on a guitar sound over the speakers.

It's not her voice that has me running when she starts to sing "You Were Meant For Me." She's got a good ear, and her tone is perfect for the Jewel song.

It's the lyrics.

Like they did every time I heard them on the radio, they remind me just how much I've lost.

EIGHT

```
Subj: Breakfast
Date: 11/7/1999 8:01:10 AM
From: makeupchick1200
To: Ford_soundguy
```

You didn't last long last night. Want to meet me for breakfast?

FORD

WHEN I WAKE at five a.m. chasing the shadow of a dream, it takes me a moment to figure out where I am.

Not that this is a new feeling. Between my on-the-road life and the series of hookups I tumbled through up until a few months ago, I'm no stranger to strange hotel rooms. The dark wood paneling and the gingham curtains finally jog my memory, and I'm hit with two simultaneous feelings.

Relief and dread.

Relief that Whitney seems okay enough to party the night away. Dread that she's doing it to cover up a hurt I can't even imagine.

No use trying to go to sleep now, so I roll out of bed and

get my ass out the door for a run in the dawn light creeping over the Appalachian foothills.

Neither Wallington nor Savannah—both coastal cities—has any elevation to speak of, so my lungs are screaming by the time I reach the first scenic overlook. The reward is pretty awesome though, because while the motel may be kitschy, the view up here is breathtaking.

Not just because I can barely catch my breath.

Mist hovers over a lake in the foreground. Purple mountains rise in the distance. But it's the bright reds, oranges, and yellows popping between the evergreens that draw people to this part of the state each autumn. Drawing in a deep breath, my sinuses fill with the aromas of fall: pine tar and musty leaves with a backdrop of wood smoke. A world away from the scents of the sea and sand, but just as enlivening.

After stretching my quads and hamstrings, I jog slowly back down to the motel, determined to be the friend Whitney needs, while doing the best job I can. My resume is a hell of a lot stronger than it was a year ago, but I've still got a lot to prove. I can't let concerns for my friend be a distraction.

A couple hours later, I've showered and read through the script again, taking notes as I go. When I check the one-line, I find we've got six pages to shoot Monday, including one scene with heavy dialogue and another in a car. It's clear me and the boys will have to hit the ground running.

Just as my stomach growls, reminding me I need to find breakfast, my phone rings too.

"Hey, Ford, it's Whit."

"I'm surprised you're up so early." After stretching its cord so I can grab my boots by the door, I cradle the phone between my ear and shoulder so I can put them on. "You looked like you were just getting started when I left last night."

"I was home and in bed by midnight, so you don't have to call Violet and tattle on me."

Her comment hits a little too close to home, so I redirect. "Listen, I'm starving. Is there anywhere good to get breakfast around here?"

She tells me about a diner in the next town over and asks if she can join me. We agree to meet in the parking lot in fifteen.

Whitney would be late to her own funeral, so I'm not surprised when she's nowhere to be seen at the appointed time. When I locate Gertie, it occurs to me I should make sure she's doing okay in the cooler temps and higher elevation.

Gertie, not Whitney. I've got an extra set of keys, so I decide to use the time to take a listen.

When I slide into the driver's seat, I suddenly feel like the guy who invented the Reese's cup. Who knew that Whitney's sweet and salty fragrance would go perfectly with the earthy scent of Gertie's leather seats? As I crank the engine, a flash of what it'd be like to lay Whit down on this butter-soft surface has my dick hardening with need. Closing my eyes, I let myself imagine burying my nose in the space behind her ear, my hands cupping her every curve. I picture her blond waves fanned out over the seat, her eyes dark with lust.

A knock on the car window jolts me back to reality. When I open my eyes, the star of my fantasy is scowling at me from outside the car, instead of moaning my name inside the car.

"Are you checking up on me? Making sure I didn't break Gertie?" she asks.

Cranking down the window, I sputter, "No, no. It's just—you know..." My hands flap in the air, trying to clear my head of the haze of desire. Or at the very least, distract her from the bulge in my jeans.

Hands on hips, she frowns. "I *don't* know, but I'm sure you're gonna tell me what I've been doing wrong to your precious girl."

"No, no. I was just making sure she was adjusting to the cold. And the, uh, mountains." Hoping against hope that she won't notice the erection still tight behind my zipper, I pat the dash and slide out of the driver's seat so she can climb in.

Crossing her arms, she shakes her head. "Uh-uh. No way am I driving her with you watching my every move."

A brief standoff ensues, until we agree that it'd be better to just take my truck. After she gives me directions to the diner, she turns to face me, eyes narrowed. "Did you loan Gertie to me so I would owe you?"

"What? What does that even mean?"

"I don't want to be beholden to you," she says, not really answering my question.

Confused, I wait until I've parked in front of the diner and turned off the truck before turning to face her. The look on her face is both fierce and fearful. Hands up between us, I keep my tone even. "Like I told you back in Wallington, I'm not driving her much these days. I need the truck to pull my trailer for work. You needed a car. That's it. That's why I loaned her to you."

"Then why were you checking up on her?"

"She's an old girl, and she's temperamental. Just making sure she doesn't need any extra attention."

Her plump lips flatten into a line. "Damn, Ford. If you'd only treat women the way you treat this car, you'd have a harem."

"Who says I don't?"

This gets an eye roll out of her. Hoping I've successfully broken the tension, I hook a thumb towards the diner. "Ready to eat?"

As we walk up the sidewalk, she says, "Still, I never thought I'd see the day when you'd willingly let a girl drive your car."

"Well, you're not just any girl." The words ride more feeling than I'm ready to admit, so I bump shoulders with her lightly and add, "I promise I won't do it again."

"Do what again?"

I open the door to the restaurant and gesture for her to precede me inside. "Check up on her without asking you first."

Shaking her head slightly, she blows out a breath. "She's your car. You can do what you want with her. I probably just overreac—"

A wall of sound swallows her words as we step through the second set of doors. The diner is packed, and it looks like we'll have a long wait. But before I can ask if there's another place we can try, Whitney threads her way through the crowd to an occupied table. After a brief conversation with its occupant and a passing waitress, she waves me over.

"Ford, this is Barbie. She's the script supervisor. I thought it'd be a good idea for y'all to meet."

"You sure you don't mind us joining you?" I ask.

"Not at all. Take a load off."

Barbie is, I'm sure, a lovely woman. Curvy, with a head of dark curls. A year ago, I would've flirted her into my bed, and it seems like Whitney knows this, because she just keeps pointing out things Barbie and I have in common. But that's not where I am right now.

I'm happy to talk shop with her, because you can never have too many allies on a set. But I don't know what to do with the way she's literally batting her eyes at me or touching my forearm when she laughs at something I say that isn't actually funny. Or the way Whitney looks at us. Like we're a car accident and she just can't keep herself from rubbernecking.

But when Whitney excuses herself to use the restroom, Barbie lets out a long sigh and shifts in her seat to face me. "It's painfully obvious that you're not interested in me."

Before I can come up with some lame excuse about not dating people I work with, she holds up a hand. "That's on me. But if you're the guy that hurt her, you'd best watch your back."

It seems strange that Whitney would've shared more of her story with a pack of strangers than she would with her closest friends. In any case, I don't spread gossip on a set. I hear more than I probably should when people are mic'd, but I've never taken advantage of that.

Barbie continues without my input. "She hasn't said what she's running from, but it's pretty obvious that she left trouble back home. She's all sweet social butterfly on the surface, but there's something about her that's got the whole crew—especially the teamsters—protective of her."

"That's Whitney for you."

Barbie tips her head to the side to study me. "So, *are* you the trouble she's trying to leave behind?"

"I am not, I promise you."

But when the woman in question catches my eye as she makes her way through the crowded space, turning heads as she goes, I have to remind myself of the promise I made to our mutual friends.

I won't be the trouble she's walking into, either.

Whitney makes up some excuse about needing to do errands and catches a ride with Barbie instead of returning to the motel with me. Left alone, I walk off breakfast with a stroll. It's a cute little town, and lots of people bustle in and out of gift shops and such. When I stumble upon a music store, I admire the instruments the owner has on display but leave with just a new set of strings. Back at my room, I spend the afternoon noodling around on my guitar.

I often lose track of time when I play, so when a sharp rap sounds at my door, I'm not surprised to note that it's already dark outside. Thinking it's one of my guys dropping off a finalized call sheet, the last person I expect to find out in the breezeway is Whitney.

She pulls the call sheet from where it's taped to the door and hands it to me.

"You making sure I'm not late to work tomorrow?"

She lifts her chin. "Wasn't sure if you knew this is how they get delivered."

"I have worked a few out-of-town jobs before, you know."

"Okay, Mister Know-it-all. I was just trying to be neighborly."

I'm still pissed at the way she tried to fix me up with Barbie at breakfast, and by her expression, she's not too happy with me either. "Did you have something else to say to me?"

She hesitates a beat before asking, "Can I come in?"

I step back and gesture for her to enter. After I close the door, I wait. She takes her time surveying the space. "Your room is just like mine, but backwards."

This doesn't seem to need a response from me. Before I can ease past her into the room, she turns to face me. "What is wrong with you?"

"What are you talking about?"

She groans at the ceiling, hands on hips, before facing me full on. "Barbie is perfect for you. She's smart. Great complexion. Has better hair than me, even. She knows her shit and has it together, too. Not only that, she wants kids and y'all would make gorgeous ones."

"What the fuck does any of that have to do with me?"

"Ford, she even owns her own condo in Atlanta, so y'all could have a base both there and Wallington."

"What is wrong with *you*?"

"Uh-uh, I asked you first."

I roll my eyes. How is it that this woman always has me behaving like a teenager? "Okay. Why were you trying to set me up with Barbie?"

One shoulder lifts and drops. "Maybe I'm tired of you trailing after me like a puppy I kicked."

"Whit, you're the one who told me about this job."

"Uh-uh." She ticks a finger back and forth in the air. "I asked if you knew anyone who was available."

"And I am. Available."

She flicks a hand in the air. "I thought you were booked in Savannah."

"Are you saying you don't want me here?"

"What I don't want is distraction."

"Is that all I am to you?"

She shakes her head, blowing out an exasperated breath. "All right. I didn't want to have to do this, but I can't see any other way out of this mess."

When she kicks off her shoes and unbuttons her blouse, I grab her hands to stop her. "What the hell are you doing?"

"I'm going to prove to you once and for all that the princess you've always wanted doesn't exist. We're gonna have sex. One time. Then you'll know."

She tries to wrest her hands away, but I hold tight until she meets my gaze. When she does, the intensity in her eyes discombobulates me to the point that the only thing I can think to ask is, "You think I think you're a princess?"

Her mouth twists slightly before the corners of her mouth lift in a smile that seems as forced as her argument. "I don't just think it, I know it."

Did I fall asleep? Is this some strange dream? "I don't get it."

"No girl can live up to the ideal guys build up in their heads. But especially not this girl." Jerking her hands free, she gestures up and down her body. "Let's just have the sex, and get it over with, and you'll see. I'm not the perfect woman."

I open my mouth to argue that I don't expect her, or any woman, to be perfect, but before I can begin, she holds her hand like a stop sign. "This is a one-time offer. Now or never Ford."

It's only then that I notice the ragged friendship bracelet on her wrist. Needing to know if it's the one she gave me twenty-odd years ago, the one I gave back to her in the hospital, I take her hand again. When she doesn't pull away, I turn it over until I spy the cowry shell braided into the bracelet. When I look up again with a raised brow, she blinks a few times before snatching the hand away.

Two fingers on the bracelet, she asks, "Do you want it back?"

I just shake my head. The fact that she's wearing it shifts something in me. The tiny part of my heart that won't give up on something between us throbs with hope. Maybe all these years I've been doing this wrong. Maybe instead of telling her how I feel about her, I need to show her.

She didn't say that she'll never sleep with me again if we have sex. She's just assuming that I won't want to. Since that's not going to happen, my job in this scenario is to make her want to "have the sex" with me again.

Challenge accepted.

I cross behind her to make sure the door is locked before gesturing for her to step all the way into my room. "Do you want anything? I've got beer and water in the mini fridge."

"This isn't a date, Ford." She shucks off her blouse and has the top button of my jeans undone before I've taken another breath.

"Whoa, whoa." Stepping back, I hold up a hand in the air. "What's the hurry?"

"We have an early call tomorrow. I figured we should cut to the chase."

Dropping to her knees, eyes on the prize as it were, she unzips my fly, and shoves my pants and boxers to my ankles.

Stepping back, so my dick is out of reach, I pull my pants back up. "Jesus, Whit. What the hell do you think you're doing?"

"Have you never had a blow job before, honey?" She looks up at me, eyes narrowed. "Or is it that you don't think I know how to suck a guy off?"

I thought I hated that particular turn of phrase, but my erection begs to differ. "Neither of those things is true. But if you were to take me in your mouth, it'd all be over quick." When she rolls her eyes, I get it. "Wait. Was that your plan?"

She shrugs. "Nobody's complained in the past."

I don't want to think about the past. I mean, neither of us are virgins. I have a lot of respect for a woman who enjoys getting as well as giving pleasure. But I'm pretty sure that's not what Whitney is talking about.

Maybe my friends' Spidey-sense about something being off in her marriage is warranted, because this feels like an act. If that's the case, the only way I can think to uncover the truth is to play along. And hope I don't fuck things up even worse.

I place a single finger under her chin and lift it until she meets my gaze. "If I only get one chance, I'm not gonna waste it."

NINE

Subj: News from Charlotte?
Date: 11/7/1999 4:30:25 PM
From: VioletCastingCarolina
To: Ford_soundguy

____

Ford, I can't wait for the group chat tomorrow night. What's happening???

WHITNEY

WHEN FORD HOLDS OUT A HAND, I let him pull me to my feet. When he leads me toward the sitting area of his room, however, I resist. "You want to have sex on the couch when there's a bed right there?"

He picks up my shirt and hands it to me. "I don't ever want to *have sex* with you, Whit."

"Why?" I can't help the venom in my tone, even as I shrug into the sleeves of my blouse. "Because I'm used goods? I didn't think you only slept with virgins."

"That's not what I meant."

"I wasn't exactly returned in the original packaging. You know I can't have kids now, right?"

He gestures at the shirt. "I heard you've been shopping at second-hand clothes stores for the first time in your life. If you can do that, I reckon I can handle a few scratches and dings."

I step back so fast I bump into a piece of furniture.

"Oh, jeez, I'm sorry, Whit. It's just a metaphor. Like, you know, a used car comes with—" Breaking off, his face pales and he takes a step back. "Shit. That… that isn't the case, is it? Did Hardy hurt you? Because I'll drive to Wallington this minute and beat the shit out of that guy if he so much as broke one of your fingernails."

Suddenly feeling more naked than I did without a shirt, I cross my arms over my chest. "I don't have scars unless you count the one from the hysterectomy. And anyway, he let you go at the hospital, but I doubt that'd happen again. He knows an awful lot of lawyers and cops."

"Who told you what happened at the hospital?"

"Who do you think?"

He runs a hand down his face. "You know what? I don't want to talk about that asshole. I want to just… spend time with you."

"You don't want to—" I unbutton my blouse again.

He holds up a hand. "If I didn't make it obvious when I was nineteen or when I was twenty-nine, I'm into you. But listen—we've never spent time together, not just the two of us. Plus, we've been apart for years. Formative years. Can we just… sit on the couch and talk?"

His eyes track to my mouth, where my frown must speak volumes. "I know you're up on all the gossip on this set. You can fill me in, so I don't hit any potholes my first week."

"Are you sure that's what you want?"

"I want a lot more, Whit, I always have. But I won't be a rebound guy."

"So, what? You want me to hook up with someone else on the show? While you watch?"

His glower gives me the answer I expect. "No, I don't want that. But I also don't want you to run from Hardy to me. If it's ever going to happen between us, I want you to walk into my arms free of him."

As I stare into his eyes, my heart pounds loud in my ears, and beats against my rib cage like it wants out of here. But it's a different fear than I'm used to.

When I showed up tonight, I came loaded for bear. Yelling at him didn't work. Lobbying for Barbie didn't work. Nor did the offer of a quickie. I'm not sure what to do now that those attempts missed the target.

It feels weird to sit next to him on the couch, so I skirt around him to sit on a chair instead. He offers me a drink again, and I say no again. When he asks if I've had dinner, I just shrug.

I'm sure my lower lip is pushed out like a toddler, but he ignores the pout. He just nods and starts talking to himself as he pokes around in the room's kitchenette, which I'm surprised to see he's already stocked.

"Well, I'm having a beer, and I'm pretty hungry. I don't really feel like going out, so I'm just going to make my famous hotel room Snackeroo."

He sticks a package in the microwave and dumps a bunch of stuff in a big bowl. After the oven dings and the room fills with the scent of popcorn, he plunks the bowl and two plastic cups on the coffee table. "In case you're tempted."

My curiosity gets to me, and I lean forward. "Snackaroo, huh?"

He waggles his eyebrows, blue eyes glinting with humor. "Came home starving at the end of a workday with nothing to eat one too many times."

"Don't you eat on set?"

He takes a long pull of his beer. "I try. But sometimes I just get too busy. So, I created this snack. Salty and sweet. Some protein, some fruit. Help yourself. There's plenty."

I lean forward and inspect the mix. "Where'd you get the bowl?"

"It's part of my kit."

"Huh."

He hands me his beer and picks up the bowl, shaking it. "Popcorn, peanut M&M's, almonds, coconut, pretzels, cranberries, and raisins is the usual recipe. If I can find some other interesting nuts or whatever, I'll add those too."

I take a sip of the beer as he talks, appreciating the complex flavors. When we were in college, Ford was into foreign beers like Heineken and Molson's. No Bud or Michelob for him. It seems he's now caught the microbrew bug, because I don't recognize the brand name on the label.

He leans back on the couch with a sigh and asks questions about the show. How many pages we're actually shooting a day versus how many we're scheduled to get through. Whether there are any feuds between departments. Whether the DP and director are in sync or in a power struggle. Things like that. Before I know it, he's opening another beer, since I didn't return the one he shared with me. I've also eaten two cups of his tasty snack mix.

Even better, I'm laughing.

Once he's gotten all the set gossip, he steers the conversation to memories.

"You remember the first time we all went to the beach in Gertie? Grabbed burgers for a picnic at Wrightsboro on a Sunday night?"

"Damn. We were so young then." I've migrated to the couch, and I lean my head back on the cushion, my feet up on the coffee table as I picture the five of us as teens. "I remember you wanted to go cruising in her like they did in that movie. You know, with the guy who played Opie."

"Oh yeah. *American Graffiti.* What a classic."

I let myself look at him and am rewarded with the view of his perfect profile. His firm jaw softened by his wide smile.

"But it was too hot to do that in Wallington. So, we made you go to the beach. Even though you didn't want to get sand in the car."

He shakes his head, his eyes still on the ceiling, like there's a movie of our childhood adventures playing there. "I was more worried about the burger grease and ketchup staining the seats, but yeah. I don't know how I thought I could keep sand out of her. I guess my grandma never went to the beach."

Drawing my legs up underneath me, I shift to face him. "Nobody got any food on her, but I spilled my sunscreen."

His head tips to face me and he shakes his head slowly. "I remember that. Then the car always smelled like you."

I poke his thigh with my foot. "Which you gave me no end of grief about."

He grabs my foot before I can withdraw it. "Want to know a secret?"

I just raise a brow.

"I loved that smell. Still do."

I'm not sure what he means by this. He doesn't want to have sex with me, but he loves the scent of my sunscreen? Before I can decide whether or not to poke into this, he steers the conversation to safer topics.

We talk for another hour or so about movies, and TV shows, and music until we're both yawning so much that it's getting ridiculous.

Still, I don't want to go. It's a bizarre feeling, just hanging out with a guy. Every time I was alone with any other man, things got hot and heavy pretty darn quick. Afterwards, before I got married, I'd either leave or the guy would. Once I got married, I just pretended to be asleep.

Now, I *need* to go to sleep, so I push myself off the couch. My room is only one floor down, but he insists on walking me back.

"See ya tomorrow," he says, after I unlock my door. "And thanks for hanging out. I had a really good time."

And then he just walks away.

TEN

Subj: FedEx
Date: 11/10/1999 4:55:01 PM
From: LoveLost_production_office
To: Ford_soundguy

Ford,
Somehow FedEx lost the DAT tapes you sent
last night. Hopefully you have backup you
can send again??

FORD

MOST PEOPLE THINK my job is just about getting the words from the actor's mouths onto tape with as few extraneous sounds as possible. That is the endgame, but besides being a team leader, almost everything I do is problem-solving.

What problems are we solving? Everything from dealing with boom shadows, to revealing costumes that give us very few spots to hide a body mic, to sometimes minor and sometimes major equipment failures.

My goal is to avoid disaster. If I can't prevent an issue, I aim to solve it as quickly as possible. And I'm pretty good at it if I do say so myself.

Except when it comes to women, apparently.

When the gang convinced me to take this particular job, I figured I'd ride in on my white horse and get Whitney to confess what happened with her marriage and I'd somehow make it all better.

Stupidly, I ignored my own unrequited feelings for the woman. Not to mention the slew of fantasies I'd nurtured from age fifteen to one year ago, where she starred as the love of my life.

I'm still confused about what happened in my room three nights ago. Despite getting her to relax a bit, despite having a truly good time talking and laughing with her, it wasn't until after I walked her back to her room that I realized I was no closer to finding out what went down between her and Hardy.

Her out-of-the-blue sexual proposition supports the theory that there *is* a problem, but as to what it is, or how to fix it, I'm still lost. And you could argue, I suppose, that the problem is me.

Between feeling like a failure in that department and a boatload of unrequited desire, I may be grumpier than usual this week.

Whenever Walt avoids the cart and Ronnie mutters to himself—his Brooklyn accent getting thicker by the minute—I know I need to at least try to be nicer.

But when I put on my headphones and hear Walt trying to negotiate with the director in his Kentucky-born-and-bred drawl, I'm up and out of my seat in two shakes of a lamb's tail.

"Hal," I say to the director. "I hear we've got an issue here?"

It only takes a few minutes for me to come up with a way we can cover the shot without it having to be looped later.

When that conversation's done, I take Walt by the elbow and steer him to a quiet corner. "Walt," I growl. "Why didn't you call me in?"

Walt flinches at my harsh tone but meets my gaze, which I'm sure is blazing. "For just this reason. I don't know what's got your panties in a twist this week, but you could start an argument in an empty house." He flaps a hand toward the lighting crew. "I just thought I'd fix the problem myself."

Eyes on the ground, I rub the back of my head and blow out a breath before facing him again. "You're right."

He grins. "I think I'm going to need you to repeat that. Did you just say that I'm right?"

I roll my eyes. "Yes, you asshole. You are right. About this one thing. I've been in a mood, and for that I apologize. But" —I raise a finger—"do not make a habit of sneaking around behind my back. If there's a problem, I want to know about it. We can work together to fix it. No secrets."

He nods slowly. "Got it, boss."

The AD calls for last looks, and Walt hurries back to set while I get back to my cart as fast as possible.

"Everything all right?" Ronnie asks when I sit back down.

"Yep. All good," is what I say out loud. But in my head, I have to admit that no, everything is not okay. I need to stop obsessing over Whitney if I'm going to avoid fucking up this job. I am in way over my head, and I have no idea how to fix it.

Or her. Or me.

I just hope I haven't already blown my one and only chance.

ELEVEN

Subj: Thanksgiving
Date: 11/12/1999 9:30:45 AM
From: VioletCastingCarolina
To: SullyCallaway999, DanielleGoodwin856,
makeupchick1200, Ford_soundguy

Hey gang, just checking in to see who will
be in town for Thanksgiving because my
grandma wants to throw us a baby shower.

Subj: RE: Thanksgiving
Date: 11/12/1999 5:14:53 PM
From: SullyCallaway999
(Reply All)

Me and Helen will be in town, but is this a
girl thing or an everybody thing?

```
Subj: RE: RE: Thanksgiving
Date: 11/13/1999 7:40:56 AM
From: VioletCastingCarolina
(Reply All)
```

This is an all-hands-on deck baby party!
Ford and Whit, I know you're probably
working crazy hours, but we are thinking of
having it on the Friday evening after
Thanksgiving—our usual game night—if y'all
can come.

FORD

THE SATURDAY after our first full week of work, my crew just cannot accept the fact that I won't go out to the bar with them.

"Seriously?" Walt asks. "You turn thirty and you're too old to have a good time?"

"I went out last weekend," I grumble. "I can't handle karaoke two weekends in a row. My ears haven't recovered."

"We found out about a different place. No karaoke, and it has pool tables."

I don't feel like going out. I don't feel much like doing anything. "I think I might be coming down with something. I'm gonna go to bed early."

"Bullshit. You never get sick."

I just shrug.

Ronnie, the third man on my crew, sticks his head in the doorway. "Saw that blond makeup chick from Wallington at the laundromat. She asked me if you were coming."

My heart beats double-time at his words, but I just double down. "Not gonna go out and spread whatever I've got to the rest of the crew."

"I don't think love sickness is catching," Walt says, chucking something at me.

I nab the balled-up socks before they hit me in the face and sling them right back. "What are you talking about?"

"You're a horn dog who won't even look at a girl. Only time that happens is when a horn dog falls in love."

"With a girl he can't have," Ronnie adds.

"Y'all are barking up the wrong tree. Now get outta here and leave me and my germs alone."

"Okay if I hit on the makeup girl?" Ronnie asks.

"You?" Walt says, knocking him playfully in the shoulder. "Why do you think she'd be interested in you when I'm—"

"Goodnight, gentlemen," I say, heading toward them to cut off the argument. "Have fun. But not too much fun. And leave the makeup girl alone."

Before they can reply, I shut the door. Not quite in their faces, but a little more rudely than I should to the two guys who have my back on set day in and day out.

WHITNEY

After Ford's boom guy told me they were going to play pool instead of doing karaoke on Saturday night, I talked my department into joining them. As long as it's not a cocktail party where all anyone can talk about is real estate, or a fancy dinner where all people do is try to one up each other, I'm in.

Until last year, being around people has always energized me. It's why I love my job. Our trailer is like a slumber party every day. Sometimes it's low key if there's a big dramatic scene coming up, but even then, it's a special kind of intimacy.

I'm a little disappointed when Ford's crew shows up

without him, but I stick around for a couple hours. It's fun making people laugh at how terrible I am at pool. I don't even have to play the dumb blonde. When someone tries to explain that billiards is all physics, my mind is literally blown.

After a bit, I get worried about Ford. It's not like we can call in sick. Especially someone in a key position like his.

So, I bow out early and stop by the convenience store on the way back. Supplies in hand, I knock softly on his door, thinking I'll just drop my little care package outside if he's gone to bed early. When I hear music coming from the other side, I knock a little louder.

Moments later, the door cracks open.

"Everything okay?" Ford asks.

"Heard you were sick and brought you some supplies." I lift the plastic shopping bag. "But something tells me you're just having an introvert night."

He huffs out a laugh. "Guilty as charged."

We just stand there staring at each other for a few moments. Sunday's cozy evening sharing memories and snacks on his couch seems far away. Even though we're working together, I hardly saw him all week.

Ford's very good at finding a hidden corner for his mixing cart. He practically growled anytime anyone tried to hang out there to watch the filming on his monitor. So, my department hung out at video village instead.

"Do you want to come i—" he begins at the same time that I say,

"Well, I guess I'll just leave you—"

We break off at the same time and then start up again in unison too.

"Oh, sure I'd love to—"

"Yeah, I should probably get to bed."

He laughs and steps back, making way for me to enter. "Come on in."

"You sure?"

Instead of answering, he asks, "What's in the goody bag?"

"I don't know if I'd call it that," I say, moving past him and catching a whiff of his comforting scent. Pretty sure it's the same English Leather aftershave he's worn since high school. I prefer its woodsy, leathery smell to the expensive cologne that Hardy doused himself in. If I ever encounter that blend of cedar and sandalwood again, I swear I'll barf.

I set my offerings next to his TV. "I got you the essentials: Emergen-C, Tylenol, and Cup-a-Soup. If you do get sick, you'll be set up."

It's only when I turn around that I notice the guitar sitting on his couch. "Is that yours?"

He picks it up and sets it in a case. "It is."

"Since when do you play the guitar? How do I not know this?"

"I started when I was on the road a few years ago. And I don't really play, I just fuck around." He meets my gaze and one side of his mouth lifts, but it's not quite a smile. "I guess there's a lot you don't know about me."

I shake my head. "That's just wrong."

He shrugs. "There's probably a lot I don't know about you."

"Fair enough," I say, realizing that this could be dangerous territory. There are reasons I never share anything deeper than my moisturizer choices. "Would you play for me?"

"Not sure your ears are up for it."

"You suffered through me singing karaoke last week, I think I owe you."

"Yeah, but you're good."

"Am not."

"Are too."

"Not."

"Are."

Laughing at how quickly we revert to the schoolyard antics, I plop down on his couch, lean back, and set my feet on the coffee table. "Not leaving until you play me one song."

He considers me for a moment. "All right. But I'm going to have a beer first. You want one?"

He keeps his eyes on what looks like a cheat sheet of chords on the coffee table after he returns with two beers, which makes me think he's nervous to play for me. Ford's not one to hang out in the spotlight, so I'm blown away when he begins to sing.

Because it's a male voice and a guitar instead of a piano and a female singer, it takes me a moment to recognize Sarah McLachlan's "Do What You Have to Do," but once I do, the words hit me in a way they never have before.

After he plays the last chord, he sneaks a look at me. "That bad, huh?"

I swipe a hand under my eyes. "The opposite. That was beautiful, Ford. You should be on the other side of the mic."

"Pfft. I'm surprised you recognized it."

"I mean, it doesn't quite match you on the recorder in fourth grade, but…"

"Hard to top 'Hot Cross Buns.'" He laughs and shakes his head before putting his guitar in its case and stowing it in the closet.

I'm about to excuse myself, unsure if he wants me here when he says something I can't quite understand.

"Sorry, I couldn't hear you."

Returning to the seating area, he perches on the arm of the couch. "I said, do you remember the first time we met?"

"In preschool?"

"Well, yeah. That's when we met."

I shake my head. "How can you remember that far back?"

He scoots down into the couch and puts his feet up on the table, mirroring me. When he crosses his arms over his broad chest, biceps bulge inside his flannel shirt. Definitely not a fourth grader anymore. In fact, Ford wasn't even this built in college.

Eyes on the ceiling, he murmurs, "I just have this image of you at the top of the big slide. The one we weren't supposed to go on."

The picture of this very sexy, very grown-up man within arm's reach clashes with the memories his words bring up. Safer to focus on the past. "I do remember that slide. It seemed so huge. I think that awful girl Ellen dared me to do it. Ellen Hamster Killer."

"Ellen what?"

"Ellen Hamster Killer. That's how I always think of her. She had a hamster and then decided she wanted a bunny instead. Her parents said she couldn't have more than one pet, so she stopped feeding the hamster until it died."

His head whips toward me. "Jesus. That's awful."

Nodding, I press my lips together as another set of incongruous images vies for space in my head. Ellen then and Ellen now. "She's the current president of the Junior League in Wallington."

"I'm horrified." His expression is so full of shock, it's almost funny.

"Obviously, nobody asked me for a referral."

Not wanting to get into my life over the past year, I redirect him to the past. "What else do you remember?"

He swivels his head back to face the ceiling. "I just remember your eyes being big and round. I thought you were too afraid to slide down, so I climbed up after you. By the time I got to the top, you were sliding down, cackling the entire way."

That feeling—the whoosh of going down the slide—has me laughing all over again.

Ford points at me. "Just like that."

"Yeah, I got in trouble for going on that slide a bunch of times. Once I tried it, they couldn't keep me away from it."

"Little rebel."

"That was me."

"Was?"

"Yep," I say, hopping up from the couch. "I'm a good girl now who goes to bed on time, so she gets plenty of rest. Sleep is the best thing to keep your skin young-looking, you know."

He looks like he's going to say something else, but I can't deal with whatever it is, so I make a beeline for the door. "Glad you're not really sick. 'Night."

FORD

Whitney escapes from my room so fast it makes my head spin. That, and the yo-yo effect of her opening up and shutting down has me wondering if any of this is a good idea.

I honestly don't know if I can be just her friend. Getting close will just make me fall in love with her all over again. I don't want to just be a rebound for her, but I also can't imagine watching her date someone else.

It might be too late to call Sully since he gets up at the ass-crack of dawn to go surfing—even on the weekends, even when the water's cold—but I figure he can just let it go to voicemail. My cell works about as well here as it does in Wallington, so I punch in the numbers of my calling card and dial his home number.

"Whassup," he says, after picking up halfway through the second ring.

"Sorry to call so late."

"Everything okay?"

"Yeah. Well, yes, and no."

"Whitney?"

I hesitate, now not sure what to say. Not even sure what I'm feeling. If I should be feeling what I'm feeling. I promised Violet and Dani that I wouldn't get involved with her.

"That bad, huh?" he says, and I can hear the grin in his voice.

I let out a groan.

"Just tell her how you feel. For real."

I could barely get off the couch ten minutes ago but now I can't sit still. Phone pressed to my ear, I pace as far as the cord allows. "What good would that do? She's married."

"It might help." He clears his throat. "It'd help you, at least."

"I don't need help," I snap, even though that's exactly why I called him.

A laugh snorts out of him. "Yeah, you just keep tellin' yourself that, brother."

Flopping back on the bed, I rub my chest, which hurts all of a sudden. "I wish it were that simple. I mean, I don't even know what I feel about her anymore."

He's quiet so long that I'm about to ask if he's still on the line when he says, "It's just, I mean, I get it. You've loved her forever. And I'm truly sorry if I got in the way by thinking I wanted her too. But I have to ask: do you really know her?"

"Of course, I know her. I've known her as long as I've known you."

The image of that tiny little girl, cackling as she flew down the slide hits me right between the eyes.

"But you and me left for seven years after college," Sully says, shattering the picture. "A lot of life can happen in that time."

On my feet again, I argue, "I don't know about you, but I'm the same person I was back then."

"Are you though? I mean, jeez. I hope I've grown up a bit since I was a teenager. I feel like I matured a hell of a lot just in the last year."

Like Whitney, Sully went through some challenging life

events in the past year, but I push back anyway. "Growing up and changing your entire personality are two different things."

"I don't know if we ever knew the real Whitney, though." I can almost hear the wince in his voice. "I mean, we definitely put her on a pedestal, compared to other girls."

"Well, she kind of deserves that pedestal. Her family's in Wallington's society pages on a weekly basis and we're all from the other side of the tracks."

"Not Violet. Not me. We're not high society but we're not exactly…"

"You can say it. Trailer trash like Dani and me." Violet's parents are engineers or something, and Sully's parents are both academics, while Dani was raised by a single mom and my family runs a garage.

"That's not what I was gonna say. I guess it doesn't really matter, though. Town and gown are pretty far apart in this town. I mean, Whitney was a freakin' debutante!" Sully laughs. "Who even does that anymore?"

"People like Whitney's parents who treat their daughter like any of their other expensive possessions. Something to show off."

"And sell to the highest bidder?" He blows out a breath. "You think that's why she married Hardy?"

"I wouldn't put it past them." Bile rises in my throat at the thought. "But she married him because of us."

Sully coughs, but I can't tell if it's in disbelief or surprise. "Do you seriously think that's why she married him? Because of that fight a year ago?"

"Why else would she finally cave to her parents? She'd been dodging their list of so-called 'suitable young men' since we graduated college."

"I don't know," Sully says, his voice dismissive. "Maybe she just wanted that lifestyle. She always did like nice things."

"I don't buy that. She was getting regular work on local shows. Earning union rates."

"That girl could go through money like a duck through water." He sighs heavily. "I mean, I get it. I blamed myself at first. But she's an adult. Nobody held a gun to her head."

Emotion blocks my throat as the memory surfaces. Her in my arms at the wedding. Deathly pale. "They might as well have."

Sully yawns, and I realize that talking this through is only getting me more confused, so I tell him I'll see him in a couple weeks, over Thanksgiving.

"Are you and Whit coming together? So she can go to Violet's baby shower?" he asks before I can say goodbye and literally let him off the hook.

"What are you talking about?"

"Have you checked your email lately?"

"Uh, no. My first week's been pretty hectic."

"Well," he says, over another yawn. "You should. And in the meantime, don't do anything rash. You've got another, what, six weeks of working together? Don't want to rock the boat, shit where you eat, all that jazz."

I'll rack up his crazy mix of metaphors to the late hour. "All right, brother. Talk soon."

"Love ya, man."

"Love you too."

After I hang up, I trudge back to my bed and fall onto it face first. I'll find Whit and talk to her about Thanksgiving tomorrow. In the meantime, I pull out a book that'll remind me of where my head should be at. My current read features two of my movie heroes: Cameron Crowe interviewing Billy Wilder.

Unfortunately, I can't even get through a single chapter without my thoughts returning again and again to Whitney. But it's only when something Sully said comes back to me that I put the book down for good.

We definitely put her on a pedestal.

Is that what she meant about being a princess? Have her rejections of me had more to do with how she thinks I see her, than how she feels about me? Like I'm just infatuated with some perfect being that doesn't exist?

Am I?

And if I am, what am I going to do about it?

TWELVE

```
Subj: RE: RE: RE: RE: Thanksgiving
Date: 11/18/1999 10:55:34 AM
From: VioletCastingCarolina
(Reply All)
```

Thanksgiving is literally one week away!
Are y'all coming or not?

FORD

WITHOUT EITHER OF us saying anything, it becomes a habit. Almost every night after work, Whitney comes to my room, and we just hang out. Sometimes we eat and talk. Sometimes we watch a movie, sometimes we just watch a bit of *Letterman*. Every night, I walk her back to her room.

Good news is, I feel like I'm really getting to know her, and she's letting me in bit by bit.

Bad news is, getting closer just makes me want more. Meanwhile, I'm not any closer to finding out what the heck was up in her marriage. But I don't want to rush any of it, so even though Vi and Dani and Sully have not so subtly bugged me for the deets, I haven't pushed.

Towards the end of my second week, we have a challenging shoot day that involves live music, which requires bringing in an extra man to do playback. The guy drools over Whitney all day, so I take it upon myself to tell him she's married.

"Why's she flirting with me, then?" he asks.

"That's not flirting. That's just how she is," I shoot back.

He rears back at the growl in my voice. "What? She married to *you*?"

"No. I've just known her since we were kids."

"Well, if you haven't tapped that, then maybe I should."

Before I know it, I've grabbed the guy by his shirt. "Don't talk about her that way."

"Jesus, dude. I'm just shooting the shit," he says, hands up.

"Have a little respect. *Dude*," I mutter, after releasing him.

He stays away from her, but the incident runs on replay in the back of my mind all day. After work, I'm still so agitated that I don't wait for Whit to show up at my room; I go to her.

"Where's the fire?" she asks when she opens up.

"No fire," I grumble, shoving my hands in my pockets.

She doesn't invite me in, just scans my face. "You just whaled on my door like you were planning to break it down. Am I late for something?"

"Can I come in?"

Her nose wrinkles, and she glances quickly behind her. "My room is a mess."

I shrug. "So what?"

"Promise you won't give me shit about it?"

"I promise. Just let me in. It's cold out here."

"Fine," she says on a sigh, stepping out of the way so I can enter.

"Wow." She wasn't exaggerating. In fact, I'm not sure any exaggeration could do this room justice.

She hip-checks me as she skirts past to move piles of clothes off the sofa. "You promised."

"I just don't... how does this happen?"

She looks around the room with a shrug. "Just getting ready for work in the morning."

"Is it fun?"

"Is what fun?"

"Getting dressed and re-dressed a thousand times?"

Her head tips to the side, something she does when she takes time to think before speaking, which isn't often. Something that I admire as much as it exasperates me. "Sometimes it's a lot of fun. Sometimes it just makes me more anxious. And it usually makes me late."

I want to ask what she means by *more* anxious, but I'm on a mission here, so I take a seat on the couch.

"I don't have any beer," she says. "But I have some soda if you want."

"No, thanks. I'm good."

She perches on the sofa too. Close, but not too close. "Is something the matter?"

"Why don't you wear your wedding ring?"

The non sequitur has her narrowing her eyes, but she answers without questioning it. "Because I don't want anything Hardy gave me."

"But technically, you're married."

"Not all married people wear wedding rings."

"Yeah, well," is all I seem to be able to say to that.

"What's this about, Ford?" Her tone is laced with exasperation.

"It's just... you're so flirty with everyone and today, the guy doing playback was being gross about you and I-I wanted to punch him."

She raises a single brow. "I thought you wanted me to have a rebound thing."

"I said, *I* didn't want to be a rebound thing." What I want to say but don't know how, is, *I don't want you to have anything with anyone else but me.* Without her shutting me down again, at least.

"And what do you mean I'm so 'flirty'? Are you saying I'm being unprofessional?" The challenge in her tone has me meeting her gaze, where I'm met with defiance. "Are you trying to tell me how to behave?"

Shaking my head, I throw my hands up between us. "No, no, but… maybe you're just not aware of how people might interpret the way you treat them."

"You mean smiling? Being friendly? Being considerate? Instead of growling and practically swatting at people's hands when they come near your precious cart?"

"Even if I did smile more, nobody would think I was flirting."

One shoulder lifts and drops. "I beg to differ."

"Could you maybe just, I don't know, touch people less?"

"Touching people is part of my job, Ford." Sitting back against the arm of the couch she folds her arms across her chest and lifts her chin. "This is just like when we were in college, and you called me a slut."

"What? No, I didn't. I would never do that."

"You said, and I quote, 'Every guy in town has wiped his feet on you.'"

I just stare at her, blinking, trying to remember what the hell she's talking about. And then it hits me. "You mean when I said you needed to stop being such a doormat? Letting people run roughshod over you?"

"That's not how you phrased it."

"Well, that's what I meant. I don't remember what I said exactly."

Looking like she just smelled a rotten egg, she gives me a look that'd curdle milk. "Well, excuse me. When everyone in your life treats you like you're as helpless as a newborn lamb, you believe them."

"But that's dumb."

"Did you just call me dumb?"

"No. Believing them is dumb. Just stop it."

"It's not that easy." Her head whips to the side, her chin wobbles, and I swear all the fight just goes out of her.

"Let me help you then."

"I don't want your help. And I shouldn't need it anyway. I have to learn how to take care of myself."

"Of course, you can take care of yourself. But Whit—" I pause, wanting to be extra careful with my choice of words. "You know you're smart as hell, right?"

Facing me again, her chin lifts. "I want to believe that. I guess it's just habit. Calling myself a dumb blonde. Acting like I'm helpless."

"Can I call you on it?"

Her brow furrows. "What do you mean?"

"Well, the first step to breaking a habit is noticing that you're doing something. You practice observing until, eventually, you catch yourself when you're about to do the thing and can stop yourself before actually doing it."

"Hmm. I guess I did that with smoking. But I always relapsed."

"I haven't seen you smoking lately."

"I guess that was the only good thing to come from being pregnant."

Not gonna touch that with a ten-foot pole, and thankfully, she explains without me having to.

"When I was pregnant, even smelling other people smoking made me upchuck." She shudders. "And that has stuck with me. Can't stand to be around smokers now."

"All I'm saying is, maybe I could help in this little way. Like if you're getting down on yourself, I can point it out."

"Without, like, making it obvious?"

"I could use a code word. Like 'don't forget to take out the trash.'"

"That's a little harsh. It's like you're calling me trash."

"How about, 'I thought you were on a diet'?"

"No way. I am not dealing with people calling me fat. I had enough of that from my momma. 'None of a lady's parts can be bigger than a gentleman's.' or 'Only whores and maids have muscles.'"

"Yikes. I knew your mother was mean, but damn. No wonder you eat like a bird."

She shrugs like it's no big deal. "I'm proud of my muscles. Look at these quads from standing all day." She squeezes a thigh in a way that sets my imagination down a path it shouldn't travel. Me squeezing them while they're hooked over my shoulders, for instance.

"Ford?"

I snap to attention when she flicks a finger to my forehead. "Ow."

"Earth to Ford? I said, what are these called?"

"Triceps?"

"Triceps, right. Feel this muscle," she says, still pointing to her flexed upper arm. "From wielding a blow dryer."

Since it's unlikely I'll be grasping her quads anytime soon, I'll take what I can get. "Nice. You've got some real definition there."

"It's been a bitch building my strength back up, that's for sure."

She's stronger than she thinks, on the inside and the outside. Just one more thing on the long list of things I wish I could get her to believe.

THE NEXT DAY, WHEN WHIT WALKS BY MY CART ON HER WAY TO set, she waggles her left hand in front of my nose.

"Where'd you get that?"

She doesn't stop moving, just turns her head to mouth, "Props department."

She shoots me the bird with the same hand, but she's also got a sassy grin on her face. I avoid pointing out that the men on the crew seem to give her a bit more space the minute that thing appears on her finger, glad that she took the suggestion with good humor.

When we come back from lunch, however, she's less than happy when I get Ronnie to call her over to my cart.

"What now? Do I need to wear a chastity belt too?" she hisses, obviously still hanging on to her irritation.

"I'm trying to do you a favor," I grumble.

"Maybe you should just pee a circle around me," she says, hands on hips, loud enough that Ronnie's jaw drops open. Thankfully, he turns on his heel and walks away before she continues. "You're like a dog in the manger. You don't want me but nobody else can have me either."

"That's not what I—" Breaking off, I switch gears. This is not the time nor the place to argue about our non-relationship. Pointing to the monitor, keeping my voice quiet, I say, "I called you over because I noticed something problematic on one of the actors."

She grimaces. "Really?"

I nod, as I pull up my recording from before lunch. "I mean, it might not be a big enough thing to worry about, but the lead actor has a splotch of what looks like lipstick on his collar. And I don't think that's because he's cheating on his girlfriend."

"How long has it been there?"

"I'm not sure. I just noticed it, though. I won't tell Susan."

"If I fucked up the most important thing is fixing it. Not hiding it."

"Sure, I just thought—"

She waves my words away. "I need to deal with this. Thanks for telling me."

From what I can tell, the shirt gets changed out without too much drama, but I hate the strained look on her face the rest of the day.

After we wrap, I head over to the makeup trailer but stop before I get too close when I see her and the key in a heated discussion. I can't hear what they're saying, but Whitney's doing a lot of nodding with her eyes cast down while Susan flaps her arms around.

Not sure if I made things worse rather than better, I just head back to my digs, deciding to check in on her before bed.

She shows up at my room before I can get to hers, and the minute I let her inside, she starts right in. "I'm trying so hard to be good. To be independent. To save money. To not need anybody. But all I want is—"

She breaks off with a groan and covers her face with her hands. I wait as long as I can stand before stepping closer. "Being independent and going it alone are two very different things."

She nods, dropping her hands, but then the nod turns into a slow head shake. "I don't think I know where the line is."

"It might take some practice, but I think you'll find it."

"How?"

Shoving my hands into my pockets to keep from pulling her close, I clear my throat. "Well, you could practice with me. If there's anything I can do that would make you feel less alone, you can ask me for it."

When her eyes lift to mine, her expression is full of doubt.

"Whit. It's always okay to ask for what you need. I want to strangle your mama right now for making you feel like it's not, but as your friend, I'm telling you it's okay."

She takes in a breath and lets it out. "Can I have a hug?"

I don't hesitate. My arms fly out from my sides. With a

sweet little laugh, she steps close, rests her cheek on my chest, and I wrap her in my arms. When her arms snake around my waist, I tell my dick to keep it PG, but it snaps back with a *Fuck you man, we've been waiting for years for this moment.*

Figuring I should be honest if I want her to be, I'm about to warn her I may have to step back when she presses her hips closer and leans her upper body back to say, "I want to feel your lips on my skin."

Afraid that my lizard brain is making things up, my mouth opens to ask if she just said what I think she did, but all that comes out is, "Whuh?"

Pushing her hair away on one side, she tips her head to the side, and points at a spot between the curve of her jaw and her ear. "Right there."

I have to clear my throat as well as my frontal lobe, but I'm not proceeding without her full understanding of the situation she's creating. "Whit, you got to know that my body is going to respond to this."

"If you're good with that then I am."

I've wanted to taste her honey-dipped skin longer than I can remember so my judgment may be faulty, but this feels like it could be what I've been hoping for. Her letting me in for real.

I don't let go of her. Nor do I rush. First, I breathe her in, and the musky sweet scent takes me right back to the moment I knew I wanted her. Smiling as I brush my lips behind her ear, I can't stop the chuckle that escapes.

She jerks her head away. "Are you laughing at me?"

"No darlin', I'm laughing at *me*. At fifteen-year-old Ford, the day he noticed you wearing a bra. At the fact that I've wanted to do that ever since."

"Since the tenth grade?"

"Pretty goofy, huh?"

I'm rewarded with the ghost of a genuine smile, and it

spurs me on to tease more feelings out of her. "You're one of the few people who knows what a goober I am, you know."

"Because all most girls see is a tall drink of water with perfect hair, a perfect face and a perfect body?"

Her gaze isn't exactly hungry as it roams over my parts, and that hurts somehow. Squashing that feeling, I counter with reason.

"I hope people focus on my accomplishments. Boss of my own crew before I turned thirty and all. But it sounds like you're just as guilty of objectifying me as you think I am of you."

She just lifts a shoulder, her gaze skating to the side. It suddenly occurs to me that while I've asked her to run off with me, twice, I've done nothing to make it clear how I feel about her.

No more talking, Ford. Time for showing.

My hand trembles right up to the moment my finger contacts her skin, but by the time I've turned her to face me again, every single cell in my body is on board.

"Can I kiss you, Whitney?" I ask, even as I lean in close, catching her nod of assent only moments before my lips land on hers.

It's not just our first kiss. It's *the* first kiss. Like every other kiss in my life was something else entirely. A peck, a graze, a simple meeting of lips.

This kiss is the one I've been waiting for. The doorway into a world my imagination didn't—couldn't—do justice.

She's as strong as she is soft. Fierce in a way that makes me wild. Makes me want to burrow inside and never leave. Want to fuse my every corner with her every curve. Our gears turning in perfect harmony.

I have to force myself to go slow. To hear each sharp intake of breath from her parted lips. When my teeth scrape the side of her neck. When my fingertips trace the curve of her waist. When my palms cup her round little butt cheeks.

Breath releases on moans that grow in intensity even as they fall in pitch. It takes all my self-control to keep from stripping her clothes away so I can feast on the sight of her. Stilling my hands, I brush featherlight kisses along her jaw until I reach her lips again. Like coming home. Nuzzling at the seam, I tease them apart. When she lets me in and takes my upper lip into her mouth, sucking it between her teeth, I'm the one moaning and gasping for breath.

And stepping away.

Her eyes blink open, dark with lust. "What?"

"If I don't stop now, I won't be able to stop at all, and we… I don't know what we are. I don't know if this is a good idea. We're working together, you're still married…"

I don't know if you're still fucked up in your head from whatever happened in that marriage.

She tips her head to the side and tucks her hands in her armpits, looking both world weary and vulnerable in equal measure. "Is this because of Dani and Violet?"

"Huh? What do you mean? I told you; I never had a thing for Vi. Or for Dani, for that matter."

She shakes her head. "I mean, don't you think they'll be mad? Worry that I'm not good for you?"

"If anything, I think it's the other way around. That I would be bad for you."

"No way," she scoffs.

"Way," I bat back, happy to get a grin out of her. "I'm a skirt-chasing Casanova."

"So? They all think I'm a dumb blonde and a slut." Her smile is rueful. "Sounds to me like we're made for each other."

"I do want you, Whit. I've always wanted you. Since I was fifteen years old, like I said. But it just feels wrong. Like you need my friendship more right now."

Before she can argue I add, "And the same for me."

She looks away, nodding silently, before picking up her

jacket and heading for the door. Before she leaves, she turns back to ask, "Back then. In high school. Why didn't you ever…?" She breaks off with a half shrug.

"Do anything about how I felt?"

She nods.

"Dang, Whitney. Why do you think? I was a gangly, pimple-faced gear head, while you had every jock in school after you. Not to mention the fact that your momma literally wrinkled her nose every time she saw me. I knew she thought an auto mechanic wasn't good enough for you."

Her pink lips press into a hard line, mumbling something that sounds like, "Turns out, my momma's a bitch."

On a roll, I continue. "I couldn't believe you ever spent time with me and Sully and Vi and Dani. You were so classy, and we're all rednecks."

She shakes her head slowly, her eyes never leaving mine. "I had to make up all kinds of reasons to be allowed to hang out with y'all, but it was worth it. It was the only time I could ever relax. And even though I was a jerk half the time, I knew y'all loved me, anyway."

"And we still do."

"Love me?"

I nod.

"Even if you don't *love* me, love me, it's okay."

I open my mouth to protest, to tell her I do, that I've always loved her, but she wags a finger back and forth in the air between us. "Don't say anything you'll regret later."

And then she disappears before I can.

THIRTEEN

Monday, 11/22 9:05 PM
SullyCallaway999: Ford, we're
all wondering what the heck is
going on out there.

DanielleGoodwin856: Yeah, you
guys have gone radio silent.
Meanwhile, Violet's going nutty
with the game plan for her baby
shower.

VioletCastingCarolina: I am not.

Ford_soundguy: Sorry, y'all.
It's been a bear of a job. Long
hours and all.

VioletCastingCarolina: You had
all weekend to respond to the
email.

Ford_soundguy: As far as I know,
we are both coming to Wallington
for the holiday and to your
shower, but I'll confirm ASAP.

FORD

THE NEXT TIME we get a relatively short day—that is, wrapping before sundown—I decide to run back to the motel. I always keep running gear on the trailer and the location's less than five miles out, so I get Ronnie to drive my truck back and I take off, needing to get my blood moving after a day of sitting on my ass behind my cart.

And needing to clear my head of a certain person in the makeup and hair department.

Some mixers like to be party central. One I worked for in LA even kept a hard drive on his cart that he'd loaded with just about every song imaginable. Whenever we had a long break, he'd take requests and blast the music. It kept people energized and happy during the mind-numbing changeovers, but I can't be that guy.

It's not just that I don't want people leaving coffee cups on my cart that'll inevitably spill on my equipment. I do my best to hide from the action because I am not what you'd call a social butterfly. I get my fill of human interaction even without having a ton of people hanging around my cart all day. Plus, I need quiet to do my job.

On this show, though, I find myself wishing the makeup and hair people *would* hang out near my cart. Hearing Whitney's laugh in the distance or catching a glimpse of her as she rushes to touch up an actor's face or a whiff of her sweet scent when she brushes by me under the meal tent just isn't enough.

To have her so close without actually having her close? It's killing me.

She hasn't been back to my room since I kissed her days ago, so obviously that was a mistake. Even though she said she wanted the kiss, she probably wasn't ready. Or I pushed for too much. Or not enough. One way or the other, I obviously screwed up.

They say that the third time's the charm, but that doesn't seem to be the case for me.

When I make myself sprint the last half mile and then power up the stairs to my room, I'm surprised to find the woman I've been obsessing over idling outside my door, like I conjured her with my thoughts. My smile is wide when I run up, even though I have to double over with my hands on my knees to catch my breath. But when I finally straighten and meet her eyes, she's not smiling back.

In fact, she looks as if she might have been crying, which has me placing a hand on her arm. Friendly, not intimate. "Hey, Whit. What's wrong?"

"Ugh. It's stupid." She digs around in her purse for a tissue and blows her nose before fanning her hand in the air. "You know what? I'm probably just hungry. I didn't have time to eat lunch today."

One hand still in contact with her, I pull my room key from my shoe and unlock the door. "Come in for a sec. I need water and you know I've got snacks. You can eat something before you hike all the way back to your room."

This gets an eye roll out of her, but she doesn't resist when I usher her inside.

I grab a couple of water bottles from the fridge, and after she takes one, I pull out the basket of goodies. "You can have my usual mix, or one of these."

"Wow. Very Martha Stewart of you," she says, gesturing at the way I've arranged the rows of dried fruit and nuts and protein bars.

"I'm not an animal." When this gets a grin out of her, I feel like I won the lottery, and when she takes a bag of peanuts and shakes a handful into her palm, I'm even happier.

After chasing the nuts with a swig of water, she says, "Kind of makes me want a Coca-Cola."

The memory of pouring a sack of peanuts into a frosty

bottle of Coke makes me think of summers at the beach when we were young. "I have a *can* of coke…"

She shakes her head. "Wouldn't be the same."

"Dang," I say. "Now I'm jonesing for that sweet and salty crunch."

"Nothing like it."

We're quiet for a few moments, as she gets calories in her and I re-hydrate. When she balls up the wrapper and looks around for the trash, I take it from her, the brush of her skin making me wish I weren't in sweaty running clothes.

"Would you want to hang out? Maybe watch a movie?" I ask.

She looks uncertain, but I barrel on. "I need a quick shower, but I can be done by the time you pick out a movie. There are some good ones on HBO right now, like *Runaway Bride*, or, uh…"

Realizing that it might hit too close to home I try to remember what else I saw on offer last I looked. "There's a cute kids movie called *Stuart Little*."

Dammit, now I've brought up kids, another sore subject. "Oh, there's a remake of *The Out of Towners* that looks hilarious. Goldie Hawn, Steve Martin, and John Cleese."

Pulling clean clothes from the drawer and backing toward the bathroom I add, "I'll even make popcorn," and then disappear before she can say no, hoping politeness will have her waiting for me if nothing else.

True to my word, I'm done in minutes. But when I return to the main room, she's not in the sitting area where I left her.

Instead, she's in my bed.

WHITNEY

The look on Ford's face when he comes back from the bathroom is priceless. But it also makes me mad. "What? You can watch movies in bed with Violet but not with me?"

The expressions that cross his face in response to this are harder to read. Before I can parse them out, he drags a hand down his face, erasing them.

Then I see what he's wearing. On most guys, a t-shirt with a Panavision logo and plain old gray sweats would be the opposite of sexy. But on this man... the fabric stretching across broad shoulders and defined pecs is just a prelude to the gathered cotton draped teasingly from his hips.

Today was a bad day. Not because I fucked anything up. In fact, Susan thanked me for staying on top of every mascara drip, every mussed hair. But I barely made it through listening to the scene we shot at the end of the day. At first, I thought I'd successfully blocked out the words. The way I would when my mother would start in on me.

I never said that. You're making it up like the liar you are.

You just don't know how to think, do you? You can't even make a simple decision.

But the minute I hauled out the last bag of trash from the trailer, I couldn't hold it together anymore. I had to rush to the honey wagon—ironically named, as portable toilets draw flies like honey—where I sat on the toilet sobbing. By the time I'd let it all spill and fixed my own makeup, I barely caught the last crew shuttle back to the motel. But when I found myself knocking on Ford's door, he didn't answer.

The thing is, I truly don't know why I'm so upset. It's not like I have to live with my parents anymore.

The mattress dips next to me. "Hey, hey," Ford croons. "What'd I do?"

His thumb swipes a featherlight caress across my cheek, but I bat it away before it can comfort me.

"You know Vi and I were never a thing, right?" he says. "She just had cable, and we didn't. Plus, we liked all the same movies."

"But you slept there," I say, hating how whiny my voice sounds.

"Not on purpose. Conked out halfway through some film. It was always so frustrating."

"Because you wanted more?"

"More movie, yes. More of Violet, no."

"But she's beautiful. And good. And smart."

"Sure, I guess she's all those things. But I just never felt that way about her."

When I open my eyes to read his, he's on his side, head propped on a hand to face me. My gaze goes right to the gap between his shirt and waistband, but I force them back to his eyes, which are dancing with something that looks an awful lot like… glee.

I shove him. Hard. But he doesn't move. "Are you laughing at me?"

His smile widens and his dimples deepen into caverns. "Nah. I just like that you're jealous."

"Am not." This time when I shove him, he rolls onto his back, pulling me on top of him, right onto one very hard, very large, erection.

His palm spreads over my lower back, pressing me into him. "I never had one of these when I was in bed with Violet."

His pupils have blown to where his sky-blue irises are just a thin ring around them. "Swear it," I whisper.

"I swear. On my DAT machine."

Even though I know the Digital Audio Recorder is the piece of sound equipment he can't function without, my heart's pounding and my head's full of this-is-a-bad-idea, as I reach up to trace the edge of his jaw. For one long moment, I think he's going to kiss me, but then he groans and scoots out from under me.

"Where are you going?" I point at the tent in his sweats. "I can see that you're turned on, dummy."

Rolling onto his belly, he turns just his head to face me. "I am. I'm always turned on around you. But you were upset when you came over. Tell me why, and we can, uh, talk about… other stuff."

I poke him in the side, but he just scoots away. "No touching before talking."

Groaning, I roll onto my back and flop a hand over my eyes. "Forget it. Let's just watch a movie."

He takes one of my hands and gently tucks it under his arms and over his heart. "Tell me what happened."

I shrug. "It's dumb."

"Hey." He squeezes my hand. "This is me pointing out that habit of yours."

"I said *it's* dumb, not *I'm* dumb."

"Just tell me," he says, his voice a low growl that has me wishing I were still on top of him so I could feel the vibrations on my skin.

"Fine," I say, letting the word ride a dramatic sigh, even for me. "The scene at the end of the day was tough."

"What was that about again?"

"How can you forget?" My eyes whip to his face again. *Is he making fun of me?* "The things her father was saying to her? Picking her apart bit by bit? It was just so…" *Familiar*, is what it was, but I can't say that, so I go with, "Ugly."

"Right," he nods, sounding sympathetic. "She was crying. That was a lot of work for you. Keeping the makeup straight."

"Yeah, that was a lot." Remembering the awful words the male actor spewed, my throat aches all over again. "But it was the things he was saying. It was all so mean and hurtful."

He squeezes my hand. "You know they're just acting, right? And it's a romance, not a Shakespearean tragedy."

I sit up, too agitated to be still. "This story is no romance. They don't have a happy ending. The girl dies."

His eyebrows come together, and he stares at the ceiling. "She does?"

"Are you for real right now? I know you read the script. You're too well-prepared not to."

His spine straightens. "Of course, I read the script. And I read all the new pages every day. I can tell you how many actors are in each scene, the page count and the location, and what the background sound issues are going to be."

I send him my best disbelieving look. "But you can't remember how the movie ends."

"No need to waste brain cells on a silly thing like the plot."

Instead of gracing this with an answer, I hug my knees to my chest, wondering how I got from an almost kiss to an argument about work habits. Wondering why I opened up this can of worms.

"Hey," he says, nudging my shoulder. "Are you saying that the scene brought up something for you? Like, personally?"

You mean like some of his lines were word-for-word things my mother has said to me?

"No. I mean... I don't know." Scrambling, because we don't talk about things said in our home, I go for a more general approach. "Maybe I was just, like, letting it all in too much and it wore me out."

"Why?"

"Why is it exhausting?"

"No. Why would you do that to yourself?"

"It's not like I can control my emotional responses."

"That sounds awful."

The look on his face is so horrified that I have to laugh. "I guess you're saying you don't feel what the actors are feeling?"

"God, no," he says, looking even more alarmed. "I don't even like to feel my own feelings. I mean, it's probably not healthy. I hear it's good to feel things."

Pushing all the things I've managed to not feel over the years back down where they belong, I give him a sly smile. "And now we're back where we started. There are some things I bet you like to feel."

He squeezes his eyes shut and withdraws his hand. "Whit, we talked about this. I don't want to be your rebound or a quick lay. I *do* want to be a good friend."

Needing a distraction, needing closeness and comfort, just all over needy, I drag a fingernail along his wrist. "We could be friends with benefits. Isn't that a thing?"

He snorts out a strangled laugh. "I doubt it's a thing that actually works."

"What if we had rules?"

"Like what rules?"

"Well, how about, what happens here"—I draw a triangle between the two of us and the door—"Stays here. No telling anyone else."

He nods slowly, his eyes never leaving mine. "That makes sense. We both want to keep things professional. Speaking of which, if being together is causing any kind of problem at work—"

I hold up a hand. "It'll be over, I get it."

He shakes his head. "No, no. I was going to say, we talk about it. Figure it out."

"Oh," I say, a little thrown. "I figured because your career is so important..."

"Yours is too, isn't it?" he asks, and I suddenly realize it is. Not just to make money, but because it makes me feel good.

"It is."

"Anyway," he says with an eye roll, "I've made more mistakes since we kissed than I've made all year."

"Oh," I say, deflating. "Isn't that a—"

"What I mean," he says, interrupting me by taking my hand. "Is that I'm distracted wondering if and when I'd get to do more."

"Ohhh," is all I'm able to say at the moment because the word *more* releases an entire flock of butterflies in my belly, each and every one of them wanting more too.

Squeezing my hand, he adds, "Above all, we promise to stay friends, no matter what."

My friends have always been my lifeline, so I add, "Exactly. We don't sacrifice friendship—ours or with the rest of the gang—for... you know."

"And if either one of us wants out of"—he draws the line between us like I did—"*you know*, then we stop. No questions asked."

"Right."

His smile is wicked as he releases my hand to tuck a lock of hair behind my ear. "And what exactly do you mean by *you know*?"

Eyes closed, my attention on his touch, now moving from behind my ear, to the back of my neck, words fail me again. "Y-you know. Uh, sex things."

"And if there's a *sex thing* you don't want to do, you'll tell me?"

One finger trailing over my shoulder to my waist is setting my pants on fire. Not even sure if I can handle more, I hold out my hand for a shake. "I will if you will."

"I will if you will," he repeats.

When his hand leaves my hip to take my hand, I'm relieved and devastated in equal measure. Then his eyes drop to my lips and that hand slips behind my neck again, fingers sliding through my hair. He eases me closer, until we're breathing each other's air, until I can feel the heat of him.

"Thank god," he breathes. "I've been wanting to kiss you again so bad, I can barely tie my shoes, let alone keep up with the log sheets."

I lever back slightly, so I can meet his gaze. A lot of emotion flits across this face for a guy that says he doesn't feel things. Desire, longing, and finally, hope have me closing the distance between us. Easing out of his grip, I place a hand on each side of his face, and my lips find his.

And just like the first time we kissed—a kiss that's been on replay in the back of my mind for days—I am over-whelmed by what I get in return. Talk about *more.* Every touch demands more. Everything our mouths are doing is more. The rest of my body wants in on all of it. I kneel up on the bed, needing to press closer, feel more of him.

But when I reach for the waistband of his sweats so that I can caress the part of him I've been dreaming about since it pressed against my belly a week ago, he takes my hand and brings it to his lips. "You don't have to do that. I just want to… feel you."

I'm a good actress when I want to be. Not a full on *When Harry Met Sally* at the deli performance, mind you. That'd just be exhausting. Most guys will buy a few whimpers and shud-ders. But the fact is, I've faked an orgasm so many times that I'm not rightly sure if I've ever had a real one.

When Ford first showed up last week, I tried to push him for sex, so he'd learn, once and for all, that I'm not worth the effort. If any guy could see through my act, it'd be him. When he couldn't make me sigh and shiver with pleasure for real, he'd finally give up on me.

But now, instead of the usual feelings I experience when a guy touches me—my own special cocktail of disgust blended with self-loathing and garnished with dread—Ford's hands have me instinctively leaning in for more. Chasing a feeling I truly didn't think I was capable of.

Real-life, actual desire.

When his tongue darts into the corner of my mouth for a taste, instead of having to suppress a gag, my lips close around it, pull it deeper inside, which has my sex squeezing with need.

The only time those walls ever squeezed anything was when I had a tampon that needed changing, or my bladder was about to bust, and I needed to hang on tight until I could get to a bathroom. But now, they want a very specific organ to hang onto.

Before I know it, my heart rate is up, I'm breathless, and my skin feels weird. Almost like I have a fever. I try to move away but end up grabbing onto his shirt and pulling him with me, so that we end up sprawled in a tangle across his bed.

And he laughs. Not at me. But this delighted, silly laugh.

Like he's having fun.

This is a mistake. It's going to totally backfire. Because if he kisses me one more time, I'm going to fall even further for him. And if it doesn't work out, what happens then?

I can't lose him.

But when I open my mouth to say so, he captures it. And then my body—my stupid, needy, hungry body—does an override on my brain and takes over.

As easy as slipping into the waves on a perfect beach day, my hands push his t-shirt up so they can skate over soft skin covering taut muscles. When he reaches back to pull the shirt all the way off, my eyes roam greedily over the hills and valleys of his chest and shoulders. Before I know it, my jeans and sweater are gone, leaving me in a plain white Jockey for Her cotton bra and hip-huggers. I can no longer afford fancy lingerie, but that doesn't seem to matter to Ford.

He looks like he wants to have me for dessert.

It's only when his hungry gaze lingers on my abdomen, that I remember the scar. Covering it, I whisper, "Don't look," and try to pull him up my body, so he'll just move on to the business at hand. When he resists, I realize maybe I will get what I originally intended. He might not get bored or frustrated with my lack of response, but he could be disgusted. Disappointed. Reminded that I can no longer have children.

He lifts my hand away from the scar to study it. "Does it hurt?"

"Not anymore."

When his finger traces the puckered skin, he frowns, and I hate that I still want him to want me. Because now it's definitely over. I'm so lost in that circle of hell that he's got me flipped over so I'm straddling him before I know what's happening.

"What are you doing?"

I haven't had intercourse with a ton of men. I wasn't lying when I told Ford that most guys were good with a blow job and a see ya later. Hardy's position of choice was missionary, which I was fine with. Less work for me.

I'm not sure what I'm supposed to do sitting here on top.

"I want to know what turns you on," Ford says softly.

I reach behind me to find his cock, still erect. "Uh, don't you want to fuck me?"

"I do. I'm very much looking forward to being buried deep inside you. To feeling your walls hug me the way your thighs are hugging my hips. But right now—" He reaches behind my back and unhooks my bra before easing the straps over my shoulders and down my arms. "I want to see you."

Unnerved by all the ways his touch makes me feel, I take him by the wrists and place his palms over my breasts, his large hands dwarfing the piteous little things. "I know they're small."

Instead of pinching and kneading like I'm biscuit dough, his thumbs circle tantalizingly. "They're perfect."

"There you go again. I'm not perfect." I roll my eyes, but even as I struggle to hang onto sense, my nipples have a dirty conversation with my cunt about all the things they want done to them by these hands.

"Do you not like them?" His voice is hushed, gentle.

"They're fine. I kind of liked it when I was pregnant because they got bigger." I look down at them, cupped by his hands like he's my bra. "I swear they shrank after I lost the baby."

He winces.

"Sorry if that turns you off," I add, lifting my chin in challenge, because I'm actually not sorry.

He growls, pulling my torso down so that I'm stretched on top of him, and then runs his hand over my hair and back like I'm a cat. "Listen, if you just want to lie here and snuggle with me, I'm good with that. If you don't feel up to having sex, that is."

Turning my head to the side, so my cheek rests over his hammering heart, I let out a sigh. "I don't understand you. What do you want from me?"

His arms wrap around me, and I've never felt so... held.

"I just want you. That's all, Whit. Just you."

WE DON'T END UP HAVING SEX AND HE STILL DOESN'T LET ME give him a blow job. Which has me worried that the man is suffering from some serious blue balls. But when I wake up next to him, having slept more deeply and soundly than I have since, well, ever, he's got a shit-eating grin on his face, even in sleep.

I have a much earlier call than he does, and he was smart enough to set an alarm for me last night, but I'm up before it goes off. Resetting it for a half hour before his call—how he can get ready for work in under thirty minutes is beyond me —I throw on my clothes and hustle back to my room in the pre-dawn light.

And in the shower, I do something new. I touch myself

while thinking about him. When I come, my heart pounding and my sex clenching, I'm determined that the next time it happens, it'll be around him.

FOURTEEN

Subj: Friends or Seinfeld?
Date: 11/23/1999 11:01:01 PM
From: VioletCastingCarolina
To: makeupchick1200, Ford_soundguy, Sully-
Callaway999, DanielleGoodwin856

I've been wondering: are we more like the
group of pals on Friends, or the ones on
Seinfeld?

Subj: RE: Friends or Seinfeld?
Date: 11/23/1999 11:24:21 PM
From: DanielleGoodwin856
(Reply All)

I thought women in their third trimester
went to bed early. What are you doing up?

Subj: RE: RE: Friends or Seinfeld?
Date: 11/23/1999 11:36:01 PM
From: VioletCastingCarolina
(Reply All)

Between my bladder and the heartburn, I can hardly sleep.
Why is no one answering my question?

Subj: RE: RE: RE: Friends or Seinfeld?
Date: 11/23/1999 11:57:35 PM
From: SullyCallaway999
(Reply All)

'Cause we're no more like those TV friends than we are like the characters on Lawson's Reach. Even though they're supposedly based on us. Though maybe not so much anymore, since the show runner stopped talking to Ford's brother.
And anyway, your math is off. There are 4 friends on Seinfeld and 6 on Friends, while there are 5 of us.

Subj: RE: RE: RE: RE: Friends or Seinfeld?
Date: 11/24/1999 10:37:45 AM
From: VioletCastingCarolina
(Reply All)

You're being too literal, Sully. I meant the vibe. And of course, we're not like the

Lawson's Reach kids. We are so much more mature than them. I think I was more mature even when I was in high school.

I'm thinking Friends. But thank goodness none of us are like Ross and Rachel. Too much damn drama!

Subj: RE: RE: RE: RE: RE: Friends or Seinfeld?
Date: 11/24/1999 1:23:24 PM
From: DanielleGoodwin856
(Reply All)

Don't forget Monica and Chandler. They're a thing now. But I think they have a chance to stay together long-term.

Do Nate and Luke and Helen count in this comparison?

And don't forget, we have Lawson's Reach writers George and Tina mining our adventures for plot lines. Not to mention Luke's buddy Max. It's dangerous to be friends with writers, y'all.

I guess Ford and Whitney are working too hard to check email…

Subj: RE: RE: RE: RE: RE: RE: Friends or Seinfeld?
Date: 11/24/1999 1:55:03 PM
From: VioletCastingCarolina
(Reply All)

Yeah! I haven't even heard if they're coming to my baby shower.

Subj: RE: RE: RE: RE: RE: RE: RE: Friends or Seinfeld?
Date: 11/24/1999 7:25:45 PM
From: Ford_soundguy
(Reply All)

Sorry about that Vi. We are coming but we probably won't get into town until Thursday afternoon. We'll be working late the day before the holiday. Definitely be there for Friday though so this is my official RSVP and I guess Whitney's as well.

Subj: RE: RE: RE: RE: RE: RE: RE: RE: Friends or Seinfeld?
Date: 11/24/1999 7:57:05 PM
From: makeupchick1200
(Reply All)

Yes, I will be there, Violet. My apologies for being tardy with my reply. This shoot is keeping me busy!
Sorry to hear about the heartburn. That's a bummer. Maybe it'll get better.
Love,
Whitney

FORD

IT PROBABLY WASN'T a good idea to read the emails from Vi and Sully and Dani after work, because now it's like they're here, witness to the hard-on I've had since last night, only temporarily relieved by jacking off in the shower. But not even the specters of nosy friends are going to deter me tonight. The only thing that'll keep me from doing my damnedest to have Whitney panting my name in pleasure is if she doesn't show up.

An hour after wrap, I've had a snack and a beer, I've showered, and I'm still waiting for her.

Should I call her room?

Go check on her?

Or take the hint and accept that she regrets the deal we made last night?

I can't just let her go this time around. I'm not going to assume she knows how I feel, and I'm not going to give up without a fight. Shrugging on my jacket, I grab a handful of condoms from my nightstand drawer and practically run to her room.

But when I get there, I hesitate.

My friends' words echo in my ear, damn them. *What she needs right now is friends, not someone who can't decide if he wants to risk his heart.*

What am I doing?

Am I pushing for intimacy when I should give her space?

Are we like Ross and Rachel? Or Chandler and Monica?

If I'm honest, the answers to these questions are I have no idea, yes, and probably the worst of both. So instead of knocking, I duck under my hoodie and force myself to head back to my room with my tail between my legs.

"Ford? Is that you?"

I haven't made it farther than two doors away, but her voice would have me turning around if she were calling across a football field. "Yeah. I came up to see—uh, well, I wasn't sure if, well, you wanted to, uh…"

She leans out and looks up and down the breezeway, I guess to check and see if anyone from the crew is around, and then one corner of her mouth curves up. "If I wanted to… *you know*?"

Despite the autumn chill, my face is so hot it could melt an iceberg. "Yeah."

"Do you want to come in?" she asks.

"If you want me to."

Hands on hips, she says, "What happened to the rules? Didn't I promise to tell you if I wanted out?"

I wince. "Guess it's harder to play by the rules than I thought."

She waves a hand. "Get in here. Don't worry, I cleaned up."

Still not sure if I'm doing the right thing, I obey her order, but when I step inside, I stop short. It's like a different hotel room. The bed's made, and there isn't a stitch of clothing or trash on the floor. I open the door and pointedly look at the number on it. "Huh."

"What?"

"Wasn't sure it was the same room."

Groaning, she pushes me all the way inside and closes the door behind me. "Very funny."

"You didn't straighten up for me, did you?"

Tipping her head to the side and pursing her lips, making me want to kiss her, she takes a beat before answering. "Honestly, I did it for me. I can't think straight when my place is a mess."

"I didn't know you knew how to clean."

She whacks me on the arm. "I worked as a chambermaid one entire summer, remember?"

"What I remember is that Violet almost fired you about ten times."

"Pfft," she says, waving an arm. "Do you want anything? I also went to the store and stocked up."

"I do want something. But it's not something you can get at the Piggly Wiggly."

"Well, it's a good thing I cleaned up everywhere then," she says with a sly smile.

"Everywhere?"

She shrugs one shoulder. "Things needed a bit of trimming."

"Perhaps I should check your work." Stepping closer, I hook a finger inside her waistband, to find skin a thousand times softer than the velour of her fancy sweats.

When her hands reach for my shoulders, I realize she's practically on tiptoe. Our height difference means I've got to stoop, or she's got to strain to reach me. Using that as an excuse, I scoop her up in my arms. Two steps and we're faced with two choices.

"Bed or sofa?"

She tips her head to the left. "Bed, please."

When I toss her onto it, she bounces, giggling.

"It's good to hear you laugh," I say, shucking off my shoes.

She does the same, as her eyes rove over my body. "Take off your shirt, Ford."

Reaching back, I pull the t-shirt over my head and toss it away. When I step to the end of the bed, she reaches for my pecs. My nipples harden as her fingernails scrape over them.

Balancing a knee on the bed, I tangle one hand in her soft hair, and trace her lips with the thumb of the other. Her hands skim up and down my sides and she angles her neck to give me access.

"I don't think I could ever get enough of you," I whisper between kisses.

"Shhh," she says. "Don't think about that."

Not sure what *that* is, I slide my hands under her blouse.

As her skin ripples beneath my fingers, only the knowledge that she'd probably make me sew it back together keeps me from ripping the damn shirt open. Thankfully, she makes quick work of the tiny buttons, and my patience is rewarded when she shrugs out of it.

Just like last night, a simple cotton bra cups her breasts, the white fabric with a start contrast to her golden skin. Even though I've seen her in a bikini more times than I can count, this is different somehow. I'd always imagined Whitney in lace and satin, but the unfussy Jockeys are really the perfect package for her classic beauty, so when she reaches behind her back like she's going to take it off, I stop her. "Hang on."

A wrinkle appears between perfectly shaped brows. "You want to stop? Again?"

Taking her hand, I shake my head. "I just want to enjoy this view before I get another."

She lifts her chin. "I'm ready for a new vista myself. How 'bout you lose those pants?"

"As you wish," I say, echoing her laugh as I remember watching *The Princess Bride* with her and the gang. Before thoughts of what the gang would think about what we're about to do can intrude, however, I shimmy out of my jeans and dive onto the bed, making it bounce.

By the time I turn over, she's lost her sweats, and is lying on her side. Mirroring her, propped up on one hand, I stroke my way from shoulder to waist and then back up to trail a finger across the swell of a breast.

I still can't quite believe I'm finally getting to do this. In fact, I feel more like that shy, gangly teenager than a guy who's slept with more women than he'd like to admit. Somehow, having Whitney in my bed makes it all new again.

"Are you gonna kiss me or what?" she asks, bringing me back to the present.

"And what, is what I'm thinking," I grumble, pulling her flush so we're skin to skin except for our skivvies.

"I don't even know what that me—" she begins, but I stop her words with my mouth.

And just like the last two times, when our mouths meet, I'm knocked sideways.

When she squeaks, I break this kiss.

"Why'd you stop?" she asks, breathless.

"I thought I was hurting you."

"You have to stop treating me like I'm weak and breakable, Ford. I may be small, but I'm tough as nails when I need to be."

"I know, I just—" I falter, because that's exactly what I have been doing.

"And let me tell you, mister," she continues, tapping on my sternum, "When you eat the right diet, your nails can be lethal weapons. Or at least cause some painful damage."

"Are you talking about fingernails?"

"Duh."

"You know that saying 'tough as nails' is about the other kind of nails, though, right?"

"What other kind of nails?"

"The ones you use to build stuff. With a hammer?"

"You don't know that's what they're talking about," she says, with a grin that has me flipping her over to kiss her again. And again, lust is a freight train, its power surging through my bloodstream, demanding that I taste, touch, smell —fucking memorize—every millimeter of this body. The need to savor wars with the urge to rush. I mean, for all I know this could end any time.

After all, you could argue that I'm breaking the rules. Not exactly being honest. About why I took this job.

She suddenly breaks the kiss, her breath ragged. "Full disclosure?"

Dang. Can she read my mind?

"Y-yeah, of course," I force out, scrambling to frame our friends' worries in a way that won't make her feel like we underestimate her. Think she's fragile and breakable, like she said.

Circling my nipple, her sculpted fingernail has it pebbling instantly. "I made myself come in the shower this morning. Thinking about you."

Her words erase all worries like a shaken Etch-a-Sketch. "What a coincidence. I did the same."

This time, she climbs on top of me. Her hands land on either side of my head, her hair framing her face and brushing my chest as she rubs her center over my erection.

"I'd like to see a replay of that shower action," I say, palming her butt cheeks and pulling her even closer.

Her cheeks pink up and her nose wrinkles. "Really?"

"Yes, really."

"But what will you do?" she asks, seeming to truly not get how sexy she is.

"For starters, watching you get yourself off sounds hot as fucking hell. But I can also help."

"Ohh," she says, her chest reddening now too.

"Kneel up." As she rises, I drag her shorts down her thighs, but when she tries to lift one leg to extract it, she falls onto my chest, making me grunt.

"Oops," she says, wriggling as she scoots the rest of the way out of her underwear, making my own even tighter.

"You are a naughty girl," I whisper in her ear.

"Do I get a spanking for that?"

Instead of answering, I give her ass a quick slap, which just makes her giggle. Palming her lower back, I unclasp her bra before shimmying out of my boxers, all while staying in contact with her.

"Now sit on top of me again."

She salutes me, but her sassy "Yes, sir" turns into a groan when I slide my hands to her hips and arrange her so that her center rides the side of my cock.

"Use my dick to rub your clit."

Her eyes widen even as her pupils dilate further but she does as I say. Grinding up into her, my shaft flanked by the folds of her pussy, I give her other ass cheek a slap.

"Ford," she gasps.

"Okay?"

"So okay."

My hands roam, mapping curves lusher than you'd imagine considering her size. Soft as silk breasts that fill my palms, hips that flare from a tiny waist, and her well-earned arm and leg muscles are a package I want to rip open every day of my life. The little noises she makes in response to my touch and to the stroke of my cock get my engine revving. The way her face tightens as she gets close, and then the surprised little scream as she falls over the edge—my pistons are more than ready to go.

"I want to be inside you when you do that again." My voice hoarse with need, I roll her off of me and dive for my jeans.

"Where are you going?"

"Getting protection."

"I can't get pregnant, you know. And I haven't been with anyone since the hospital where I was pronounced free of any STDs."

Why she'd be worried about those when she's married, I don't want to think about right now.

"I haven't been with anyone since the last time I got tested." Dropping the string of condoms, my greedy hands return to her hips. "Do you want me inside you?"

She bites her lower lip and looks over at her dresser drawer.

"It's okay. We don't have to," I reassure her, even though it'll mean I'll be the one jacking off next.

"No, I just—I'm going to need help. Lube." Her cheeks flush, but this looks more like embarrassment than desire. "Because of the surgery, I'm a little, uh, dry."

Hugging her to me, I whisper in her ear. "I got you covered. Flavored and unflavored." Grabbing my jeans again, I pull two sample packets from a pocket and waggle my eyebrows. "I'm gonna start with the flavored."

The eyebrows get her laughing, the squeeze of liquid has her shuddering, but my tongue spreading the lube between the folds of her cleft has her uttering my name in the most delicious way. My fingers tease her opening, play through her trimmed curls before stroking inside as I lick and suck at the sensitive bud underneath. Her hips lift off of the bed so suddenly, I have to dodge out of the way.

"Sorry!" she gasps.

"Uh-uh. I love how responsive you are," I say, using my shoulders to push her back down to the bed.

"I want you inside me."

I give her an extra kiss before replacing my fingers with the head of my cock. "I want to go slow," I say, my voice hoarse, "but I'm not sure if I can."

"Don't—I mean, do, go fast." She may have lost the ability to form a sentence, but her body speaks loud and clear, her hips thrusting up to meet me, obliterating my control. When I thrust inside until my balls hit her ass, she releases a most unladylike squeak, and I'm grinning as hard as I'm pounding.

Her heels press into my ass as I ease out and slide in, over and over, focused on the friction, the heat, the slick of the lube. She meets me thrust for thrust, and when the walls of her pussy clench around me, I'm gone, fused with her as I spill, lost in her as she hugs me inside and out.

FIFTEEN

```
Subj: Holiday Schedule
Date: 11/24/1999 9:05:09 AM
From: LoveLost_production_office
To: makeupchick1200
```

Please let your leads know if you plan to stay at the motel over Thanksgiving so the staff can plan accordingly.

WHITNEY

PILLOW TALK. I truly thought it just happened in movies and books. But it's become the favorite part of my day. Even more than the sex—or the lovemaking, as Ford insists on calling it—which is rocking my world in all the best ways.

I don't want to sugarcoat anything with this man. I was raised to hide everything from the fact that I actually perspired to the mean things my momma said to me, but I want Ford to know every little thing about me so that he knows exactly what he's getting into.

One night, after what for us is a quickie, meaning that I

only come twice, he gets this serious look on his face. "I know we've both been with a lot of people—"

Interrupting him, I cut him off at the serious pass, determined to keep things light. "Ford Fischer. Are you calling me a slut?"

His face reddens adorably. "No, I, uh—"

"You know what? You can. If I can."

"Call me a slut?" he chokes out.

"Yeah. 'Cause we both kind of are. Sluts."

His look of horror shifts to a devilish grin. "In a good way?"

"In a, we were doing the best we could way."

"Huh," he says, like I've said something that really made him think. "And now?"

"Now it's different."

He nods slowly. "It is different."

"Yeah?"

"Yep." He pulls me on top of him, where I can feel an erection at work, even though he just blew to kingdom come ten minutes ago. "For me, this is the first time I've ever been with someone I love."

My heart races at his use of the L word. But it's a fight-or-flight kind of alert because that's not our deal. "You mean, love like you love Dani and Vi. And Sully."

"Well, yeah. Someone who knows what a jackass I can be and loves me back, anyway."

"Someone who'll drop everything to take you to the hospital."

"Or even who can make me laugh. At myself." Before I can add to the list, he says, "But it's also an admiring kind of love. For a woman who never gave up on herself even though a couple assholes did their best to shove her into a little box and put her on a shelf."

I should object, but there's truth to what he's saying.

"Plus, there's the way you make everything better." His

hands stroke down my back, which soothes my nerves even though I know I shouldn't relax. "Look better, taste better. The way you make me feel, like every inch of skin needs to be in contact with you. Inside and out. To the point that I can't tell where I end, and you begin. But—"

And there it is. The B word. Killer of the L word. It hurts, but I'm not gonna let it kill me, so I keep my tone light even as my heart plummets. "There is always a 'but.'"

"But. I'm afraid."

His expression says he's serious, but what does Ford have to be afraid of? "Of me and my tough nails?"

"Of *me*. Fucking up. Running away again. Losing you. Again."

Heart in my throat, knowing I shouldn't, I whisper, "You never lost me, Ford. You just never really had me."

"Do I now?"

Instead of answering, I ask another question. "Tell me the truth. Is the threat of losing me the reason you thought this was a bad idea?"

He opens his mouth, but before saying anything, he closes it and turns his face toward the ceiling. "I don't want to just agree. I mean, yes. I didn't want to repeat the past and strike out a third time with you."

When he doesn't continue, I say softly, "That makes sense."

Finally, he turns to face me again. "But I also didn't want to push you before you'd recovered from…"

Again, he leaves it hanging. "You mean from the hysterectomy?"

"Well, yeah, of course. But I imagine you'd tell me if anything hurt because of that." All the muscles of his face squeeze together like he's struggling with something and then he blows a breath past his lips, like a horse. "I don't know what I'm saying."

He seems truly disturbed, so I do what he did for me the

other night. After snuggling up next to him, I take his hand and cradle it under my chin.

"Is it that you want more than this friends-with-benefits deal we have going on?'

His eyes pop open, but they're full of something other than recognition. Guilt, maybe. "It's okay if you do. I'm just not sure I can do more right now."

Looking relieved, he turns to face me. "I can be patient. You're still married. But I'm not going to pretend I don't want you. All of you. The good, the bad, and the ugly."

Needing to lighten things before my heart makes me say or do something stupid, I poke him in the side. "Did you just say I was ugly, Ford Fischer?"

Rolling over me, pinning me to the mattress in the most delicious way, he grins. "We've all got ugly in us and on us, Whitney Moore."

I give him my most imperious look. The one you wear when you're the princess in a parade. "If you do, I haven't seen it. At least since you stopped trying to grow that awful mustache in tenth grade."

"I loved that mustache!"

I just shake my head.

Pulling me flush so I can feel that he's hard again, he dips his head to whisper in my ear. "Well, keep an eye out. I'm sure you'll find something."

I doubt I will, because as far as I can tell, he is the perfect man. But just as his lips lower to kiss me, and I hug him close, he passes gas.

Gasping, I pull back. "Ford Fischer. You farted!"

He drops his forehead to my sternum briefly, but when he lifts it again, he's laughing. "It's true, I admit it. I occasionally let one rip. Even at the most inopportune moments, obviously."

I narrow my eyes at him. "Sully used to say you were

legendary on boy scout camping trips. I always thought he meant your fire-building or tent-making skills."

"Nope. It was my tent-*filling* skills if you know what I mean."

"Yuck!"

"Don't worry. Pretty sure that had something to do with the food we were eating. However"—he waggles his eyebrows —"now you have to tell me one of your imperfections."

"How do you know I have more than one?"

"Because you may be perfect for me, Whitney Moore, but you're still human."

The words *perfect for me* make my heart squeeze dangerously, so I go for an easy lob. "You know mine. I'm pretty much your typical dumb blonde. Vain, venal, vacuous—"

"Again, with saying you're dumb? When you're spouting SAT words? Nuh-uh." He shakes his head. "I want to hear something real. Not shit your parents told you."

I smile sweetly even as I strain to vacate my mother from my head. "Wouldn't they know me best?"

His frown takes over his entire face. "I don't think they know you at all. I think they had an idea of the girl they wanted and did their best to stuff you into that mold."

When I say nothing, he rolls me back on top and gives my fanny a smack. "So come on. Give it up. Tell me an ugly. I can take it."

I'm definitely in trouble here, because right now, the way he's looking at me, his face full of delight, and fun, and challenge, I'd do anything to hang on to him. Despite all that, or because of it, who knows, I go for the gold. "If I tell you, do you promise to keep it a secret?"

He snorts. "Like my farts are a secret?"

"No. Like a real secret." *Like this thing between us has to be and probably always will be*, echoes in my head, but I push that away, keeping my brows up, expectant.

After studying me for a long moment, making me wonder if he knows more about my secrets than I'd thought, he says, "Okay. Secret."

I hold up my pinky until he hooks it with his. "Pinky swear."

"Pinky swear," he repeats, nodding solemnly.

"Okay. I have an evil chin hair."

"A what?"

I have to stifle a giggle at the perplexed look on his face, but I keep my expression serious as I point to the left side of my chin. "A wiry little hair that keeps growing back no matter how many times I pluck her. From this scar. From the time I—"

"Fell off your bike in first grade."

"You remember that?"

"Hell, yeah. There was a lot of blood." He levers up a bit, squinting. "I don't see any chin hairs."

I rub the spot, the way I always do, despite the fact that my momma used to pinch me for touching my face. "That's because the first thing I do every morning is check and pull her out if she's grown in overnight. It is amazing how big a hair can get in eight hours."

His slow nod turns into a shake of his head. "Damn, this might be a deal breaker."

Before I can sputter out an objection, though, he's tickling me, and then kissing me, and then making love to me until I forget why any of this could ever be a bad idea.

<h1>SIXTEEN</h1>

Wednesday, 11/24 8:05 PM

DanielleGoodwin856: Ford, are you sure nothing's going on between you and Whitney?

VioletCastingCarolina: I believe we agreed on no extra-curriculars.

SullyCallaway999: Normally, I would tell these two to stand down, but this is important. You promised to keep things friends-only.

Ford_soundguy: You think I have time for any of that? We are working over here. Y'all could make a preacher cuss the way you stick your damn noses in.

FORD

YOU READ ABOUT HOW, when you love someone, sex is something special, but I never really believed it.

Until now.

And it's not just the actual intercourse, though that's incredible. When Whitney touches me, it's like it goes deeper, reaching past my skin and directly to the core of me. As a result, I want to be close to her all the time, but when I am, it's torture to not touch her.

It's getting hard to keep the secret on set. Pun intended.

Thanksgiving is tomorrow, and I *really* don't know how I'll hide my rapidly developing feelings for her when we go back to Wallington. When we're with people who know us both so well, they can practically read our minds. With all this banging around in my head as we're snuggled side by side in my hotel room, I blurt, "You think we could just skip Violet's baby shower and stay here over the holiday?"

"What?" she says, turning to face me. "Why would we do that?"

When I share my concerns about keeping us a secret, she just says, "Well, we have to go. Violet's one of my best friends. I can't just skip her shower."

"But won't it, like, be hard for you?"

She rolls away from me to face the ceiling, so I take her hand and tuck it under mine, atop my heart. "I'm sure she'd understand if you didn't feel up to going."

After a few beats, eyes still on the ceiling, she says, "I want to tell you something, but I'm afraid you'll judge me for it."

Squeezing her hand, I say, "I won't. I promise."

She turns just her head in my direction. "You don't know what I'm going to say. And it might make me fall all the way off the pedestal you like to keep me on."

"Eh, don't worry about that. You lost that thing a long time ago."

Her gasp is dramatic enough that I know she's playing, but I'm dead serious when I add, "I'm in no place to judge you. You're human, I'm human. No one is perfect."

"Still…"

"Just tell me already."

After facing the ceiling, she says, "I was happy to lose the baby. I was planning to have an abortion, anyway."

"Well, that makes sense. Having his child would tie you to Hardy forever."

She nods slowly, "Yes, but it's not just that. I was relieved to lose my uterus too."

"Why?"

"You said you wouldn't judge."

"I'm not, I promise. I just... don't get it. I mean, Dani talked about not wanting to have kids for as long as I could remember, but you never did."

"I like kids. But I just don't want to pass it on."

"Pass what on?"

"The ugliness of my family," she says, so softly that I'm not sure I heard right.

Before I can ask what she means, she turns to face me. "Do you want children, Ford? Tell me the truth."

Needing to comfort her, I scoop an arm beneath her to hug her into my side. "Honestly, it's not something I've thought a lot about. It's hard to picture. I mean, I'd love to have a dog, but even that seems irresponsible with the way I have to pick up and go all the time."

What I don't say? That I now have a glimmer of hope that we could make it work, with or without kids or dogs. Sensing that saying that would spook her, I try to find a happy medium. "I just hope I can figure out how to keep a certain woman happy, even if we can't always be together like this."

Her arm snakes under me, and she hugs me tight. "I bet you can figure it out. You're pretty smart."

And then we're both quiet until we fall asleep.

```
Subj: Baby Shower
Date: 11/25/1999 7:30:45 AM
From: VioletCastingCarolina
To: makeupchick1200, Ford_soundguy, Sully-
Callaway999, DanielleGoodwin856
```

```
Do we think six party games is too many? So
far, I have My Water Broke, Baby Bump
Twister, Guess Who, Stroller Racing,
Because I Said So, and Don't Drop the Baby…
```

WHITNEY

IT'S a no brainer that I'd ride back to Wallington for the Thanksgiving holiday with Ford. It's also a given that I'll go. I wasn't going to miss Violet's wedding even though I felt like death warmed over and my husband didn't want me to go, and I sure as hell will not miss her baby shower. Even if it means a long drive on a big traffic holiday, I don't want her to think that she has to treat me with kid gloves just because I can't have children.

What's tougher is where to stay, but when I finally find

time to check email, I'm relieved to find that Dani insists I bunk with her and Luke.

The hardest thing of all will be pretending that Ford and I aren't doing this friends-with-benefits thing, so, when we're stuck in yet another slow spot on the two-lane highway, I turn down the radio.

"I thought you liked Bonnie Raitt," Ford says.

"I do. 'Somethin' to Talk About' is one of my favorite songs. But I'm a little worried about being something our friends will talk about. So, I think we need to set some ground rules."

"More rules?"

I have to squelch a giggle at the genuinely horrified look on his face. "Sorry, but in order to keep this a secret, I think we might have to avoid each other."

His lower lip sticks out so far you could set up camp on it.

"Come on, Ford. It'll be easier to keep our hands off each other if we're in the same room as little as possible."

"You don't think that'll be suspicious?"

"We can say we're sick of each other."

We're in Gertie, who has a large bench seat, so I slide close, take his free hand, and lean my head on his shoulder. "Just for the weekend. So, we can keep what's between us private."

His lips pressed together, he nods. But then he shoots me a look. "Then I want to head back Saturday. Morning."

I shrug. "Works for me. Not like I need to spend time with my family or anything."

Telling myself that this is all for the best, I turn the music back up, and get him smiling by singing and dancing along with Sheryl Crow's "My Favorite Mistake" just hoping I'm not making one.

"ARE YOU LOOKING FOR SOMETHING?"

Startled, my skull hits the edge of the kitchen cabinet I'm peering into. "Ow!"

"Yikes, you okay? Didn't mean to scare you," Dani says.

Rubbing the top of my head, I sit back on my haunches. "Sorry for snooping around, but I, uh, hid something in this cabinet. Under the big roasting pan. Which is now in the oven obviously, so…"

"Hid something? When?"

"When I was here taking care of you. After your surgery this spring."

She rubs her own head, mirroring me. "Wow. I completely forgot that you were here that week until just now."

I can't help but grin. "You were pretty loopy."

"Oh, wait. Was it kind of a"—she draws a large square in the air with her hands—"big, black envelope thingy?"

Nodding, I ask, "Yeah. Did you move it?"

"I did. This summer when we used the pan to make ribs." Reaching a hand to me, she helps me up off the floor. "Your noggin okay?"

"Yeah. Luckily, I'm pretty hard-headed."

"I wouldn't disagree." She taps her chin with a finger. "Dang it. Where did I put that thing? And why did you hide it under the turkey pan?"

"I figured you wouldn't use it till Thanksgiving, so I'd have plenty of time to retrieve it, but I forgot about it when I went to Charlotte. It's my work portfolio. You know, photos of looks I created for various shows. I want to show it to Susan when I ask if she'll hire me again."

Her finger shoots up in the air. "I remember where I stashed it. C'mon."

Following her into her bedroom, curiosity has me inspecting the space. Her new husband has added a few items to the room, but its décor is as spare as it always was. "Wish I had your willpower when it comes to buying stuff."

"It's easy for me. I hate shopping."

"We really are chalk and cheese."

She reaches behind her desk, pulls out a large black leather portfolio and hands it to me.

"Oh, thank goodness. Susan needs someone with tattoo and wound experience on the next show, and I've got some good examples here."

"Cool. Why did you hide it here, anyway?"

I meet her gaze and find no judgment, just curiosity. "I'd, uh, just found out I was pregnant, and I guess I knew I needed an exit strategy. I didn't really think it through. I just brought it with me when I came over."

She tips her head to the side. "I remember you saying you had to pretend you had a dentist appointment to even come over that day. Did Hardy hate me that much?"

I shake my head. "It wasn't hate. You just weren't on the approved list."

"There was a list? Of people you were allowed to see?"

I shrug. "My parents were the same. I just stood up to them better."

"That's fucked up, Whitney."

When her brows come together in a wrinkle, I have to keep myself from telling her to stop it, so she doesn't etch lines across her forehead. "He was controlling, I guess. But no more so than my parents. It was just harder to get around his rules."

She shakes her head slowly. "Please tell me you've started divorce proceedings from this guy."

"Well, we can't get a divorce until we've been separated for a year, so I'm kind of hoping he does it. I don't have money to hire a lawyer. All the accounts were in Hardy's name, so when I left, I lost all that."

"Jeez. That's seems kind of fucked up too."

"Well sorree. Not everyone gets to marry the perfect guy."

"Whit, I'm not blaming you. In fact"—she sinks onto her

bed like someone let the air out of her tires—"I just want to say that I'm sorry."

"For what?"

Disbelief wars with the regret on her face. "For everything I said after the hurricane. If my ugly words or kicking you out of my house pushed you to marry that man—"

A hiccup of a sob stops her words, and that stops my heart. Dani doesn't cry. Like ever. So I rush to reassure her. "Sweetie, it wasn't you or what you said."

She takes my hand. "But you left that night and the next thing we knew your engagement was in the paper. You were married within, what a month?"

Dani may be one of my closest friends, but telling her the real reason I finally caved to my parents' insistence to wed someone of their choosing… I just can't.

"I'm just so, so sorry," she says.

I dig a packet of tissues out of my bag and hand it to her. "Listen. Marrying Hardy was a mistake. I know that now. But it was my mistake. Please don't beat yourself up over it."

She lowers her chin and fixes me with her gaze, like she doesn't quite believe me and is waiting for me to fess up. I can see how it might work on her younger siblings, but I won't crack with just a look. Eventually, she lets out an aggrieved sigh, pulls out a tissue, blows her nose and gets up to cross to her desk again.

After flipping through her Rolodex, she pulls out a card and hands it to me. "This is one of my locations regulars. She does family law. You should talk to her and see what your options are. She has a real nice house off Colonial Drive she paid for herself, so I'm sure she's a hell of a negotiator."

EIGHTEEN

```
Subj: Reminder
Date: 11/26/1999 10:05:21 AM
From: VioletCastingCarolina
To: SullyCallaway999, DanielleGoodwin856,
makeupchick1200, Ford_soundguy
```

Don't forget to bring a baby picture or you won't be able to play the Guess Who game!

WHITNEY

I SPEND all of Thanksgiving afternoon and evening with Dani and Luke. A few of her random cousins join us, along with Luke's sister who's visiting from California, plus a couple of *Lawson's Reach* regulars who didn't have anywhere else to celebrate the holiday.

Ford has dinner with his family, of course, and I spend a lot of the day pretending I'm sick of him. Not just to my friends, but to myself.

Neither Dani nor Luke makes me feel unwelcome, but I'm worried about cramping their style. Friday morning I make excuses and get out of the house as early as I can. Even though I take my time picking out a baby gift, I arrive early for the shower.

Vi's grandmother ushers me into the home they moved to after selling their inn. After complimenting her harvest-themed holiday decor, I ask if I can do anything to help.

"Actually, could you finish tying ribbons on the favors?" Mrs. Kennedy says. "Violet's getting dressed and my arthritis is acting up."

"Of course. Just point me in the right direction."

She thanks me profusely as she sets me up in her craft room, but I'm truly grateful to have something to occupy my hands. Unfortunately, as I place adorable drink coasters shaped like onesies and stamped with "It's a Girl" in gift bags, it suddenly occurs to me I'll never know if the baby I lost was a boy or a girl.

I'm not sure how long I've been sitting and staring at the words on the coaster when the floor creaks behind me. When I turn around to find Nate and Vi in the doorway, I scramble to continue tying ribbons on the bags, but I guess I'm not fast enough.

"Honey, are you okay?" Vi asks, handing me a tissue.

"I'm fine," I whisper, even as I wipe my face. "I'm sorry I'm such a drama queen. God, first I turn your wedding into a circus and now I'm crying at your baby shower."

"Oh, sweetie," Vi says, squeezing my hand.

"Hardly anybody even noticed. At the wedding, I mean," Nate says.

Vi shoots him some sort of look, and he clears his throat. "I'm going to get my wife some water. She needs to, uh, stay hydrated."

After he leaves, I squeeze Vi's hand. "I truly am sorry about the wedding. I can't imagine you believe me after everything I've done, but—"

"Whitney, not even you can conjure a major infection just to get attention."

"Yeah, I guess," I say, even though it was my fault. If I'd gone to the doctor after I miscarried instead of pretending it didn't happen, I might still have a—I cut off this line of thought, because getting emotional over a hysterectomy when my friend is pregnant is just rude. But when she pulls up a chair to sit next to me, her lips press together in a line.

"Just say it, Vi. Whatever you're thinking, spit it out."

She looks to the side momentarily before facing me again. "I just want you to know that we are all here for you."

"Vi, I'm fine. I swear." I flap a hand at the party favors. "I'm just tired. I'm not really upset about—"

She holds up a hand, cutting me off. "I'm saying we love you and we care about you, and we are worried about you."

It's hard to believe her words. I've never quite understood why the group of friends I've known since kindergarten put up with me, let alone care about me. They're the people I care most about in the world, but I can't seem to stop hurting them.

Still, Vi is nothing if not a straight shooter, so I brave a true statement. "I hoped, when you invited me to your wedding, that you'd forgiven me, but I don't know why you would."

She takes my hand, scooting the chair closer. "No one is perfect, Whit. We've all had a lot of growing up to do. I won't speak for anyone else, but I never thought you were the only cause of the bad feelings between Sully and Ford. It takes three to tango, if you know what I mean."

This gets an unfeminine snort-laugh out of me. "I don't know. I mean—"

"Yeah, you're a brat sometimes, but so am I," she says, plowing past my objections. "Yeah, you've done some stupid shit, but so have I. It's not your fault those two boys fought over you. Not only that, you're also kind and talented and way smarter than you think."

I want to believe her. I need to believe her. So, I nod.

"And I've just missed you, you know?"

"For real?" I ask, my voice breaking.

"Of course, I have. I mean, nobody snort-laughs like you. Nobody can give a girl a makeover like you. And let me tell you, this hair"—she swirls a hand over her beautiful head of auburn curls—"has gotten even crazier."

"Can I touch it?"

"Do you even have to ask?" she returns with a laugh.

I run my fingers through it. "It's even prettier than usual, Vi, but it's normal for the volume of hair to increase during pregnancy. Something about it all staying in the growth phase because of your hormone levels. I can put it in a nice chignon for the party if it's driving you crazy."

She grabs my hand. "Would you?"

"Of course."

I grab supplies from my bag and stand behind her to run a wide-toothed comb through the curls before pinning it up.

"I swear this isn't the only thing I've missed about you but it's up there. And sorry for making you do this on your day off. Like a busman's holiday."

"I wouldn't have offered if I didn't want to do it."

"Well, I appreciate it. I'm sure I'll appreciate it even more when the photos come back from the printer and my hair isn't flying out of every frame." She laughs and then adds, "Of course that might be a good distraction from the fact that I'm as big as a tank."

"Nonsense. You're gorgeous. Hair like a Pantene commercial and curves to die for."

"Thank you for saying so." She squeezes my hand tight and then releases it. "Listen, I know you've got Ford up there in Charlotte, but if you need anything, you call, you hear?"

"Yes, ma'am." Suddenly feeling guilty for hiding what's going on between Ford and me, tempted to spill it so I can get her advice, I force myself to change lanes instead. "You're gonna be a good momma, you know."

"You bet your boots I am. I may have had crappy parents, but at least they taught me what not to do."

Not wanting to contemplate what I learned from my own parents, I focus on the head of hair in front of me, which always soothes me. The wonderful thing about hair and makeup is that it's easy to fix your mistakes. Even a bad haircut will grow back in.

Which reminds me, I should warn Violet that she'll probably experience hair loss after she has the baby. After I explain why it's normal, I get her talking about the pilots she mentioned in an email. Vi is the top casting director in Wallington, so she always knows what work is coming down the pipe.

"I hope both you and Ford will be on them. It'd be nice to have the band back together again, as they say, all of us working together."

I tell her yes, of course it would be great, but I don't really mean it. I don't think I can afford to work in Wallington yet.

Financially or emotionally.

I MUST'VE ATTENDED A DOZEN BABY SHOWERS OVER THE PAST year, all for women I knew from the Azalea Belles or being a debutante up in Raleigh or wives of Hardy's colleagues, but I never actually enjoyed a single one.

Today, I don't have to worry that my dress isn't fashionable enough; I don't even know what decade the second-hand thing I'm wearing came from. I don't have to field comments about when it's going to be my turn because everyone here knows I'll never have one. Best of all, today I feel accepted for who I am.

By almost everyone, anyway.

You'd think it'd be Helen frowning in my direction. Her guy Sully used to be hung up on me, after all, and I'm sure she's heard the stories. But instead, it's the man himself, glowering at me so much that I eventually drag him outside to get the yelling over with.

But when I tell him to just get it off his chest, whatever he's mad about now, his expression shifts to surprise. "You think I'm angry with you?"

"Something's got your goose. You've been shooting evil looks at me for the past two hours!"

Squeezing his eyes shut, he shakes his head. Not like he's saying no, but like he's trying to literally shake something off. He takes my hand, and when his gaze meets mine again, it's sad, not mad.

"I just hate myself every time I think about what you've been through."

A little panic flutters through me as I wonder what he's talking about. "You mean, losing the baby and all?"

"Well, yeah. But also, the way we treated you last summer. The things we said. And I feel like, if I hadn't started it by asking you to go away with me on the boat, that none of it would've happened." He runs a hand down his face. "The worst thing is, I didn't even think of it that way until Ford told me how guilty he felt. But now…"

Relief washes through me. He hasn't unearthed details about my family life. Instead, he's upset because, like the rest of my friends, Sully assumes that I married Hardy because they all pushed me out of the nest. It sure wasn't fun when Ford and Sully demanded that I choose between them, when Dani and Violet accused me of blowing up the friend group for the second time. But their words were justified. I should've cut both guys loose. I just didn't know how to do that without hurting them. Or losing them.

Unfortunately, I ended up doing both.

"Sully," I say, flipping his grip so that I'm squeezing his hand, "Look at me."

When he does, I release his hand and put both of mine on

my hips because it helps me to take up space when I need to speak my mind.

"Me marrying Hardy had absolutely nothing to do with your sweet invitation. It had nothing to do with you or Vi or Dani or Ford at all."

His eyes narrow when my words falter. "I did it for family reasons," I say, emphasizing the word family in a way that I hope will keep him from prodding further. "And, come on. You know I love you, but really? How long would I have survived on a sailboat? No blow dryer or curling iron? No shower?"

He nods, his grin wide. "Yeah, I guess I didn't really think that through."

"Of course, I'd have saved you from bonking your head and breaking your leg."

He laughs outright. "Yeah, I can see that. You single-handedly blocking the blows."

"I'm scarier than I look. I've stopped traffic. I could stop a little motorboat."

He just shakes his head, so I tip my head toward the house. "'Course, then you wouldn't have met Helen. So, it all turned out for the best."

His laughter fades and he looks off to the side for a moment. When he turns to face me again, sadness fills his eyes. "Did it? For you, I mean?"

My lower lip wants to tremble, but I stretch it into a grin. "I'm back on my feet. I'll be fine."

He considers this for a long moment before saying, "I believe you will."

I nod, like we've both agreed on something, but when I turn to go back to the party, he stops me. "Listen. It's none of my business, but I need to make sure you get it."

"Get what?"

"I know you and Ford are probably spending a lot of time together out there." He waits, brows raised, until I give him a nod of confirmation. "You should decide what you really want before tossing out a line to him. Because the minute you do, he'll bite. And he won't let go."

Too late, is what I'd say if I were being honest. But life has proved that I can keep a secret, so I just nod and do my best to keep my expression free of all the feelings his words stir up.

That it's not only too late, but that he's got it wrong.

I'm the one who's on the hook, and it won't let me go.

NINETEEN

Friday, 11/26 9:15 AM

makeupchick1200: Hope you had a good turkey day. I missed you but it's definitely a good thing that we split up. Dani's nosy enough as it is.

Ford_soundguy: Got it. Not happy about it, but I get it. Can you be ready to go by 10 am on Saturday?

makeupchick1200: Perfect. I have some things I need to organize for the Toy Drive, so it'll be good to get back early.

FORD

MY MOTHER COMPLAINED about the frown on my face so many times Thanksgiving Day that I had to promise her I wasn't sad to be home. Since I couldn't tell her the truth, I told her I was worried about a piece of equipment I needed to fix before we started up work again on Monday. I actually had something to fix, but I wasn't worried about it. It gives me the excuse I need to head back Saturday instead of Sunday.

But things were worse at the shower. No one expects me to ooh and ahh over baby gifts, but Violet looked hurt when I backed out of playing a game of Baby Bump Twister. Not because I didn't want to stretch out my shirt with the "pregnancy" balloon as I claimed, but because I didn't think I could manage my body's responses if I got that close to Whitney.

On top of that awkwardness, Vi, Dani, and Sully each cornered me during the shower to ask why I haven't figured out what really happened with her and Hardy. Not only have I failed on that front, but keeping this so-called friends-with-benefits deal a secret has me tied up in knots.

I'm lying to my family and friends about a relationship I'd share with the world if I could.

I'm lying to Whit by sneaking around talking about her behind her back.

Most of all, I'm lying to myself about what I really want.

By the time the party's over, since I can't take Whitney home with me, my second choice is to crawl into my childhood bed and sleep until it's time to drive back to Charlotte. When I get back to my house, however, I'm pulled into watching football with my brothers and uncles and father. When I'll only drink one can of PBR, my brothers give me shit about being a beer snob.

"Pabst ain't good enough for you?"

"Oooh, Mr. Yuppie only drinks beer out of a bottle."

I take their teasing without comment, like I always do, but after scarfing down a turkey, cranberry sauce, and dressing sandwich, I escape to my room. It feels like I've only been horizontal for moments when someone bangs on my door, yelling, "Phone for you, man."

When I stagger out of the room, it's dark out, and the house is relatively quiet. The phone's sitting on the kitchen counter, now cleared of the spread my mom put out for the football crowd. Whichever brother answered it must have retreated to the den. "Uh, hello?"

"Ford?" Dani asks.

"Yeah. What's up?"

"Sorry to call so late."

Checking the clock over the stove, I'm surprised to see that it's nine-thirty. "Everything okay?"

"Well, I'm not sure."

Warning bells go off in my head. Is it Violet and the baby? Or Whitney? "Dani, you're freaking me out. What's wrong?"

"Whitney went straight to her room after the shower and won't come out. She says she just has a stomachache but..."

When she doesn't continue, I ask, "You think the party brought up stuff about losing her baby?"

"Exactly. Could you come over?"

"Me?" Whit'll kill me if she thinks I let the cat out of the bag. "Why me?"

"Well, I'm not calling Vi, and Sully didn't answer the phone."

"Nothing like being your last choice," I mutter.

"Can you come or not?"

"Of course. I'll be there in ten."

I take longer than promised because I make a pit stop at the Scotchman convenience store. Dani whips the door open the moment I step foot on her porch. "Where have you been?"

I lift the plastic bag. "I got props."

"Like what?" she says, reaching for the bag.

Holding it high, I bat her hands away. "Inside joke. I'll tell you if it works."

Crossing her arms over her chest and narrowing her eyes she huffs out a "Fine. Just... get in there and find out what's wrong. I'm getting worried."

She points me toward the room Whitney used to rent from her. With a peek into the living room, I wave at Luke and his sister before heading down the hall. When I knock on the door, there's no answer, so I try again.

"I said I'm fine," Whitney mumbles, but she doesn't sound fine.

"Whit. It's me. I brought supplies," I call through the door.

There's a pause and then she says, "Cup-a-Soup?"

"And a couple other things."

I hear movement and then the door cracks open. "What are you doing here?"

I hold up the bag. "Heard you were sick."

"Dani called you?" She winces and then leans close to whisper, "Do you think she knows?"

"I was her last choice, so, I don't think so."

She doesn't respond to this or open the door, she just sighs.

"You gonna let me in?"

She just stares at the wall by the door for a long moment, but then she opens it and walks back into the room.

Which is a disaster. Clothes and makeup and piles of crumpled up tissues and papers and envelopes of all shapes and sizes cover every surface. She crawls onto the bed and flops onto her side, so I close the door behind me and follow her to sit. Close, but not too close.

"You want to talk about it?"

She grabs a tissue from a box by the bed and blows her nose. "No."

"Was it the shower? Did it bring up, like, grief about your baby?"

"God, I wish that's what it was."

"Then tell me. Maybe I can help."

She shakes her head. "You can't fix this Ford."

"Whit, you're scaring me. Even if I can't fix it, maybe telling me will help. Just getting it out there. Are you sick for real?" I scrabble through the bag, pulling out pain relievers and cough drops and the promised Cup-a-Soup and a giant chocolate bar.

Her eyes light up at the sight of the candy, but when she reaches for it, I hold it out of reach. "Tell me what's wrong and you can have it."

Her mouth falls open. "Are you holding that candy hostage?"

I shrug. "Whatever it takes."

She sinks back onto the bed and closes her eyes. The tear that escapes past her lashes pierces my heart.

"It'll be okay, I promise."

She says nothing for a long time, but when she does, she speaks so softly I can't quite understand her words.

"I'm sorry, what did you say?"

With a groan, she lurches up to sitting, looks around the room and then staggers to a pile of paper. Shuffling, she pulls out a piece of paper and hands it to me, before slumping into an armchair.

"That"—she points at the paper in my hands and then at the mess on the floor—"And all those were waiting for me in one big fat envelope when I got back here today."

When I raise my brows in silent question, she flings a hand in the air. "Go ahead, read it."

WHITNEY

Once his eyes have scanned the page long enough to grasp its intent, I can tell that Ford wants to crumple the letter from Hardy into a tiny ball. "Go ahead. Tear it into pieces. It won't change the fact that he's screwing me over."

He flings the paper across the room instead. With a frustrated "Fucking asshole" he shoves all the bills back into the manila envelope they came in.

"Ford!" I grab his hands to stop him. "You can't—I need *those*. If I'm going to keep from totally fucking up my credit score, I have to pay them."

His jaw's so tight I'm afraid he'll crack a tooth, but he releases the papers. "And like I said, this isn't your problem."

His hands go to his hair, like he's going to rip it out, and he paces back and forth, his long strides too big for the room. "You may not think so, but I'm pretty sure it's my fucking fault."

"How is it your fault that my husband has put me on the hook for all my medical bills?"

He squeezes his eyes shut for a long moment before dropping his arms, blowing out a breath, and opening his eyes again, which are full of regret. "It's my fault you married the bastard. So, I'm going to fix this."

Anger returns, pushing grief out of the way. "Me marrying Hardy had nothing to do with you. I'll say it one last time. This is not your problem. I am not a broken car or bike or piece of sound equipment that you need to put back together. I need to fix my own problems."

"How can you say that?"

"That I should fix my own problems? I am an adult, Ford. Y'all may think I'm a spoiled brat, and a pampered princess, and maybe I am. But the only way I'm gonna grow up is to figure out how to clean up my own damn messes."

"I'm talking about this being my fault. I gave you an ultimatum that blew up our friendship, and a few weeks later you were married to a guy we all knew was a bully. So, excuse me if I think it was because of what I did."

The need to calm Ford wars with the need to keep my problems to myself. Thinking that I could just tell him enough of the story to calm his unearned guilt, I ask him to sit down.

His brows come together as he studies me, his eyes a storm of emotion, but he finally does as I ask, settling on the edge of the bed. Sitting back on the desk chair and swiveling to face him, I clear my throat. "I would like what I'm about to tell you to stay between us."

He blinks several times. "Okay."

"Promise?"

"Uh, yeah. Of course."

"When I left this house that night after the big fight, I went back to my parents'. Waiting for me there, was"—I half laugh, gesturing at the papers all over the floor—"another big ole pile of bills."

When I don't go on, Ford says, "I don't get it."

It ain't easy, but I meet his gaze. "Have you ever been in debt?"

He shrugs. "I guess. I have student loans."

"How much?"

"I don't know. It's probably down to about five grand now."

"Because you pay them monthly."

"Well, yeah."

I blow out a breath, eyes back on the floor. "I didn't."

"But I thought your parents paid for college?"

"They did. Until I stopped taking their pre-approved list of courses. Which did not include theater or film or art classes. When I didn't cave, they cut me off." I have to swallow past the shame clogging my throat. "I was embarrassed, especially around my sorority sisters, so I just kept spending like my dad was still backing me."

"So you took out loans?"

"Not exactly."

"What then?"

"I used credit cards. For everything. And it just became this hole I couldn't ever get out of." With the dam of lies breached, the trickle of truth gathers momentum and becomes a wave, rushing to get out. "Even when I started making decent money, I couldn't ever catch up. The interest alone was... mind-boggling."

"How long did this go on?"

"Until I married Hardy."

His face goes ashen. "Are you saying your parents *sold* you to him?"

I cough out an ugly laugh. "Not exactly. But they wanted in on some development deal with him. Bad enough that they paid off my forty-thousand-dollar debt when I finally agreed to marry him."

"Forty?"

"Thousand." I hold up a hand. "I know, what a dumbass."

He kneels in front of me and places his hands on my knees. His expression is fierce, but his words are clear and calm. "No, Whitney. You were a kid. You didn't know, and obviously your parents didn't care enough to help you."

"But I was selfish," I grind out. "I didn't want to give up the lifestyle I loved so much. So much that I paid for it with..." The truth chokes me, and I can't finish. I paid for it with my future children. And I almost paid for it with my life.

He takes my hands, his touch so warm and I realize I'm shivering. "Whitney, let me help. I've got savings. I'll pay the bills."

"No, Ford. You can't do—"

"I can do what I want," he says, his jaw ticking again. "And I want to help. You can pay me back."

"But what I want—what I *need*—is to learn how to be responsible with money. I'll just keep getting into trouble if you bail me out." Needing to move to keep from falling into his offer, I get up and gather the papers myself. "I'll figure this out. I'm pretty sure Susan will hire me on her next job, another out-of-town one so I can save. This time, I'll talk to the"—I fumble the bills as I struggle to straighten the pile— "hospital and doctors and what all, and I'll work out a payment plan."

"But wouldn't it be easier if I—"

I hold up a hand to cut him off. "Ford, I swear, if you

offer one more time, I will get up at the crack of dawn and take a taxi to the bus station and go back to Charlotte by myself."

The look on my face, my tone, and the fact that Whitney Moore is threatening to take a bus must be enough to convince him, because he sits back on his heels. "Okay. Okay."

"And not a word about this to the others, you hear me?"

FORD

Before she lets me leave the room, Whitney makes me promise again to keep her story a secret, so I tell Dani that she really isn't feeling well—which I guess is the truth. That she's not upset about losing her baby—which also seems to be the truth. Dani doesn't seem satisfied, but she doesn't push for more either.

The next morning, when I return from an early run, Sully's waiting on my front porch. Meaning, Dani didn't believe me after all, and she called the cavalry.

"What's going on?" I ask, taking hold of a column to stretch my quads.

"Nothing."

Sully's a terrible liar, but I don't call him on it. "Have you eaten?"

"Not really."

The guy's so big and broad, he's always hungry. "Give me ten minutes to shower and I'll meet you in the kitchen."

By the time I make it back downstairs, my mother is filling Sully's plate with bacon and egg casserole. He thanks her before grabbing two biscuits from the breadbasket. "I've missed your cooking, Mrs. Fischer."

She grills him about what he's been up to while I fill my

plate, then excuses herself and retreats to the den with her coffee. "Y'all let me know if you need anything else, now."

Sully digs in, grunting his appreciation as he eats. I can't quite relax enough to enjoy it, even though this casserole is my favorite.

"Just spit it out, man," I finally say. "What does she want?"

He looks up from his plate. "Huh? Who?"

"Dani." I push my mostly full plate away and sit back in my chair.

"Dani? What are you talking about?"

"She didn't send you here?"

"No. Why would she?"

Shit. Now I've done it. "I don't know. I just always feel like the girls are mad at me."

He chews, swallows, wipes his mouth with his napkin. "I get that. But I'm here because I wanted to ask you something."

Now I'm worried that he's seen through our act. Is it that obvious that Whitney and I are sleeping together?

"Is that okay?"

I blink at him for a moment, so lost in my head that I'm not sure what he's asking. "Um. Yeah?"

He tosses his napkin on the table and turns in his chair to face me before speaking. "Is it really work that's kept you from any sort of long-term relationship? Or is it something else?"

Thrown by the question, not at all what I thought was coming, I cast my mind back to the conversation we had before I left for Charlotte. "Well, I have been pretty darn busy building my career."

He breaks off a piece of biscuit and tosses it in his mouth, seeming to think while chewing and swallowing. "Okay, I'll ask it a different way. What if there is no 'the one'?"

"Is this about Whit?" I narrow my eyes at him, even as my

heart races. "Are you trying to warn me off her too? I told Vi and Dani I'd leave her alone."

He tips his head to the side and studies me for a long moment. "If she stayed married to Hardy, would you be a bachelor forever?"

"What kind of question is that? I'm no monk. I've been dating."

"More like fishing without bait."

"More like catch and release, you mean. Nobody really stuck."

"Let's switch from fishing to shopping. You're just browsing."

"What's wrong with that?"

"Well, if you're really 'just browsing' then you're never going to buy."

"Again, maybe I haven't found the right... sport coat."

"But you'll never know if you don't try it on. See how it feels."

"Gimme a break, man. My"—I make air quotes—"'wardrobe' is fine. Just because you're all starry-eyed in love doesn't mean I have to be too."

"I'm not—" He breaks off, stuffing the last bite of biscuit into his mouth with one hand and gesturing with the other. "That's the thing. That's what I *thought* I felt for Whit. Like she was the star I was reaching for. But when life literally knocked me upside the head, and I landed in Helen's lap, I found a woman that challenges me. Every day, in every way that makes life better."

I have to bite my tongue to keep from lashing out at him. Saying something like *well, lah-dee-dah, good for you*. I am happy my friend is happy, but he's pissing me off. Or maybe it's guilt that I'm lying to him about what's really happening. Like I'm lying to myself. Either way, opening my mouth will only make it worse.

"What I have now is real," he continues. "In the trenches,

with a partner by my side. Life is richer. She doesn't let me give up, but she also doesn't—"

"Okay, okay, I get it. So, do I have to break a leg to fall in love? Is that what you're saying?"

"I hope not. But I do think you have to take a risk. On someone. Maybe anyone. Let a person really see you. Know you."

"Whitney knows me," escapes past my lips, against my better judgment.

"But does she? And do you really know her?" He sits back in the chair, tips his head to the side. "And what are you going to do about it?"

TWENTY

Saturday, 11/27 10:15 AM
Ford_soundguy: Running a little
late but I'll be there
before 11.

makeupchick1200: I'll be ready.
Dani's giving me the third
degree.

WHITNEY

I SLEEP for most of the trip back to Charlotte and when I'm not sleeping, I'm pretending to. It's cowardly, but I'm so full of so many feelings I just want to curl up and hide from it all.

When the car stops and the engine turns off, I wake up from a dream where I was riding a horse on the beach. Not in a fun way, like in that old Tampax commercial, but in a running away from scary… pirates? Yeah. It was pirates.

"Whit? Are you okay?" Ford asks.

"Uh, yeah." Dragging myself up to sitting, I see that we're at the motel. "Weird dream."

"Are you still mad at me?"

"I'm not mad, I wasn't mad. I just… need to do this on my own, okay?"

He looks like he wants to argue, but after a long moment he blows out a breath. "Okay." Holding out a hand to me, palm up, he adds, "We okay?"

"We are."

"Promise?"

I nod.

"Wanna grab some lunch?"

"Actually, I need to talk to Cyn. I promised to dye her hair this weekend."

"Cynthia Sheridan? That older actress?"

I swat at him. "Shame on you. She's only forty-two."

"Is she really?"

"That's what she says, and I will not question it."

"And keeping the gray away helps sell it."

"Whatever works."

"But you're not on the clock. It's still a holiday."

"Which is exactly why I want to do it." I rub my thumb and fingers together. "I need the money, remember?"

He scowls. "I remember."

Despite my protests, Ford helps me carry my things to my room, giving me shit the entire time for packing like we were going on a journey to Siberia. While I tease him for wearing the same pair of jeans for three days. By the time the car is empty, we're both laughing, and he's got me pressed up against my hotel room door.

"I missed you," he whispers.

I should find Cyn, go to the store, and get supplies, but I whisper, "Missed you too."

He lowers his mouth to my ear. "Time for a quickie?"

Before I can reply, he's kissing his way down my neck, making me shiver inside and out. "No fair," I whine.

"Nobody said life was fair." His words ride a growl, but when he scoops me into his arms, I can't keep my hands from cradling his strong jaw, can't keep my mouth from meeting his smile with my own.

And then he continues to not play fair until he has me gasping his name over and over again.

AFTER OUR LITTLE AFTERNOON DELIGHT, FORD'S THE ONE WHO falls asleep. I'm not going to kick him out, so I take a quick shower, quietly gather what I need, and leave him a note before going to find Cyn.

"Oh, thank god," she says when she opens the door to her room, which is way bigger than mine or Ford's from what I can see. "I was worried you'd forgotten or wouldn't get back in time."

"No ma'am, I'm so sorry I'm late."

Her face crumples. "Please don't call me that. It makes me feel even older than I am."

"Sorry. Old habit. I'm a southern girl and calling your—" I stop myself from saying *elders* just in time. "It's a term of respect."

"It's a term of, 'you're over fifty and invisible' from where I'm sitting."

"I promise I won't do it again." Holding up a hand in promise, I ignore the fact that she admitted she's over fifty *and* stop myself from ending the sentence with "ma'am."

She laughs and ushers me inside. "Relax honey. I'm not going to bite."

I've done hair and makeup for more actors and actresses than I can count, but I am a little star struck around Cyn. She was the female lead in my favorite TV show of all time back in the 80's, the one about the two detectives who were in a will-they, won't-they love affair. But I need to pack that away because her hair needs me.

I give her my most winning smile. "Do you know what colors your stylist uses?"

"Not only do I know, but I've got the product with me." Gesturing for me to follow, she leads me through the large sitting area to the kitchenette. There, she grabs a shopping bag and hands it to me. "She makes me promise not to do it myself when she gives it to me."

"She's just looking out for you." I dig through the bag's contents, mentally going through a checklist in my head. "Between this and what I brought, I think we're all set. Do you want to do this here, or—" I break off, realizing we can't do it in my room because Ford's there. "Actually, my bathroom is tiny, so that's going to be pretty uncomfortable."

She flicks a hand in the air. "We don't have to do either. I talked to Donny. We can use the trailer."

"Seriously? But how are we going to get in?" Donny is the hair department key, but the teamsters are in charge of keeping the trailers locked up and secure.

"Donny's having a nice dinner on me and the teamster on duty..." Her smile is practically feral. "Let's just say we're close."

Cynthia insists on driving, and when we pull up to the parking lot storing the trailers, she blows a kiss to the ruggedly handsome teamster who winks in return.

In the trailer, I get her set up in a chair with a cape and get my supplies in order. Even though she's wearing a wig for the shoot, the last thing I need is to fuck up the hair of one of my idols.

"Any chance you brought your shears? I could really use a trim too." When I hesitate, she adds, "I'll pay for your time, don't worry."

"Oh, you don't have to—" I begin. I had been planning to do it for free, but even though I need the money, I hate talking about it.

She slaps my hand lightly. "Honey. Your time and skills

are valuable. Don't undersell yourself. I hate it when women do that."

When I meet her gaze in the mirror, I picture myself with even a fraction of her nerve. And then I say, "Okay."

Usually, when I do someone's hair, I ask them about what's going on in their lives. Partly because I truly love hearing people's stories but mostly because it keeps the spotlight off of me. Somehow, though, Cyn gets *me* talking.

Maybe it's because Ford cracked open the floodgates last night, but before I know it, I confess that I'm separated from my husband, and that he wants a divorce because I can no longer have children. Somehow, she even gets me telling her all about the fat envelope stuffed with medical bills that Hardy dropped in my lap.

"I don't know how I'm going to pay them all off," I find myself saying. "It's, like, thousands of dollars."

"Hang on." Holding up a hand, she swivels in the chair to face me. "Does he not have health insurance?"

"I-I don't know. Hardy always said I shouldn't worry about such things."

Lips pursed, arms crossed over the cape, she shakes her head slowly. "You're still married, right?"

I nod. "You have to be separated for a year in North Carolina before you can get a divorce."

"A year? That's barbaric." She shudders. "If not for Vegas, I'd have lost half my life to those waiting periods. What does your lawyer say about all this?"

I turn her to face the mirror again. "I need to finish up with the tint in this section."

She stops my hand. "Whitney. Please tell me you have a lawyer."

"I can't afford one. Now, come on Cyn." I ease my hand out of hers. "You don't want your color to be uneven, do you?"

She sighs. "Fine. But I'm not done."

She's quiet while I finish painting on the product and wrapping the strands carefully in foil. But once I've fastened the plastic bag over her head so she can process, she points at the chair next to her. "Sit."

I wash my hands and set the timer first, but she starts right in the moment my butt hits the pleather. "I am no expert at staying married, but after going through five of them, I could teach a master class in divorce. Rule one, you need a lawyer. They pay for themselves with the money they'll squeeze out of your ex."

"I don't want anything from him. Marrying him was my mistake."

"Let me guess." Her unusual Coke bottle green eyes flash as she counts things off on her fingers. "All the accounts were in his name. He wouldn't let you work. He ran your social life. Decided who you saw and when. He gave you a credit card but had to approve every single purchase. And when he kicked you out, you left with the clothes on your back and nothing else."

After I pick my jaw up off the floor, a little freaked out that she's able to describe my marriage so specifically, I can only manage, "That's not—I mean, he let me take my clothes."

She sighs deeply and when I meet her eyes again, they're brimming with tears.

"Did you… was it like that for you too?" I whisper.

"Not any of my marriages, no. But my best friend's." Taking my hand, she leans closer. "Honey, she tried to kill herself."

After holding my gaze for a long moment, she sits back again. "Thankfully, she failed, and when she finally told me what was going on, I got her help."

Fanning a hand in front of her face, she blows out a breath. "Whoo. This is going to take some fortification."

After clearing her throat, she reaches for her handbag, removing a silver flask and taking a healthy sip, before offering it to me. My heart beating hard, knowing somehow what she's going to say next, I take a drink too.

"It was also the moment I understood everything about my childhood."

She goes on to describe a family that sounds an awful lot like mine. The way her friend's marriage sounded an awful lot like mine. For once in my life, I'm rendered speechless. When she's done with her story, we sit in silence until the ding of the timer has me jumping to my feet.

"Time to rinse," I say, my voice hoarse with unshed tears.

Instead of getting up, she takes my hand and grasps it firmly. "You can recover from this. But it'll take work."

```
Monday 11/29/1999 9:00 PM
VioletCastingCarolina: Ford, if
you're there, I need to hear
what happened after my shower.
She claimed she was fine, but I
did find her crying over the
onesie coasters.
```

FORD

WHEN I GET BACK to the motel after work Monday, there's a message on the room phone from Violet, begging me to log on to the group chat tonight. The one that excludes Whitney.

It feels even worse now to talk about her behind her back but when Violet gets something in her head, almost nothing will stop her. By the time I get the computer booted up and get the internet connected, she's already off and running.

```
SullyCallaway999: She was okay
when I talked to her.
```

DanielleGoodwin856: She said a weird thing Thanksgiving morning, so I'm kind of worried too. Ford talked to her after the shower and then they left the next morning and we've heard nothing since.

VioletCastingCarolina: It is not good for the baby for me to be worried, y'all.

VioletCastingCarolina: Kidding. But not really.

VioletCastingCarolina: FORD.

Ford_soundguy: She's dealing, okay. She's been through a lot but she's a grownup and I think y'all have to trust her to solve her own problems.

VioletCastingCarolina: It would just make me feel better if I knew she was okay. And there might be something I could do to help! There are openings on makeup crews for the shows coming after the holidays. She could work here and lean on us.

DanielleGoodwin856: Vi, you're about to have a tiny, helpless human to care for twenty-four seven.

VioletCastingCarolina: Exactly. Do you want me dropping the baby on its head because I'm so distracted worrying about Whitney????

SullyCallaway999: You got
anything Ford? So Violet will
calm the fuck down?

I can't tell them we're together, but Violet's like a dog with a bone on this.

Ford_soundguy: She seemed
relieved to have lost the baby,
probably because it would've
tied her to Hardy. She never
said she wanted kids, so maybe
the hysterectomy wasn't such a
big deal to her.

DanielleGoodwin856: I feel like
she said she wanted kids at some
point, but it would've been hard
to do her work unless she had a
nanny or something.

VioletCastingCarolina: At the
very least, her hormones have
got to be screwing with her.

They go on about hormones for a while and I think I'm off the hook, until a very different message pops up.

DanielleGoodwin856: Wait! Luke
says a package arrived for Whit
while we were at the shower. He
gave it to her before I got
home.

SullyCallaway999: What kind of
package?

DanielleGoodwin856: Hang on, let
me ask.

DanielleGoodwin856: He said it
was a big brown envelope,
stuffed full. No return address,
like it'd been dropped off.
Ford, what do you know about
this?

Ford_soundguy: Whit is a very
private person, so I don't feel
comfortable sharing her
confidences.

VioletCastingCarolina: But we're
her best friends! If there was
something I could do to help her
and she's suffering because I
didn't, I would never forgive
myself.

When they don't let up, I decide to tell them just the bare
bones of it. Not everything she told me about why she
married him. Just further proof that he's a jerk.

Ford_soundguy: I'll tell you
this: the envelope was from
Hardy. It's all the bills from
when she was in the hospital.
He's claiming she has to pay
them. And before you say
anything, I offered to loan her
the money or pay them myself,
and she won't let me.

SullyCallaway999: What an
asshole.

DanielleGoodwin856: I don't get it. They're still married. Don't they share the debt? And doesn't she get half his money? She told me she didn't want any of his money, but this is different, right. Like legally?

Ford_soundguy: Honestly, I don't know. But she told me she's dealing with it, and she is a grownup. I've got an early day tomorrow, so I'm signing off.

I hope that's enough to calm them down. Unfortunately, now I'm all riled up again. She already said she didn't want to get together tonight, so I can't exactly storm over there and demand to pay her bills. And I doubt there's a one-eight-hundred hotline for divorce law in North Carolina.

Maybe that's it. I'll just make sure she's talking to a lawyer. Help her find one if she needs that.

And then, convince her to change the rules. I don't want to keep us a secret anymore.

I MAY HAVE SUCCESSFULLY PUT OFF MY FRIENDS' QUESTIONS about Whit, but Sully's questions from Saturday morning won't let me go. To make things worse, Whitney spends the next week hiding from me.

She makes excuses for why she can't come to my room after work, mostly things having to do with the Toy Drive and Secret Santa activities she's spearheading for the crew. It feels like she's avoiding me, but when I stop by her room, it is indeed filled with toys. Half of them wrapped half of them waiting for her to gussy them up.

"It's one thing to organize the damn drive," I grumble. "How'd you end up wrapping them all too?"

"It's easier this way." She smiles and reaches for me, but instead of grabbing my shirt to pull me inside and have her way with me, she taps on my sternum. "Did you get the gift card for your Secret Santa? And write the haiku?"

Because we can't just get one gift and be done with it. No, we have to get three gifts. The gift card is easy enough, but writing the haiku, and finding something made locally, and then making something myself, all for a prop master I barely know... it's too much.

But maybe I'm just an asshole who misses getting laid every night.

Or a lost little boy who misses his best friend.

To top it all off, she still won't let me pay those bills.

In first grade, I'd give her my lunch money when hers got stolen, even though her family is rich and mine skates along the bottom of middle class. When she came crying because a girl said she was too skinny or too fat or too whatever, I always told her she was perfect. And once the boys started dogging her in high school, I took more than one beating trying to keep her safe.

But she just keeps insisting she's dealing with this problem. She also promises that she's not mad at me, she's just busy.

So, I do the only thing I can think of. Make her an offer she can't refuse.

Friday lunch break, I stop by the table where Whitney's eating with a bunch of other women and offer to help take the Toy Drive gifts to the fire station, thinking it'd at least be a way I can spend time with her.

"Ford, this is a girl thing," Susan, the lead of Whit's department says.

"Guys aren't allowed to give toys?"

Barbie, the script supervisor, snorts. "It's an ogle- the-fire-fighters thing. I mean, you can come. But you'd better not get in the way."

Now all I can picture is a hot guy wearing nothing but turnout pants, his big white teeth flashing a perfect smile, while Whitney melts into a puddle of lust.

"I'll pass, thanks," I say with a smirk that I hope covers my disappointment, and retreat to my cart. Along the way, I pass the group that plays hacky-sack every day at lunch, boombox blaring. Walt invites me to join them, but I wave him off, too grumpy to relax into the game.

But when Meatloaf starts singing that he'd do anything for love, I'm stopped in my tracks.

Suddenly, I have an idea.

```
Subj: Toy Drop Off
Date: 12/4/1999 8:14:05 AM
From: FireStation1505
To: makeupchick1200
```

Mrs. McRae,
Just confirming that we will be here, barring any emergencies, for you to drop your donations this afternoon.
Thank you for your generosity and Happy Holidays!

WHITNEY

I'M on a high of good feelings after the Toy Drive drop off. Every woman on the show—actors and crew alike—piled into a bunch of cars to deliver the goods. And boy, did the firemen deliver in return.

They posed for pictures on the truck and fire pole, hamming it up by flexing muscles as we hooted and hollered. Afterwards, we all trooped to the bar for apps and cocktails where everyone toasted my efforts.

Part of me knows I've been hiding from the problems in my life by organizing all the holiday activities, but the genuine appreciation from the firemen and the movie's sisterhood made all the work worth it.

The news from Susan that her show in Nashville starting the second week of January is a go, and that she wants me on her crew, is just the cherry on top of the cake.

I've also made some grownup phone calls over the past week, burning through calling cards. With Cyn's coaching, I made an appointment with the lawyer Dani recommended back in Wallington, and spoke to the billing office at the hospital, who agreed to put a hold on my account until I meet with the divorce attorney.

There's not much more I can do until the show's over, at least regarding the divorce. I know I need to face Ford, but I'm just not sure what to say to him. I'm afraid I'm falling for him. According to our deal, I'm supposed to tell him so we can end things and still be friends.

But I really don't want to do that.

Even though we don't have much time left together, I've been running around doing everything I can to avoid him.

As I trudge up the stairs to my room, I decide I'm going to give myself a break, at least for tonight, and wait until tomorrow to talk to Ford. We only have one more week left on this job, and then I have a yawning gap of almost four weeks with nowhere to live and nothing to do.

I've built up my savings the past couple of months, but if I have to pay for a short-term rental or a hotel over the holidays, not to mention pay the medical bills or a lawyer's retainer, I'll be back at zero or in the hole again.

All of this just exhausts me further. Head down and feet dragging, I don't notice the piece of paper taped to my door until it flutters in the wind, almost smacking me in the face. We don't usually get schedule changes until Sunday nights, but I grab it and drop it on the TV table after I've shucked off my coat and boots.

My room is a total disaster area, with wrapping paper and shopping bags and clothes strewn all over the place, but I can't deal with that now. It takes every last bit of energy to get through my bedtime beauty routine of removing my makeup, moisturizing my face, and releasing my hair from the bun I keep it in when I'm working.

I'm in my comfiest sweats, ready to flop face first onto my bed, when something about the note pricks my curiosity. Instead of the pale blue copy paper production uses, the paper was white. And it was a nicer quality, soft to the touch.

So instead of falling into bed, I pick up the paper and read.

Moments later, I'm knocking on Ford's door. I don't even stop to reapply makeup or do my hair or change out of my Juicy tracksuit, I just shove my feet into my ugly but oh-so-practical UGG boots—one of the few splurge items I kept from my marriage—shrug into my bomber jacket and tromp up the stairs.

When he opens the door, he doesn't welcome me in. Instead, he says, "Password?"

I look down at the note in my hand, scanning the hand-writing I know is his, but that seems like an invitation to a children's party, until I find the password scrawled at the bottom. "Uh, no take backs?"

He nods and then opens the door. It's dark inside compared to the bright lights of the motel breezeway. So at first, I'm not sure what I'm looking at. Once my eyes adjust, it seems like … "Is that a blanket fort?"

Suddenly, tears spring to my eyes. "Ford, what is this?"

He helps me out of my jacket as I step out of the boots. "I remembered you used to complain that your parents never let you go to slumber parties when you were a kid. I never went to one either, so I thought we should have one."

My tears turn to laughter. "But why?'

He takes both of my hands and waits for me to meet his eyes, which shine even in the dim light. "I'm not sure why you've been avoiding me since we got back from Wallington, and I don't have to know if you don't want to tell me. But I miss you, so I thought I'd invite you for a sleepover."

"I definitely wouldn't have been allowed to go to the kind of sleepover you're suggesting when I was a kid."

He shakes his head and makes a tsking sound. "Whitney Moore, you shouldn't jump to conclusions. I may not have been invited to any slumber parties, but that doesn't mean I don't know how to throw one. I heard enough stories from Dani and Vi."

Memories tighten my throat. I'd always felt left out on Mondays at school, when girls would talk about parties I wasn't a part of. But before I can dwell on that, Ford hands me a cup of hot chocolate and a bowl of popcorn and leads me to the fort he's created by putting the couch cushions on the ground and draping sheets over what look like mic stands. He's even strung Christmas lights on top for a festive glow.

After I've settled on a cushion, I take a sip of hot chocolate, which is well-fortified with some kind of alcohol, warming me inside and out. "Now this definitely would not have been served at a ten-year-old's party," I say.

"You'd prefer it without the brandy?" he says, reaching for my cup.

Carefully avoiding spillage, I move it out of his reach. "I didn't say that."

"Are you ready for the activities, then?"

My heart squeezes, but this time, it's not in pain. This man seems to have spent his day off planning a slumber party for me. "I couldn't be readier. Let me guess, look for Bloody Mary in the mirror?"

He just looks confused.

"Hmm." I tap my chin with a finger. "It'd be tough to do 'light as a feather, stiff as a board' with just the two of us. Unless we're talking about me being light while you're stiff...?"

"I have no idea what you're talking about." He reaches under his cushion. "I also don't know what you call these, and I'm not sure they can really tell your fortune..."

After I take the folded paper he hands me, I nod in mock seriousness. "Hmmm. A Cootie Catcher doesn't have that much power. Only a Ouija board or a Magic 8 ball can really see into the future."

"We'll see about that. Cootie Catcher, huh? Like the cooties that boys have?"

"I guess? I never thought about why it's called that. Some people call it a snapdragon, I think."

"That makes more sense." He takes it from me to move the folded paper like it's a mouth. "Anyway, I think you start by picking a color, right?"

I pick blue, and he spells the word, opening and closing the catcher along with the letters. Then I pick a number, and he repeats the action as he counts, then I pick another number from what's inside. He flips up the panel of my choice and reads, *One foot massage.*

"Oooh!" I clap my hands excitedly. "This is way better than telling fortunes. Am I really getting a massage?"

He pulls a plastic tub from the space next to the couch and flips open its lid. When I try to peek inside, he waves me away. "Ah-ah. You'll ruin the surprises."

When he turns back, he's got a bottle of oil in his hands. "Take off your socks."

"Lucky for you, I showered after today's toy delivery."

He pulls my feet into his lap, pours oil into his palms,

warms it by rubbing his hands together, and then grasps both of my tired dogs with his large, capable hands. When his thumbs dig into my arches, I let out a groan.

"Too much?"

I sink into the cushions. "It's perfect."

I'm a puddle by the time he finishes. But not sleepy. Just relaxed, loose. "You missed your calling, Ford."

"I coulda been a contendah? As a masseuse?"

"Nah." Giggling, I lift my almost empty spiked chocolate. "I'm happy not to have to share your magic hands."

He waggles his eyebrows, but instead of kissing me, he holds up the Cootie Catcher again.

There are eight possible landings, and you have to make sure not to repeat a color-number combination in order to get to them all. I'm tempted to go for that foot massage over and over, but curiosity has me choosing different colors and numbers.

Next, I end up with *Do face masks*, which I naturally make Ford take part in. While we're waiting for them to dry, I pick the next one, which is *Do karaoke together.*

Gasping, my hand goes to my chest. "For real? You'd do that with me?"

"I know you love it, so I'll give it a try. Once." He points to the drying paste covering his face. "I get to take this off first, right?"

"Definitely. We'll do it Tuesday, without masks." Taking his cheeks in both hands, I give him a kiss.

He kisses me back, but when I try to climb into his lap, he sets me back on my cushion. "Nope. This slumber party has a PG-rating."

Suddenly, I'm worried about the purpose of tonight's festivities. "Are you… are you ending our friends with benefits deal? Is that what this is about?"

He presses his lips together, like he's trying to decide what to say.

Earlier this week, I tried to talk my*self* into ending this thing between us because I was afraid of getting hurt when the show was over, and we had to go back to reality. Back to Wallington, where I have to do all the adult things to end a marriage I never should've started in the first place. Where I have to get my finances in order. Where it's impossible to keep this secret from our friends.

Anyway, after the holidays, we'll no longer be working together. I'll be in Nashville, and he'll be… wherever his next job takes him. This deal always had an expiration date, but now that it's only a week away, I don't want it to end.

But I don't know how it could continue.

Before I can figure out how to say any of this, he says, "I think we have to trust the Cootie."

Which means I have to trust *him*.

I know Ford loves me. He may not be *in* love with me, and he may not be interested in a long-term relationship, but I'm not exactly available for one either. Maybe we can figure out how to keep this going, even if it's just between jobs.

"Okay then."

After we wash off the masks, the next activity I land on is braiding hair. Ford makes a valiant attempt at doing mine, while I of course do a bang-up job putting his in French braids. "Ugh. It's not fair."

Eyes closed, face completely relaxed, he asks, "What's not fair?"

"Your natural hair color. These highlights are perfect. Are they really just from the sun?"

He shrugs. "I guess. I didn't do anything to get them there."

"Totally not fair," I repeat.

The next number leads me to the message, or question, really: *Be my date at the wrap party?*

Staring at it, I say, "But… we're supposed to be a secret. That's what we agreed on."

He closes the flap and takes my hand. "Show'll be over at the party. We won't have to worry about being unprofessional anymore. I never got to take you to prom or a formal or anything. I'd like to take you to this."

My parents had considered every high school or college public function as a run-up to my coming out as a debutante, so if I wanted to attend, my date had to be someone on their list. Which never included Ford.

In his face right now, I can see that vulnerable, awkward teen. The guy that hid his interest in me right up to the moment that he got into a fistfight with Sully over me.

That summer, I did everything I could to push both of them away. I didn't want either of them hurt, so I pretended I wasn't interested.

Maybe right now, by saying yes, I can undo some of the pain I caused.

"I'd love to."

TWENTY-THREE

FORD

THE GODDESS of slumber parties must be cheering me on because I couldn't have planned the progression of surprises any more perfectly. Well, maybe braiding hair *before* face masks would've been better, but my skin is still softer than ever, and my floppy hair is out of my face for once.

I always knew women were the smarter half of the species.

We're down to the final two choices. Not sure if I'm worried about it being too much, that she'll shut me down, or if I just can't stand being close to her without being tangled up in her, but whatever the reason, I set the fortune teller aside and pull Whitney onto my lap.

"Can I kiss you now?" she asks. "There should be two more fortunes in there, if I counted right."

"They can wait," I say before brushing my lips across hers. "I, however, cannot. Ready to switch to the R-rated version of this party? Because I sure as hell am."

"I vote for triple X," she says with a grin. "Or at the very least, NC-17."

I guess Whitney has gotten comfortable being on top. Even once we're naked and on the bed, she doesn't try to pull me into the missionary position. I'm not complaining. I love watching her ride me, as well as taking her own pleasure. But this time, I decide to switch things up and I pull her up my torso until she's straddling my face.

"What are you doing?"

"Hang on to the headboard and I'll show you." Grasping her luscious hips, I scoot down until her sex is where I want it and then I part her folds with one hand and pull her to my mouth with the other.

When her back arches, I've got the perfect view of her tits as she rocks into me.

"Are you sure this is what you want?" she breathes.

"Does it feel good to you?" I ask between laps along her seam.

"Y-yes. So good."

"Then this is what I want." I experiment with angles and pressures and strokes until her legs tremble and her ass clenches. "Fuck me, you're hot."

She arches into me yet again, and I press my lips to her tight bud before sucking it into my mouth.

"I'm gonna come," she cries. Sliding two fingers inside to curl them into her wet heat, I press on her G-spot while flattening my tongue against her clit.

Her walls shudder around my fingers, her hips buck at my mouth and the sounds coming out of her have me so hard I can't wait to get inside her.

So I don't. After quickly sliding out from between her legs, I flip over and pull her hips to me.

"Do you still want me to hang onto the headboard?"

"Whatever you need, hon," I say before impaling her.

She drops to all fours as I stroke in and out, in and out, going as slow as I can manage. "Touch yourself, Whit. I want to feel you come again."

Bracing herself on one arm, she reaches between her legs to do as I ask. Instantly, her walls squeeze. "Hang on baby, too much of that and I'll be done before you know it."

She laughs, and instead of easing up, she clenches harder and circles her hips.

Groaning, I clamp my eyes shut, riding the feeling as long as I can, letting her drive the pace until I can't stand it anymore. Shoving a pillow under her chest, I flatten her under my torso so I can pound into her while I hit the crest and tumble over.

It takes some time for me to reboot. "I'm sorry, Whit. Can you even breathe?" I ask as I lift my torso off her back.

Pushing her hair out of her face with one hand, she flails around to grab me with the other. "Don't move. I like it."

I'm a much bigger person than she is, but the mattress is soft, so I ease back down, half on and half off her back, pulling the covers over us and nestling my nose into the space between her neck and shoulder.

I love you, Whit, is what I want to say right now, but I think I need to wait. Instead, I'm going to do everything I can to continue to show her how I feel.

And hope like hell that she'll eventually catch up.

I WAKE UP SUNDAY MORNING TO A DREAM COME TRUE: WHITNEY asleep in my arms, in my bed. She has slept over when she doesn't have a super early call, but she usually sneaks back to her room before dawn, and she always kicks me out of her place.

But the fact that she's still here makes me think she's really okay with letting this cat out of the bag. And it gives me hope that she'll say yes to the last two items in the Cootie Catcher.

I must be thinking too loud, because before I can sneak out of bed to pee and brush my teeth, her eyelids flutter open. Watching her take in her surroundings, my gut clenches, hoping that she won't regret sleeping over.

When she smiles, I can finally breathe.

Running her hand over my chest and then under the covers to find my morning wood, she raises a brow. "I guess you're not over friends with benefits."

Even though I'd go for round three—or four? I kind of lost count at some point last night—right now I want to finish the game before I lose my nerve. "Thing is, I kind of am."

Her hands stills and she coughs out a laugh. "Don't tell me last night was the last time we're having sex."

Taking her hand in mine, I turn to face her. "Could we add on to the friends with benefits deal?"

Her brows come together. "You want more benefits?"

"I'm not doing this right," I mutter. "Hang on."

Rolling out of bed, still needing to pee but not wanting her to shut me down, I scrabble through what's left of the pillow fort until I find the folded paper that worked its magic last night.

When I return to the bed, she's sitting up and has pulled the sheet to cover her chest. Probably not a good start, but I hold up the Cootie Catcher with what I hope is a charming smile. "There are still two fortunes left."

She narrows her eyes at me for a long moment before seeming to come to a decision. "Okay. Yellow."

As I spell the color, my heart pounds, hoping that I continue to be graced with good fortune. When Whit picks the number, I'm relieved as I open the flap and read the message. But her response is another wrinkled brow.

"Huh? What does that mean?"

"Well, I figured you might not want to camp out at Dani's or Sully's or Vi's over the holidays, nor would you want to stay with your parents." I don't even bring up Hardy, because if she said she was staying with him, I'd have to knock her upside the head and drag her away from that bastard. "I haven't heard you mention any other plans, so when my mom called saying friends at Carolina Beach were looking for a pet sitter for a month, I said yes."

She doesn't respond, so I tap the message. "And I'm asking if you want to do it with me."

"Live with you?"

"Well, me and whatever pets these people have. At the beach."

"But what about..." She sits back, hugging her knees into her chest. "Keeping this a secret?"

Her expression is hard to read, but I don't think it's a hard no, so I unfold the Cootie Catcher all the way to reveal the final triangle, the one that all this has been building to. Then I hold it out so she can read the question and the multiple-choice answers with little boxes next to them.

Clearing my throat, where my heart seems to have taken up residence, I read, "Will you be mine? Yes or no."

Then I hand her a marker. A permanent marker.

TWENTY-FOUR

Subj: Dog and house sitting
Date: 12/5/1999 7:45:45 AM
From: TheSwansonFamily
To: Ford_soundguy

Hi Ford,
Your mom gave me your electronic mail
address, so I hope it's okay to contact you
this way.
We are so grateful that you're able to stay
at our Carolina Beach place over the holidays. The dogs just go crazy if no one's
there overnight and I hear you like to run
on the beach, which they do too!
I'll send more details soon and get the
keys to your folks this week.
Happy Holidays!

WHITNEY

WHEN I DON'T IMMEDIATELY ANSWER, Ford's
face falls. All the hope that had his eyes bright and the

corners of his mouth lifted just drains away. And then he gets out of bed.

"Are you leaving?"

"No. I really have to pee."

The minute he mentions it I have to go too, so when he emerges from the bathroom we do a silent, awkward little dance in the doorway. When I come out, he isn't back in bed. He's got clothes on and is cleaning up.

I know I've hurt him by not answering, but it's a big fucking question. It's one thing to out ourselves to a crew we may never see again but a whole other thing for me to prance around Wallington with him. I'm still married, after all.

Silently, I put my own clothes back on. I say nothing while I help him fold up the sheet, put the cushions back on the couch, and carry the dishes to the kitchenette. While he does the dishes, I make the bed. When the room is clean, he says, "I think I'm going to go for a run."

"Ford—" I begin.

He holds up a hand. "It's fine. I obviously pushed too far too fast."

"You did. But—" I gesture around the room where the evidence of the magical night has been erased. "Last night was amazing. Just what I needed."

"Except for the part where you don't want me to touch you in public."

He's standing in the middle of the room, looking anywhere but at me. Every taut muscle in his body says that he's in pain. Even though my instinct is to run from what feels like a trap somehow, I sit on the couch and pat the spot next to me. "Can we talk about this?"

He doesn't say anything for a long moment but finally blows out a breath and settles on a cushion as far from me as possible.

"I just don't know if I can do what you want," I begin. "Be who you want. It's one thing to go public here, with people who aren't all up in our business. But to live as a couple in Wallington… that's a whole other thing."

"Why? We're already more than friends. Friends plus lovers equals partners."

"Come on, Ford. It's not that simple."

"I think it is if you want it to be. I want more. If you don't, then—"

"First of all," I say, cutting him off. "I am still married. And I have a lot of shit to do to get out of that marriage. I don't want Hardy to have any ammunition against me. Like accusing me of having an affair."

He opens his mouth to argue, but I roll on. "Then there's Violet, Dani, and Sully. I don't want to lose their friendship. And when you and I break up, I have a feeling I'll be the one to go."

"What? Why do you say that?"

"That's what happened last year."

"From what I heard, it was you avoiding them, not the other way around. But what I really mean is, why do you assume we'll break up?"

"I've never hung on in a relationship long term. Neither have you. Seems like a pretty clear track record."

"I don't know about you but—" he breaks off, looking like he wants to put on his running shoes and sprint out that door instead of continuing this conversation.

But when he turns to face me again, something has changed. "I don't know about you, but I've never felt for anyone else what I feel for you. And before you start, it's not just that we've known each other forever. It's not the puppy love I felt for you at fifteen or eighteen or even twenty-one. It's not that you're even more beautiful now than you were then. Or how much I admire your courage, your resilience. Or how good you are at your job."

He takes my hand, but it's the vulnerability in his eyes pinning me in place. "When something happens to me, or I have an idea, you're the first person I want to share it with. When I wake up in the morning, you're the first person I want to see. I want you to be the last person I see when I go to bed at night. You're my person, Whitney, and I want to be friends with all the benefits. Your partner in all the things."

I have an argument for every single one of these statements, including the fact that our chosen careers will probably have us separated more often than not, but the love radiating from his heart to mine banishes those perfectly logical thoughts. I can't let go, even if it won't last.

So, taking his hand, I say the scariest thing imaginable. "I want those things too, but I don't know if I know how."

His eyes light up like a Christmas tree. "Obviously, I don't either. But I want to figure it out. With you."

Hope balloons in my chest, and I float right off the couch.

"Are you leaving?"

I hold out a hand. "If we're going to the wrap party as a couple, we need to go shopping."

FORD

Monday is a crazy day. I barely get to see Whit. She's covering the background actors and from what I hear, not a one of them came camera ready. Either they had way too much makeup on or none at all.

My department's busy too. One scene has so many bodies there's no way we can cover them, even if both Ronnie and Walt boom. The combination of boomed and planted mics plus a few wired actors means that the mix requires my constant attention, to keep everyone sounding like they're in the same room.

On top of all that, there's a weird whistling sound that

takes half an hour to pin down, meaning that half the takes are garbage, anyway.

All of this puts me in a rare mood. When I hear "check the gate" all I want is to wrap my arms around Whitney and a beer, in that order.

Unfortunately, she's still got a giant mess to clean up in background holding so I have to be satisfied with just the beer. And when I wake up in my bed at three in the morning, still wearing all my clothes, I'm alone. Too late to call Whit, but I find a note on the carpet by the door.

I knocked but there was no answer, so I figured you went to bed early.
See you tomorrow.
XOXO, W

Kicking myself for missing out on a night with her, I struggle to get back to sleep. Until I remember that after this week, we'll have almost a month together.

THE NEXT DAY, WHITNEY CARRIES A CHAIR OVER TO MY RIG AND for the first time, asks if she can sit with me. Grinning from ear to ear, I make room so she can watch the monitor.

"No background duty today?"

"No, thank god. I got to do Cyn's makeup instead." She juts her chin at the actress now on screen. "You're closer than video village for once. Can I, uh, have headphones?"

Makeup rarely cares about listening to the actors because their job is all about the look, but I just push the talk button on my mic. "Hey, Ronnie. Can I have another Comtek?"

My cable guy doesn't hide his surprise when he rounds

the corner and sees Whit sitting next to me. "For you?" he asks her.

"Yes, please," Whitney says, flashing a smile that has the man blushing when he hands her the wireless headphones.

"Fresh battery in there, so you should be good."

"Thanks, Ronnie."

I suppress a growl, but Ronnie's saved by the bell, literally, as the loud ring that tells everyone to shut the hell up because we're about to shoot echoes through the stage. He beats it back to his own cart while I play my part in the pre-shoot count-down, answering "Rolling" when the AD says, "Roll sound" and recording "Ten Baker, Take One"—the scene, setup and take IDs—before the AD calls "Background" and "Action."

Whitney leans close, eyes glued to the image on the monitor as Cynthia and the female lead argue. We're shooting Cyn's POV first because she's number one on the call sheet, but the younger actress doesn't phone it in like some people do when the camera isn't on them. She's giving it a hundred percent.

"Cut. Back to one," the AD calls. "Going again."

We go through a few takes before there's a pause while the director gives Cyn a few notes.

"She's so good," Whitney says quietly. "She gives me chills."

"She's a pro, that's for sure."

Whitney laughs. "High praise coming from you. I've only ever heard you say, 'a loud actor is a good actor.'"

"Unfortunately, that's a bar that most of them don't even reach. But yeah, it's cool to see how her performance changes slightly with each take. And she's obviously aware of the camera moves, but she doesn't lose her connection to the other actress. That's not an easy tightrope to walk."

"She's so generous too. She's been helping me with the bills."

This has me turning to face her. "You let a stranger pay those hospital bills, but you wouldn't let me?"

"No," Whitney hisses, looking around to make sure no one heard what I said. "And keep it down."

Shaken, I force my attention back to work. "Sorry."

Whit places a hand on my arm. "Ford. She's been divorced multiple times, so she knows the rules. She coached me on what to say to the lawyer Dani recommended. I have a meeting with that attorney in Wallington next week. Best of all, the lawyer's already dealing with the hospital, so I don't have to."

Thankfully, I have no experience with divorce, but it still rankles that Whitney asked for help from the actress when she wouldn't accept anything from me. Before I can say anything, though, the AD calls, "Resetting. Back to one. Lock it up."

I really don't want to fuck this job up in the last week. I need a good recommendation from this director and UPM. Forcing my frustrations to the back burner, I turn all my focus onto the job at hand.

Making me wonder if what they say is true: that business and pleasure don't mix.

TWENTY-FIVE

Subj: Last Karaoke Night
Date: 12/7/1999 1:05:01 PM
From: LoveLost_production_office
To: makeupchick1200

Apparently, Buddy's wants to celebrate our crew's last week in town with a free drink for everyone on the Love Lost crew, so be sure to thank them if you're able to go tonight!

WHITNEY

IT SEEMED to make Ford happy that I sat with him on set today, while nobody said boo about it. Still, the more I think about facing the judgment of Violet, Sully, and Dani, it seems like a terrible—and unnecessary—idea to go public back in Wallington.

As is often the case, Ford finishes for the day before I do, since he's the head of his crew, while I'm just another peon who has to do the final packing up and prep for the next day. Not that I mind. I'm grateful for the work and I actually enjoy putting the trailer back in order, knowing that it'll be ready to go when we're all bleary-eyed and half-asleep tomorrow morning.

Tuesday night is karaoke Night at Buddy's, however, and this is our last week in town, so I promised that I'd meet my crew there. I don't bother trying to talk Ford into it. I can hardly expect him to follow through on his sleepover promise when I'm not planning to.

But just as I'm getting settled with my department at our favorite table, Ford walks into the bar.

Even though I didn't say yes to staying with him at the beach. Even though I balked at checking off the box that I know would make him happy, at least in the short term. Instead of joining me, however, he sits on the other side of the room with his guys.

He doesn't look angry, but he's definitely avoiding my gaze. Poor guy, he's probably nervous to get up there. But on my way to tell him that he doesn't have to torture himself by performing, I get waylaid by a nice woman who worked as an extra, and by the time I finish writing a list of product recommendations for her, Ford's no longer in his seat.

Figuring he's getting another beer or visiting the restroom, I continue towards his table. When I get there, Ronnie tips his chin towards the stage. "This your doing?"

Turning around, I find Ford talking to the guy setting up the karaoke equipment. Laughing, I ask, "What? Is he up there telling them how to do their job?"

"I wouldn't put it past him," Walt says, pointing toward the stage. "But he brought his guitar."

My head whips around so fast I make myself dizzy. Grabbing the back of the chair Ford left empty, I ease into it as I watch the stage.

Ford opens his guitar case. The stage tech adjusts the mic stand and brings him a stool. The strum of the guitar sounds through the speakers, followed by Ford clearing his throat.

"Don't worry," he begins. "Karaoke'll start as soon as I'm done here. If you'll humor me, I'm just going to play a song by another Carolina boy. He's a hell of a lot better at this than I am, but… when a friend asks, you gotta deliver."

As the familiar chords of "You've Got a Friend" echo through the room, I'm transported back to the seventies when James Taylor was constantly on the radio. When Ford begins to sing, I swear I can hear women—and probably men— swooning from one end of the room to the other.

I can tell he's nervous from the sweat on his brow, and the gaze that's glued to the floor. Despite the nerves, he's all in, and his surprisingly sweet tenor wraps around my heart and ties it up in a bow.

When he gets to the chorus, the audience joins in. Softly at first, but by the second chorus, the entire room is singing along with him. Until he stops, with a flourish of the guitar. "Y'all don't need me for this. But thanks for listening."

FORD LEAVES THE BAR RIGHT AFTER THAT AND I'M NOT FAR behind. He doesn't lock his door until he goes to bed, and he told me weeks ago that I don't have to knock. I still feel a little weird just barging in, so I announce myself as I walk in.

"Hide the valuables, Whitney's here!"

He startles, eyes wide, and slams his laptop shut.

"Everything okay?"

Nodding quickly, he gets up, drying his palms on his jeans like they're sweaty. "How bad was I?"

I just shake my head. "You didn't have to go through with that, but I'm glad you did. I think it made everybody happy."

"It definitely could've gone worse." He turns to unplug the doohickey that connects the computer to the internet.

At my touch, he relaxes, but not completely. "You're sure everything's okay?"

He sighs. "Yeah, just—you know—trying to get through these last couple days without fucking up. I don't have a job lined up like you do, and I could use a good reference from these people."

"Do you want me to leave so you can go to bed?"

In answer, he steps behind me to peel off my coat. "Nope. I want you to stay so I can go to bed."

After kicking off my shoes, I turn to face him. "Thing is, I'm not that tired."

Arms encircling me, he walks me backward until I run into his bed. "I think I have a solution for that."

Hands to my chest, eyes wide, I ask, "Whatever could that be?"

He proceeds to show me.

LATER, WHEN MY BODY FEELS WORN OUT IN THE MOST DELICIOUS way, after we've washed up and brushed teeth and returned to the bed, we settle into our favorite going-to-sleep position.

When I wake, we'll inevitably be on our sides, either me spooning him or being spooned, or even backs pressed together, and feet entangled. But for whatever reason, Ford always starts out on his back, one arm around me, while I use the space between his shoulder and chest for a pillow.

As his lean muscles relax and I breathe in his musky, masculine scent, it hits me. I don't want this to end. Or even to change. I know it has to. This job will be over at the end of the week. This carnival will pack up and we'll all move on.

I'm grateful that Ford arranged a house-sitting gig for the two of us, but the worry that's been niggling in the back of my mind is suddenly knocking loudly on the front of my skull.

"You awake?" I ask as softly as I can.

"Unh" is his answer.

When I don't say anything more, he squeezes my shoulders. "Whassup?"

My heart racing, I take a deep breath and just jump. "Yes."

He turns to face me, his eyes flashing in the dim light. "Yes, what?"

"To everything. To being together over the holidays. To being yours."

"Are you sure, Whit?"

"I'm not sure it's the best thing to do but... I want to try."

"That's good to know." He pulls me in again, holds me tight. As I drift off to sleep, I don't think I've ever felt so happy.

TWENTY-SIX

Wednesday 12/8/1999
Ford_soundguy: Heads up, y'all.
Just going to cut to the chase:
Whitney and I are together and
will live together in a house
down in Carolina Beach over the
holidays.

FORD

WHITNEY'S CONCERN about the gang's reaction to the two of us getting together isn't entirely unwarranted, so I decide to head drama off at the pass with a warning message in the group buddy chat.

Ford_soundguy: She doesn't know
I'm telling you but I'm doing it
so y'all don't overreact. Please
act surprised but don't judge.
Especially her.

VioletCastingCarolina: WHAT???
How long has this been going on?

DanielleGoodwin856: Um, that was
not part of the plan, Ford.

SullyCallaway999: What they
said.

Ford_soundguy: Tough noogies.
Things happen.

DanielleGoodwin856: But she's
still married, right?

VioletCastingCarolina: Were
y'all together over
Thanksgiving? Cuz I thought
something was up.

Ford_soundguy: Yes, she's
married, but they're obviously
separated.

Ford_soundguy: I'm not getting
into details. All I'm going to
say is that we are happy, so I'm
hoping you'll be happy for us.
We'll be back in WAL late
Sunday, and we'll probably see
you next week. Gotta go.

The minute I disconnect and shut off the computer—
hoping the action snuffs out whatever fire I started—I hope
telling them was the right thing to do.

TWENTY-SEVEN

```
Subj: Checkout
Date: 12/11/1999 12:25:04 PM
From: LoveLost_production_office
To: makeupchick1200
```

Just a reminder that while we do have a late checkout from the motel on Sunday, everyone MUST BE CLEARED OUT by noon at the latest!

Meaning, have fun, but not too much fun at the party tonight.

WHITNEY

MY MOTHER DOESN'T LIKE me to wear pink. She thinks it's tacky, especially hot pink. But I love how certain pinks make my cheeks look rosier, my eyes bluer. So, when I found this hot pink, sparkly off-the-shoulder dress at the vintage store last weekend, I knew I had my outfit for tonight's wrap party.

I would've taken it home and begged the costumer to tailor it for me, but I didn't need to. The minute I saw Ford's eyes when I walked out of that dressing room, roving over the new curves it showcases, I would've bought it for a hundred dollars.

Lucky for me, it was only twenty-five, because that's all I had.

Things with Ford have been on a bit of a roller coaster since Thanksgiving. As usual, all the drama starts with me. But while I'm terrified of facing the music back in Wallington, I want to shine at this party, with Ford right by my side.

With that in mind, I take my time getting ready. My locks aren't bleached blond like Cyn's, but I do help nature along on a regular basis, so I give it a nice mask treatment before putting it in fat rollers. No butterfly clips and messy buns for me tonight. I'm going for classic red-carpet.

I have fun with my makeup, too. First, a light application of matte foundation and powder. I skip blush and put the spotlight on my eyes and lips.

Thinliner is all the rage right now, but this outfit screams Posh Spice, so I start with an ultra-sculpted cat-eye liner in black. Then I add baby blue frosted shadow on the lids, shimmery pink on the brow bones, and finish the look with plenty of black mascara.

I line my lips in a dark burgundy, fill in with a slightly lighter shade, and top it all off with my favorite lacquered lip gloss.

After tucking the gloss and lipstick into my treasured Fendi baguette, I dig through my Caboodle for the body glitter, because if any outfit or occasion calls for sparkle, this one does. Grinning at the image of Ford covered in the stuff later tonight, I pouf it on my cheeks, collarbone, décolletage and arms.

And then it's time to get dressed. Heroin chic may be all the rage, but Ford has said multiple times that he's glad I've gained weight. Still, this dress hugs in all the places, so Wonderbra and waist-cinching Playtex Secret it is.

My mom offered to pay for breast enhancement as a high school graduation present. She was getting them, and I guess she thought it'd be a fun mother-daughter activity, but with all the bad news about the silicone implants, I'm glad that I said no and that she didn't push for once. Still, my boobs are tiny and I'm not too proud to wear a padded bra.

I've just stepped into my favorite sparkly heels when there's a knock on my hotel room door. I open it with a flourish, hoping to see Ford and watch his jaw drop, but it's Susan.

"Wow!" she says, *her* jaw dropping. "Va-va-voom, girl. You look amazing."

She turns a finger in the air, like she wants me to turn around, and I comply, preening, before inviting her in.

After I close the door behind her, she says, "Now you've got me rethinking my little black dress."

"I'm going to be the one with regrets," I say, patting my flattened belly. "I won't be able to eat in this thing. Do you want anything to drink?"

"Nah, I'll wait for the free stuff at the party. I just wanted to stop by and tell you it's official. You are on my crew for Nashville."

Clapping my hands together, I jump up and down. "Yay! I'm so excited. Thank you!"

She shrugs. "It was a no-brainer. You're a hard worker, you're talented and easy to get along with. I'm looking forward to working with you again. I just had to talk them out of hiring a local. Thankfully, they saw the wisdom of my arguments."

She gives me more details on the dates and rates and travel. Just before leaving, though, she asks, "I heard you're going to this shindig with a date. Our sound mixer?"

Not sure where she's going with this, I just nod.

"And you're sure he'll be okay with you taking off halfway across the country?"

I wave that idea out of the way. "It's only a few hundred miles. Anyway, he gets it. Ya gotta go where the work is."

She nods, but her lips press into a flat line, and I'm reminded of our conversation about showmances the first week of production, so I add, "And really, we're just close friends."

"Good," Susan says. "I'd hate to have you back out at the last minute because your heart gets in the way."

"Not this heart." I point to my chest. "It may look sparkly pink, but inside it's as cold as stone."

This has her laughing all the way out the door.

Leaving me to break the news to Ford. That we need to go back to just friends.

FORD

I'm just buttoning my jacket when there's a knock on my door. Checking my watch, I realize I'm a little late to pick up Whitney, so I open it, planning to put off whoever's on the other side.

Until I see who it is.

The dress Whitney picked out when we went shopping last weekend at a vintage place looked awesome on her, but I couldn't have pictured this complete transformation. She looks like a fucking movie star. From the heels to the hair, she glows. In fact, some sort of sparkly stuff highlights her elegant shoulders and the rise of her breasts above the neckline of the dress.

But it's her eyes and lips that I keep going back to. I love Whitney's face free of makeup, but she is a pro, and her artwork showcases those big blue eyes and full, pouty lips.

"Aren't you going to invite me in?"

My brain seems to have reverted to its Neanderthal roots,

because all I can think about is peeling her out of the beautiful dress.

"Ford?"

Literally shaking myself, I manage a "No."

Perfectly shaped brows come together. "You're not inviting me in?"

"No. I, uh…" *Deep breath in, deep breath out. Redirect the blood flow from the penis to the brain.* "If you come in, that dress won't last long."

She laughs. "Ah, okay."

But then her expression shifts. She looks up and down the hall before leaning closer. Unfortunately, this has her scent wafting into my nose. Something new, but just as hormone activating. "Before we go to the party, I need—"

I hold up a hand. "Sorry to interrupt, but if you want to actually get to this party, we need to get away from my room."

She laughs again, but there's something brittle about it.

"We can talk in the car, okay?" I reassure her.

Once I've bundled her into Gertie, because really, she's the perfect coach for this Cinderella, I blast the heat and head for the party. Glancing over, I find my princess's gaze out the window, and even from this angle she looks pensive.

"Is everything okay?" She takes my free hand and I immediately envelop it in mine. "Are you warm enough? Your hand is freezing."

"I'm sorry to go back on my promise from the other night. Again. But we can't go as a couple to this party."

"Is this because I didn't actually do karaoke?"

She laughs, but it's not the cackle of delight I love so much. "No, I think you did one better than karaoke. It's something else. Good news is, Susan stopped by to tell me I officially have the Nashville job."

Even though this isn't exactly good news for me, I'm man enough to congratulate her. "What's the bad news?"

"I guess she's had crew abandon her at the last minute because of relationship stuff, so I had to reassure her that wouldn't be the case with me."

"You know I wouldn't stand in your way."

"Yes, but *she* doesn't know that." She flips our hands over to squeeze mine. "I told her we were just good friends. I'm sorry, but I really need this job, Ford."

My first instinct is to argue. To say that Susan isn't treating her like an adult. That Whitney's love life is none of her fucking business.

But I can tell how worried she is. Determined not to let Whitney pull away completely, I bring her hand to my lips and give her knuckles a kiss. "If I promise to play your friend this evening, do I get to be your lover back at the hotel? And in our house over the holidays?"

She breathes out a sigh of relief. "Yes, please. And thank you for understanding."

"That's what friends are for," I say, almost but not completely extracting the bitterness from my tone.

WHITNEY DOES ME A SOLID AND KEEPS HER DANCING WITH other men to a minimum. I don't think I could stand to watch any of the guys in the room press themselves up against that dress and her soft curves. But the ones who've been salivating over her the whole shoot, the ones that make their interest obvious, I stalk them like a tiger, practically growling as I step in whenever any of them get too close to her.

Mostly, she dances in a circle with her crew and then returns to me on the slow songs. Each time, I'm ready with hydration and a snack, like a good wingman.

It's a blast watching her let it rip with "U Can't Touch This" and Haddaway's "What is Love." No one's ever going to see me out there throwing my body around and whooping it up, but I get the need for catharsis.

Working inhuman hours under constant pressure to create something great—or as is the case with this movie, something pretty good—creates a special camaraderie. We need to celebrate that it's over and mourn the people we'll miss. Sometimes I think the closeness results from knowing it's going to end. That's definitely been the case with any flings I've had during a shoot.

I am not anywhere near ready for things to end between Whitney and me, however. I just need to figure out how to convince her I'm in it for the long haul.

As for this wrap party, my clock is ticking. After I watch her and her crew belt along with La Bouche as they dance to "Be My Lover," I decide it's time to be her lover again. The next time she retreats to our table for a break, I can't keep myself from leaning close to growl, "The sooner we get out of here, the sooner I can make you come."

She leans away to catch my gaze, and I love seeing my desire mirrored in her eyes. When she turns to scan the room, her teeth catching the plump plum of her lower lip, I whisper, "All over my face."

A shudder runs through her. "Sold."

WHITNEY

Ford does exactly as promised. I swear I've had more orgasms in the past month than I've had in my entire life. Mind-blowing sex, dancing my ass off, and the compliments I got all night have me on the top of the world. I leave Ford in my bed so I can shower off the makeup and sweat, and when I return to snuggle in next to him, I have what seems like a really good idea.

"I'm just wondering if we could keep things the way they are when we go back to Wallington."

His arm tenses. "Uh… what do you mean?"

Shifting away so I can see his face, I say, "Tonight went well, so maybe we should just do it on repeat. I'm also still worried about going public."

He flops a hand over his face but says nothing.

"Maybe we could share part of the truth? That we're sharing the pet sitting gig because we both need a place to stay—which is obviously true for me. You've said your parents' house usually fills up with out-of-town relatives over the holidays, so it could be true for you. I mean, it's probably why your mom hooked you up in the first place, right?"

He's quiet for so long that I wonder if he's gone back to sleep, but the tense muscles in his arm and shoulder tell me it's that unlikely.

"Are you embarrassed of me? Of us?" he finally asks.

I nestle closer, needing the contact. Wanting to keep this from going awry. "No. It's the other way around. I'm the one who brings the drama. As usual."

I try to lace my words with humor, but even in the dim light, I can see frustration building in the hard planes of his profile.

"Plus, Violet is about to have a baby and it's the holidays, so everyone will be busy. And this"—still not exactly sure what to call this, I circle my hand over his chest in a way that I hope will communicate affection—"is still so new. I don't want to share it or you."

His lips press together like he's trying not to say something.

"I mean, we'll be heading off in different directions in January, so can't we just enjoy each other in private? Keep it just between us?"

He shifts away from me, moving his arm to fold it behind

his head. "Are you saying you want to break up after the holidays?"

The anger in his tone has me sitting up. "No, Ford. I'm just being realistic. We're living in a bubble here. It's like we've had this awesome time at sleep-away camp and now we have to go home, back to the real world."

"So, you *are* saying you want to end this."

"You're the one who keeps saying that. Do *you* want to break up?"

He rolls over, turning away from me, and mumbles something into his pillow.

"I can't hear you," I practically shout at him.

He turns his head to face the ceiling. "We can do whatever you want. I'm exhausted. Let's just go to sleep." And then he rolls back to his side, facing the door again.

"Don't fucking turn away from me Ford."

I shove his back. Hard. And then he finally rolls over and sits up. "What do you want from me, Whitney? To say, hooray, I'm so excited to think about the fact that this thing between us, the love I feel for you, has to have an expiration date? Like it's doomed to go bad?"

The word love catches against the sharp edges of my heart, but I won't let it stop me from facing reality. "We are living in hotel rooms, away from our friends and families, away from the fact that I have shit-ton of details to deal with in order to extricate myself from my mistake of a marriage. In addition, you have said multiple times that your career is your priority."

He opens his mouth to protest, argue, who knows what, but I stop him. "And I have to make my career a priority. I need to work. Need to get enough hours in so that when my marriage ends, I have health insurance. Need to save money so I can afford a car, and first month's rent on an apartment."

His face is stone, not agreeing or denying now, so I just barrel on. "And you've only been mixing exclusively for a year, right? You need to be free to take the next job no matter where it takes you."

"Can I speak now?"

"Of course."

"Everything you're saying adds up to, you want to break up."

"I'm not the one using those words. You are."

"Then I must be the dumb one here because I don't understand."

Anger flares at his reference to me being the dumb one, but I blow it away. "I don't want to be involved with anyone but you, Ford. I'm just asking if we can protect what we have for the next month by keeping it private."

"And after that?"

"I guess we just take it one step at a time."

He stares off into space for a long time. So long that I'm worried I've pushed too far, that he feels like I'm saying no again, but just as I reach out for his hand, he catches it and holds on tight.

"Okay. If that's what you need, that's what we'll do."

TWENTY-EIGHT

Sunday, 12/12/1999 8:12 AM
Ford_soundguy: RED ALERT.
Whitney has asked that we
continue to keep our
relationship secret. So you
DON'T KNOW about it. Okay?

SullyCallaway999: What happened?

VioletCastingCarolina: This is a
relationship now? Not just a
fling?

DanielleGoodwin856: Maybe it's
for the best.

Ford_soundguy: She got cold
feet, I think. And things are
more complicated in Wallington
with her still being married
and all.

    Ford_soundguy: Officially, we
    are doing this house-sitting gig
    together as friends because we
    both need a place to stay. And
    you know nothing about any of
    it. Got it?

    SullyCallaway999: OK. Whatever
    you want, man.

    VioletCastingCarolina: I'm going
    to need an in-person discussion
    about this, but OK.

    DanielleGoodwin856: Yep.

WHITNEY

SUNDAY MORNING, it's a scramble to check out of the motel, even though they've given the entire crew a late checkout time. I don't know about Ford, but it took me a long time to fall asleep last night, so I'm pretty groggy when the alarm goes off. He doesn't say much before grabbing his stuff and heading back to his room to finish packing.

My own process takes longer than it should, partly because I keep going over the fight from the night before, trying to figure out where it went wrong. Partly because people keep coming by to say goodbye with promises to stay in touch and exchanges of phone numbers and email addresses. By the time I get on the road, I'm exhausted, so I crank up the tunes and sing along the entire ride back to Wallington.

Our plan is to meet at Ford's parents' house to get the key from his mother. He drives faster than I do—heaven forbid I get Gertie into an accident, so I'm even more careful than usual—so when I arrive, he's already there.

After I park behind his truck, reality hits. The Thanksgiving visit was in-and-out, so I didn't worry about running into Hardy or my parents or people from that part of my life. But being here a whole month means they'll be tougher to avoid.

A knock on Gertie's window startles me and has me flinching away from the glass. I roll down the window to find a man that looks a lot like Ford. "You lost, miss?" he asks, his accent much thicker than Ford's.

"Oh, no. I'm meeting Ford."

The guy points at the truck. "Looks like he's arrived. Come on in the house."

He opens the door for me and helps me out of the car. "I'm his older brother Fred. The good-looking one with the normal name."

"I see that. We've met, I think. Back in high school?" Back in high school, Fred was close with the writer who created *Lawson's Reach*. I'm pretty sure he stayed at home to work in the family business. "I'm Whitney. Whitney Moore."

His brows shoot up and he looks me up and down. Not leering, just curious. "Right, Whitney."

A little unnerved, I wave my hand at him like a dork. "That's me."

"After you." He gestures up the walk. "Heard a lot about you."

"All bad, I'm sure."

"Pretty much the polar opposite, actually. The kid worships you."

"Well, there's no accounting for taste."

He opens the front door without knocking and ushers me inside. "I can't fault him myself."

"Do you live here?" I ask.

"Nah. I live over in Brunswick County. I'm here for Sunday dinner too."

I wasn't aware we were here for Sunday dinner, but before

I can say anything, Fred hollers, "Ford! Your girlfriend's here!"

"Oh, I'm not—" I begin to say, but before I can finish Fred gets tackled out of nowhere. He staggers into me, and I land on my butt.

"Goddamn it, Pete!" Fred turns around and offers me a hand. "You okay, hon?"

"I'll live." I smile to let him know I'm fine, but I squeak as he hauls me to my feet. "Damn, girl, you're so light a strong wind'd blow you away. We got to get some meat on these bones."

Ford appears and there's a lot of yelling and back slapping between him and Fred and Pete and what seems like a dozen other people. Eventually, I'm pulled into a small kitchen in the back of the house, where an older woman is barking orders and pulling food out of the oven that smells amazing.

Her face lights up when she sees me. "You must be Whitney. So glad you could join us."

"Yes, ma'am, that's me." Ford rarely talks about his family, and I've never been invited over, so this warm welcome is not at all what I expected. I was raised with good Southern manners, though, so I add. "So nice to meet you, Mrs. Fischer. Dinner smells amazing. Is there anything I can do to help?"

She swats at a hand trying to steal cheese off the top of a casserole, and barks a few more orders to the young men hovering in the doorway. To me she says, "You're fine, honey," which in Southern means "We're all set, thanks."

I ask Ford for directions to the powder room, which makes one of the younger guys snicker, and he guides me out of the chaos and down a hall. He knocks before opening the door, but before I can step inside, he says, "Guess we're staying for dinner. Sorry for the ambush," and then pulls me in for a kiss.

A good long kiss. What I hope is an *I've-forgiven-you* kiss. So good and so long that my knees are weak, and my brain is mush when he breaks it.

When he's done undoing me, he gently pushes me through the door. Closing it behind me, he says, "Lock don't work but don't worry, I'll guard the door."

BY THE TIME WE'RE FINALLY HEADING TO CAROLINA BEACH, I'M exhausted. But in a good way. The muscles of my belly and my face ache from all the laughing over the past couple of hours. The feeling in that house is the polar opposite of what it was like growing up in mine.

I have to make myself pay attention to follow the directions Mrs. Fischer wrote down for us, because my mind just keeps comparing moments from tonight's dinner with scenes from my childhood.

By the time I pull into the driveway and haul my weekend bag up the stairs to the door, Ford has already let the dogs out —top of the to-do list we'd received—and the three of them are lounging together on the sectional couch.

"Is dinner always like that at your house?" I blurt, unable to contain myself.

"If you mean loud as hell and too much food, then yes," he says.

Ford has developed pretty good Whitney-dar, so when I don't say more, he gets up off the couch and pulls me into a hug. "Were they too much for you?"

Tears spring to my eyes for some reason, so I keep my face buried in his chest and just shake my head no.

"Did you hate the food?"

I shake my head again.

"Did somebody say something rude? Who was it? Because I'll go back there right now and punch him in the face, the asshole."

I blow out a breath, ease out of his arms, and drop onto

the couch. The smaller of the two dogs immediately crawls into my lap and I stroke its soft fur.

Ford pushes the big dog out of the way to sit next to me. "What's going on?"

"I just—" I begin, but I'm just not sure how to explain.

He tucks a curl behind my ear. "I know you grew up in a much nicer house. I'm really sorry if the bathroom was gross. And the food was so basic. It's one reason I never invited you over. That, and you made it pretty clear that you wouldn't have been allowed."

"Ford, it's not any of those things. I mean, the bathroom" —I stop myself, because that's my mother talking. When a whole family shares a bathroom, it's got to be hard to keep it clean. "What I mean is, it was a lot different at my house."

"Well, duh. Y'all are rich."

"Not in a good way." Hugging the dog to me, I shift to face him. "Was it like that at your friends' houses, too?"

He shrugs. "Everybody's different. Like, at Sully's house, they have these intellectual debates. I actually preferred it there. I never really spent time at Dani's or Vi's, except for parties her grandparents hosted and sneaking into her room to watch TV."

He tips his head to the side, considering. "But my other guy friends, I mean, I guess. Loud people giving each other shit or competing to do stupid shit. Food that fills you up but isn't fancy. You know, normal stuff. Regular people."

I'd figured that because we had money, I was lucky.

But I think I'd have preferred poor and happy.

"Talk to me, Whit. What's upsetting you?"

My mom's voice echoes in my mind, drowning out Ford's.

You're about as useful as a steering wheel on a mule.

Good Lord. If this girl had an idea, it would die of loneliness.

For god's sake, Whitney, I was just joking. Why do you have to be so goddamned sensitive?

Ford shakes my shoulder, breaking through the end-of-the-night TV static in my head. The place I'd disappear to when my mom wouldn't stop yelling at me. Picking at me. Criticizing every little thing about me. "Whit? Are you okay?"

My heart pounding in my throat, feeling like I've been caught in the act of something bad, I force a smile. "I'm just tired. I think I'll go to bed."

FORD

Whatever spooked Whitney at my house seems to have disappeared after a good night's sleep, but I can't shake the feeling that she's hiding something from me. Everything that went down the last couple of days up in Charlotte taught me that pushing her doesn't work, however, so instead of demanding definitions or answers, I plan to do my best to make our time together fun.

This morning, I bring her coffee in bed and then spend the next few hours loving every soft, sweet-smelling inch of her body.

Once we've both been thoroughly satisfied, she announces that she'll make breakfast. "Hope you like toaster waffles, because that's the only thing they left us."

"Love 'em. But maybe we should do a little grocery shopping?"

The Piggly Wiggly tempts us into making festive holiday purchases, as well as breakfast and lunch basics for the next few weeks. Neither of us is much of a cook, but we figure even we can make Christmas cookies with Slice 'n Bake cookie dough and cocoa from a mix.

On the way back to the beach house, Whitney makes me stop at a church where Christmas trees are on sale, and then talks me into buying the scraggliest, most pitiful looking little tree they've got.

"They have other ones that're small." I point to an entire aisle of cute trees under two feet tall.

She holds up the sad tree. "But this one needs us. It'll be our Charlie Brown tree. Please?"

We stop at the hardware store and Whitney grabs a string of lights, a roll of thin wire, and a can of gold spray paint. Back at the house, while we take the dogs for a long walk on the beach, Whitney collects shells in a bucket she found in a storage shed under the house. When we get back, she spreads newspaper on the deck's picnic table, and spends an hour making ornaments with the paint, wire, and seashells.

Meanwhile, I nestle the tree in a bigger beach bucket and do my best to string it with lights without knocking the poor thing over. I get some cookies baking while Whitney adds her decorations, and then we toast our tree with spiked cocoa and sugar cookies.

"He's perfect," Whitney says with an appreciative sigh. "This is perfect."

I hug her into my side. "We're a pretty damn good team."

"We are," she agrees, cuddling closer. But then she sits up, sniffing. "Is that   "

"Shit. The second batch of cookies." Leaping to my feet, I bump into the coffee table. I watch in horror as the mug I'd just set down tips over, and a stream of hot cocoa spreads across the glass, heading for the white shag rug.

And then the fire alarm goes off.

"You get the oven, I've got this!" Whitney yells, whipping her shirt off and diving to stanch the spill.

After I've removed the blackened cookies from the oven, opened the kitchen windows to let the smoke out, teetered on top of a kitchen chair so I can turn off the blaring alarm, answered the phone to reassure the fire department that there's smoke but no fire, and then called my mother so she can tell the Simpson's that all is well, I return to the living room.

To find Whitney sprawled across the couch, her shirt a chocolate mess, laughing her ass off.

"So much for perfect," I growl.

Two sparkling eyes meet mine. "That was better than perfect. It was fun."

THE NEXT DAY WHIT HAS AN APPOINTMENT WITH THE DIVORCE lawyer, so I call around until I can find someone to go Christmas shopping with me.

When I ask Dani if she's interested, she says, "Why didn't you ask Violet? She's much better at this shit than I am."

"She's too busy quote-unquote 'nesting.' Says she did her Christmas shopping in October."

"Of course, she did." Dani clears her throat dramatically. "You sure it doesn't have to do with the fact that Violet will get the four-one-one on your relationship status out of you faster?"

I stifle a groan. "You know what? Forget it."

"Wait, wait," she says, before I can hang up. "You know we're all just concerned. About both of you getting hurt."

"I appreciate that, but you're just going to have to let us figure it out ourselves."

When she doesn't say anything, I ask, "Do you hear me bugging you about whatever the hell is going on between you and your so-called-fake husband?"

She does not stifle her groan. "Fine."

"Will you call off Violet as well?"

"You know I can't control her."

After a long moment where I weigh the pros and cons of getting shopping help versus dealing with nosy friends I finally ask, "So, any ideas? For a present for Whitney?"

She doesn't hesitate. "She's used to expensive shit, Ford.

Designer stuff. You want to go that route? A five-hundred-dollar handbag or whatever?"

"I can't compete with Hardy's money, or her parents, but I don't think that's what she'd want, anyway. I'm thinking something handmade."

"Ooh, I know," Dani says. "There's this cute little shop downtown that has stuff made by locals."

"Sounds perfect."

She gives me the address and thirty minutes later we're browsing through the store, smelling candles, and laughing at snarky messages on t-shirts.

"I hear Whit's headed to Nashville in January," Dani says.

"I thought we weren't talking about this."

She throws up her hands. "What? I'm talking work here. Do you know where *you're* working next?"

"I've got a line on a couple things, but nothing solid." Usually, I work the phones to nail down the next job before the current one ends, but I guess I've been distracted by whatever you can call this thing with Whitney.

"You should definitely talk to Helen. She knows the Line Producers on both the pilots coming to town. If you booked one of them and the show got picked up, then you could work here instead of running all over the country."

"Good idea," is what I say, but I wonder how it'd feel to work here, to hang out with my friends on the weekend if Whitney's not around.

At the same time, does it make sense to plan my life around her when we have nothing solid between us? I've never wanted to do that for a woman. Not even for Whitney, really. But getting so close to having an actual relationship with her… I don't want to give up yet.

Dani raps on my forehead. "Earth to Ford. Hello?"

Swatting her hand away, I snap, "Jesus. Leave me alone."

"I've been standing here talking to you for, like, five minutes. Did you not hear a word I said?"

"I've got a lot on my mind," I growl.

"Mm-hm." Her expression is suspicious as she dangles a necklace in front of me. "How about this for Whit?"

I take it from her and study the tiny sea-green bottle attached to a delicate silver chain.

"It's hand-blown glass, and the sand inside is from Wrightsboro Beach. Might be nice for her to have a reminder of us when she's out of town."

Appreciative that she truly seems to have let her curiosity go, I give her a genuine smile. "Thanks. Good find. Now what about Luke?"

TWENTY-NINE

```
Subj: Your appointment
Date: 12/14/1999 9:15:34 AM
From: Wallington_Family_Law_PLLC
To: makeupchick1200
```

Hello Whitney,
This is a confirmation of your appointment with Rebecca Edelman on Tuesday, December 14 at 1:00 PM.
Rebecca looks forward to meeting with you. Please reply to this email with any questions.

WHITNEY

MY MEETING with Rebecca Edelman was only supposed to last an hour. When it turned into two and I apologized for taking up so much of her time, she reassured me that Hardy will pay for it.

That wasn't the only good news. Rebecca thinks it's an open and shut case in terms of what I'm owed monetarily, although Hardy's apparently now claiming that a self-induced abortion caused the infection. That claim scared the crap out of me, but Rebecca called it a Hail Mary pass.

"If he's spewing that kind of bullshit, he's desperate or crazy. Abortion is legal. No woman would induce one unless she was afraid of her husband. Either way, we win."

Then things got sticky. My face must've revealed something, and before I knew it, Rebecca had a whole new game plan, which includes me seeing a therapist. "Listen, from the little you've told me so far, this sounds like an abusive relationship."

"What? But he never hit me or anything."

"Physical abuse isn't the only kind of domestic abuse. Financial abuse and emotional abuse can be as damaging to your psychological well-being, if not more. The things you've mentioned, just in passing"—she ticks items off on her fingers—"the bank accounts in his name only, he didn't allow you to work, isolated you from friends, controlled what you ate and wore... this is all classic abusive behavior."

Her casual use of the term abuse has me pinned to the chair.

Rebecca comes around the desk and takes a seat in the empty client chair next to me. "I'm sorry if this is upsetting to you, Whitney."

"I-I guess I just feel like an idiot. How did I let this happen to me?"

"I'd imagine he's a pretty successful man. Charming, well-respected, especially in his line of work?"

"Um, yes. He makes a lot of money, anyway."

"The veneer of social superiority is all part of the guise. It makes it easier to convince you and everyone around you that everything is normal. To make you doubt your own sense of reality when you question the one he presents."

My stomach churns, and I'm afraid I'm going to hurl right here on her beautiful walnut desk. A cup of water appears in my hand and Rebecca encourages me to sip at it. "Are you staying with someone? Someone you trust?" she asks.

Not with this, is my first reaction, but I nod anyway.

"I just want to make sure you won't be alone right now. Again, I'm sorry if this comes as a shock." She returns to the other side of her desk to search through a tiny file box, then hands me a business card. "If it's all right with you, I'm going to have my secretary set up an appointment with Laura Robinson. She'll be sure you get in as soon as possible."

I stare at the card, which reads, *Laura Robinson: Marriage and Family Therapy*. "But I—"

"It will help to talk to her. Just give it a try. If you don't gel with her, let me know and I'll help you find someone else. It's important. Not only for your mental health, but for this case."

After I leave Rebecca's office, I do my best to pretend that everything's okay. Meanwhile, I'm walking around feeling like my skin's been peeled back and everyone can see what a freak I am.

Because if Hardy's behavior makes him an abuser, then my mom is one too.

Has it always been obvious to everyone but me that my family was messed up, as well as my marriage? I never felt like I fit in with the debutante crowd or Wallington's inner circle. But maybe everyone kept me at arm's length because they knew my secrets. Judging me for marrying my husband, for putting up with mistreatment from my parents.

But that makes no sense. And if my real friends knew, wouldn't they have helped?

I'm so disturbed that I'm tempted cancel on our dinner plans with Nate and Vi. But then Ford would just spend the night asking me what's wrong. Like he's been doing all day.

After he parks in front of Vi and Nate's house, Ford turns

to me. "Are you sure everything's okay? Hardy's not turning the screws again, is he?"

I keep telling him that the news is all good on the divorce front. Which is the truth. But he obviously knows that I'm upset, so I make something up. Something that might be just a little bit true. "Maybe the reality of Violet actually being a mom is hitting me."

"I'm sorry." He takes my hand and squeezes it. "Just tell me if you want to leave. We'll say we have to let the dogs out on a certain schedule."

I nod, unwilling to take the lie further, and we go inside.

Violet greets us with hugs, but her belly's so big she can barely get her arm around me. "I am so damn ready to get this baby out of this body."

Despite working full-time running her own casting business, Violet has somehow decorated her home from stem to stern for Christmas. From the enormous tree in the front window to the garland and lights draped artfully across the mantle and up the stairs to the cinnamon scented candles burning everywhere, it's like a magazine spread in here, and I tell her so.

"Nate did all the work."

He puts an arm around her and kisses the top of her head. "She told me what to do, of course."

I do my best to keep my feelings at bay throughout dinner, which includes a course Violet calls "The Salad," which she claims is famous for getting women to go into labor in Los Angeles.

"I really don't want this baby to be born on Christmas. It'd be such a terrible birthday. And we've tried everything else. Long walks, spicy food, lots of"—she cups her hands around her mouth to stage-whisper—"sex."

"Gross," Ford says. "I don't want to hear about that."

"Anyway, I was complaining to Nate's sister about it, and she told me about 'The Salad.'"

"What is 'The Salad?'" I ask.

She holds up a forkful. "Apparently, it's famous out in LA for jump-starting labor."

Ford leans away from his plate and pokes at it, like it might bite back. "What's in it?"

"Just romaine and watercress with walnuts and gorgonzola, but it's the secret recipe dressing that makes it all work. Nate's sister talked the restaurant into giving her a jarful of it and she FedExed it to me. Bon appétit!"

Violet plate is heaped with the stuff, and she dutifully cleans it as we all talk about plans for the coming year.

"Hard to believe it's going to be a whole new century," Ford says.

"As long as the world doesn't shut down on January first," Nate says. "You think this Y2K thing is for real?"

While the three of them talk about backing up computers, I clear the plates. Even though I insist on cleaning up, Violet follows me into the kitchen and settles on a stool while I fill the dishwasher. "Hope the salad works," I say when I notice her studying me.

"Tastes better than cod liver oil, which is the next method on the list."

"Ugh." I shudder. "My mom used to dose me with that stuff."

"It is supposed to be good for you. My grandmother swears by it for her rheumatism."

"I just thought it was one of my mother's more creative punishments."

When I turn to ask if she wants the salad bowl in the dishwasher, she's got a funny look on her face.

"You doing okay?" she asks.

I shrug the question off. "Of course."

"You want to tell me why you're staying at some place way down in Carolina Beach over the holidays instead of at your parents' house?"

I busy myself with arranging the silverware just so in the rack. "They didn't invite me."

"What? Why?"

"I guess my parents are still mad that I won't beg Hardy to take me back."

"You guess? You haven't even talked to them?"

"Not everyone has a family like yours, Vi."

She snorts. "You mean parents too busy to show up for the birth of their first grandchild?"

I blow out a breath. "Sorry. I meant your grandparents. I guess I always think of them as your family."

"Me too, to be honest." She narrows her eyes at me. "But you didn't answer my question."

"I can't—I don't want to talk to my parents, okay? I don't think I ever want to talk to them again. Turns out my childhood was pretty fucked up if you really want to know."

"What do you mean?" Violet's gasps. "Oh my god. They didn't—I mean, your father didn't—"

I wave a hand in the air. "No, nothing like that. But"—my chin wobbles and I have to swallow back the emotion clogging my throat—"I think the way they raised me set me up to be a perfect victim for a man like Hardy."

Violet narrows her eyes, and it's clear I've said too much. "It's not a big deal. Just something I have to, uh, deal with."

"I'm still confused."

"Oh, shit." I point at the clock. "It's later than I thought. We have to get back to let the dogs out before they pee all over the floor."

"But—"

"I'm fine, Vi. Don't worry about me. You've got a full plate as it is."

And then I get out of there before I spill any more shameful details about my fucked-up existence.

<h1>THIRTY</h1>

Wednesday, 12/15/1999 9:34 PM

VioletCastingCarolina: Ford, what the hell is going on with Whitney? Are you not telling us something we should know?

Ford_soundguy: I mean, she met with the lawyer. That was all good. What are you talking about?

VioletCastingCarolina: At dinner tonight, she said something about her childhood being fucked up. And not like her being a spoiled, overprotected princess, but that they "set her up to be a victim." Do you know anything about this?

DanielleGoodwin856: Victim? Of what?

Ford_soundguy: You sure you're not overreacting?

```
SullyCallaway999: Not a good
thing to say to a woman, Ford.
Especially a pregnant one.

DanielleGoodwin856: Vi, it's
good she went to the lawyer. It
sounds like she's dealing
with it.

VioletCastingCarolina: I guess.
It just really creeped me out. I
felt like there was a lot more
that she didn't want to tell me.

SullyCallaway999: So maybe we
let her tell us when and if
she's ready?
```

FORD

AFTER THE LATEST Buddy List chat with Vi and the others, I'm left in a quandary. While I'm relieved that they're no longer fixated on what's happening between Whit and me, I really don't know what to say to them about Whitney's frame of mind. She has seemed distracted since meeting with the lawyer earlier in the week. She's been out almost every day, either with another appointment—I assume something having to do with her divorce—or doing what she calls "errands." Every time I ask if everything's okay, she either changes the subject or gets defensive.

I don't want to waste the time we have together, so I resolve to back off, hoping that she'll tell me if there's anything I can do. Instead of prying further, whenever I can, I swoop into the living room, scoop her into my arms, and haul her off the bed to show her how much I care about her.

DURING A QUIET BREAKFAST THE NEXT MORNING I IMAGINE BEING able to sit across a kitchen table—or island, or peninsula, because it's likely the location will change—with Whitney for years to come. Even if it doesn't happen every single day, as long as I know it'll happen again, I can be content.

After she leaves to do yet another errand, I get dressed for a run. Before I make it out the door, the phone rings.

"The famous salad worked," Nate says without preamble. "Violet's in labor."

"Wow. That's great. Right? It's good news?"

"She says it is."

"Should we come to the hospital?"

"*We're* not even going to the hospital yet. It's the early stage. We went to see her OBGYN, and she wants Vi to wait until she's further along. We'll keep you posted, though."

Before I can ask if they need anything else, he says, "Oh, that's the call waiting, probably my mom calling back."

I tell him I'll call the rest of the gang. "That'd be great, man."

After leaving messages for everyone, I attach a note for Whit to the refrigerator, and head down to the beach with both dogs in tow.

By the time I get back, Whitney has returned. "She's having the baby?"

"Yes, and no. Sounded like it could take some time."

The phone rings and Whit snatches it up before I can. "Oh hey, Sully. Yeah, no more news yet."

They continue to chat, so I whisper, "I'm gonna take a shower."

I've just lathered up when Whit walks into the bathroom, so I stick my head out. "Want to join me? Plenty of room in here. As yesterday's experiment proved."

Instead of stripping, she leans on the counter, arms crossed. "Did you tell Helen I was looking for work?"

I duck back behind the curtain. "Why? Does she have a job for you?"

"Can you answer my question, Ford?"

Not sure how this went wrong, I ask if I can finish my shower before discussing it. Minutes later, dressed but hair still dripping wet, I find her in the kitchen, opening and closing cabinets fueled by what sounds like anger, if the slamming is any sign.

"What's the matter?"

She wheels to face me. "The *matter* is that I have work lined up in Nashville, which you very well know, but Helen just told me she called in a favor with the UPM of one of those pilots shooting here in January, to get me on the hair crew. Did you ask her to do that?"

I scan through my memory of my conversation with Helen. "I asked her to put in a good word for *me*. I might have said something about how nice it'd be if all of us could work in town again."

"Well now, I have to at least talk to this department key, or it makes Helen look bad."

I scrub both hands through my hair. "But wouldn't it be nice if we could work together again?"

She just glares at me. "You can't do this, Ford. I don't like you running around behind my back and fixing things. It makes me feel like you think I can't take care of myself."

"I hear you." Hands up, I go to her slowly. "I'm sorry. I won't do it again."

"Promise?"

"I promise." I hold my arms out and after a beat, she walks into them.

"I'm sorry to snap at you," she mumbles into my chest. "I'm just—I don't like being blindsided like that."

WHITNEY

Christmas is a tricky season when you're trying to save money, but it's especially hard to avoid shopping when one of your closest friends is about to have her very first baby.

After my first therapy appointment, which was just as surreal as the first one with the lawyer, I wander in a daze until I find myself standing in front of one of my favorite Wallington gift shops. Staring at the window display, debating whether I should splurge on the cute little hand-knit teddy bear for Violet's baby, I hear a familiar voice.

My husband's.

I don't even think. Self-preservation has me ducking inside the shop, my heart pounding in terror.

Which should probably tell me that the therapist is right. Before I can sort that out, however, the little bell over the shop door jingles and I hear him again.

This time it's his laugh.

Grabbing two items of clothing from the rack in front of me, I duck into one of the tiny changing rooms and pull the curtain across, my hands shaking.

Hardy hates shopping, so I hold my breath, expecting him to be in and out quickly. But then I smell his cologne. Right outside the curtain.

"Bet you're missing that wife of yours now," a different man says. "Since you have to do all your Christmas shopping yourself."

"Nah," Hardy says. "I've got my secretary doing all that. I just need something for the other woman in my life. You know, the one I told you about this summer?"

Feeling woozy, I ease down onto the bench, my heart pounding loud in my ears.

"You're still seeing the hostess down in Myrtle Beach?"

"She can't get enough of me."

I have to swallow past rising bile to keep from gagging as he goes on to describe his latest encounter with this woman. I can just picture the self-satisfied smirk on his face.

"Your wife never suspected about your sidepiece?" the other man asks.

"Nope."

"She really must've been an airhead."

"She ain't the brightest bulb on the tree, but I also kept her on a very short leash. The housekeeper reported on her every move—told me where she went, with whom and for how long—and I used that knowledge to my advantage."

"For real?"

"Women need to be controlled, Steve. In fact, they prefer it that way."

"Not sure my wife would agree with you," Steve says, with a hollow chuckle.

"Then you need a new wife."

I'm not sure how long I sit in that dressing room after they walk away, but when a clerk knocks on the outer wall to ask if anyone's inside, my voice feels like it's coming from outside my body. "I'll be out in a minute."

Struggling to my feet, embarrassed to find that my armpits are drenched with sweat, I do my best to arrange my face into some sort of normalcy.

When I emerge, the salesperson is hovering nearby. "How'd you do?"

It takes me a beat before I figure out what she's talking about. Realizing I'm still clutching the items I grabbed before hiding in the dressing room, I hand them over to her. "I'm sorry, they're not going to work for me."

"Maybe next time," she says, taking the wrinkled shirts from me.

"I sure hope so," I say before brushing past her. I pause in the doorway of the shop, looking up and down the street to make sure Hardy isn't lying in wait for me, and then I beat it back to Gertie.

It's only when I'm wrapped in her comforting scent that I'm able to take a full breath.

Guess that therapist wasn't so crazy after all.

FORD

Poor Violet is in labor for two whole days, which Nate reports is not unusual for a first pregnancy. Still, I think we're all relieved when the baby finally arrives, and the doctor pronounces both mother and child healthy.

Whit and I plan to make a brief hospital visit the next day, but Nate calls to tell us they're actually going home. "Vi just wants to get out of here. We can't get any sleep with all the poking and prodding."

We decide to wait until the following day to visit, since Vi's grandmother has moved in to help out. When we show up, we're not the only ones. The whole gang is here. After we take turns peering at Kennedy Davenport Fowler—a pretty big name for such a small human being if you ask me, but of course no one does—Violet tells us Nate needs some exercise. Translation: she needs space.

The guys and Dani head out to play basketball in the driveway while Helen and Whit help Vi's grandma organize all the gifts and food we brought.

After a rousing three-on-three game, we head for the sunroom, where Nate fills us in on the delivery and how it's going with being a parent so far.

"Sounds like y'all are doing great," Dani says.

Their baby is pretty darn cute, but I can't even imagine being responsible for such a tiny, vulnerable thing. Hell, I can't even talk a grown woman into letting me keep her safe.

Luke asks me a sound equipment question, which has me off and running. I'm happy for distraction from the talk of domestic bliss, but there's also nothing I love more than geeking out about the latest innovations in recording technology.

But just as I'm getting into some really cool stuff, Sully interrupts me.

"Do you ever relax, Ford?"

Thrown by the non sequitur, I take a sip of beer before answering. "Uh, yeah. When I'm sleeping."

He just frowns, which has me adding, "I need to keep moving. That's why I prefer running over being out on the water like you."

Both Sully and Nate are surfers. I'm a little jealous of how much time they spend together, but I never could get into the lifestyle.

"But what's all the effort for?" Sully asks.

"Well, you get in shape, for one. Healthy heart and all that. But running helps me think more clearly."

"I'm with you on that," Luke says. "If I'm stuck on a problem with a script, a run usually helps me sort things out."

"Honestly, I don't know how y'all can just sit out there on the water for so long, waiting for the perfect wave," I continue. "And then half the time, it seems like another guy gets it, anyway."

"Maybe he got the perfect wave for him, but yours is coming."

Sully has definitely gotten more Zen in the past year, so I'm not sure if we're talking about preferred exercise routines, work, or life. He's always been less ambitious, less of a go-getter, though. "I just feel like you get to it sooner if you're not sitting around waiting."

"The wait is part of it," Sully says. "Just like in life."

"But if you just wait around for shit to happen to you, you miss out," I argue.

Part of me envies Sully. He doesn't seem to have anything to prove, but part of me can't even imagine what that would be like.

"I think it's the opposite. I think if you're never still, that's when you miss out."

"On the best wave?"

He tips his head to the side, studying me in a way that has me feeling uncomfortably exposed. "No, man. On what happens while you wait. Like appreciating the heat of the sun on your face and the cool of the water on your arms and legs. The lap of the water beneath you and the birds calling overhead. The movement of the water and the air."

I shake my head slowly. "I think I'm too impatient for all that."

"Maybe," he says, but his tone says the opposite. "Or maybe you're running away from something you need to pay attention to."

Before I can ask him what he means by that, the door leading to the main part of the house opens and Helen says, "Nate, Vi's asking if you can head out to pick up the smaller size diapers."

"Like right now?" he asks.

Helen winces. "Her tone had a desperate edge to it."

"Copy that," Nate says with a salute, before turning to us. "Vi wants everything to be perfect, but the woman could take a page from Sully's book." His face gets all dreamy as he continues. "I can just sit with that baby. Marvel at her little toes and fingernails. The way she takes in the world like it's all new. Which I guess it is."

Nate grabs his car keys, and Luke says, "We should probably head out too."

"Give them some space," Dani adds.

As we all head inside to say goodbye, Sully stops me with a quick squeeze on the shoulder. "I know you and me are made differently."

He seems like he has more to say, so I prod, "But?"

One side of his mouth lifts. "I just don't want you to get twenty years down the road and wonder what it was all for."

THIRTY-ONE

Subj: Food delivery schedule
Date: 12/19/1999 5:05:20 PM
From: DanielleGoodwin856
To: makeupchick1200, SullyCallaway999,
Ford_soundguy

This is something Violet would do so I'll probably screw it up, but I think we should make a schedule and bring them dinner for the next few nights. Luke and I will take tomorrow.

Sully - can you and Helen take Tuesday?

Then, I guess, Ford and Whitney can you put something together for Thursday? You can do takeout if that's easier.

FORD

LATER THAT NIGHT, when I'm cuddling with Whit after we've made love, Sully's words just won't leave me be. Thing is, I'm not sure if he was trying to tell me to go for it with Whitney because I need more than work in my life or to be patient and wait for her to come around.

I know now that I fucked up in the past by asking for too much too soon, but I was also reacting to the threat of losing her. Now, I want her to know that she won't lose me, because I'll wait as long as it takes. "Can we talk about the future?"

She stiffens in my embrace, so I add, "I want you to know that if it were up to me, I'd want to spend every night like this."

She doesn't reply, so I just keep going. "But I'm not asking you to change your plans. I get that the Nashville job is the best option you've got."

"Then what *are* you saying?"

"That I'll miss you, I guess. I'll miss this. Sleeping next to you. Seeing your face every morning." My heart accelerates, but I press on. "These past few weeks have been like a dream come true for me."

She sits up and shifts to face me. "What if you get lonely while I'm gone?"

I tuck a curl behind her ear so I can see her entire face. "I'd rather be alone than be with a person I don't care about."

She frowns. "From what I've heard, that's not how you've been in the past."

"True. I have had my share of flings. But they're like junk food. When I was younger, I could eat it all the time. Now, even if it tastes good, my body is not happy with me afterwards."

She raises a brow. "So, you're looking for a healthier diet?"

"I don't know about that." I trail a finger along her thigh. "Time with you is not like eating my vegetables. It's more like savoring a meal made with the finest ingredients."

She smiles, but it doesn't reach her eyes. "I'm not sure I can live up to that expectation."

"I'm not asking you to do anything or be any certain

way, Whit. I just want you to know where I'm at. And I guess I hope you'll give us a chance. Whether we're physically together all the time or not. I want to spend as much time as I can with you wherever and however that can happen."

I take a deep breath. "And I'd like to spend the rest of my life doing that."

She squeezes her eyes shut. "You're ready to commit to a woman who's attached to someone else for another nine months? Who can't create a family with you? You looked pretty smitten with little Kennedy today."

"Who wouldn't be?" I trail the back of a finger down her cheek and her eyes flutter open. "But there are all kinds of ways to make a family. We could adopt. We could be honorary aunt and uncle. We could do more toy drives and other stuff that supports kids in need."

She sits up, shifting away from me. "You say that now but—"

I sit up too, eager to put this topic where it belongs. On the shelf. "Having kids has never been high on my list of priorities. I can't see giving up on my career to stay in town to raise kids, and I definitely wouldn't want to have kids and then be leaving them all the time."

"It's not the life most people have," she argues.

"We're not most people. We love our careers and to pursue them, we have to go where the wind takes us."

"And if that wind blows us apart?"

"It's going to happen. But there's always the little man."

"What little man?"

Like the old Yellow Pages commercial, I let my fingers cross the distance that has opened up between us, until my hand lands on her knee to do a little dance. "You know. The little guy in the computer, the one who delivers the email. Who will bring you all my love notes."

Snorting, she captures my hand just as I'm about to tickle

her. "Would you send me a real love note every once in a while?"

"Hmm," I say. "With flower petals inside and everything?"

She sighs. "I've always wanted one of those."

Pulling her hand to my lips, I give them a solemn kiss. "Then love letters with petals you shall have, my lady."

WHITNEY'S MOOD CONTINUES TO ROLLERCOASTER OVER THE DAYS leading up to Christmas. She spends a lot of time visiting Violet, walking Skye with Dani, and just hanging out with me at the beach house. She begs off of going to Christmas dinner with my family, assuring me she really wants the time to herself.

Christmas morning, though, we indulge in cinnamon rolls from the can that pops when you open it—as homemade as either of us gets—before opening presents. I totally forgot about stockings, but Whit must've found some in the house somewhere, and either she or Santa filled them with tangerines and chocolate in the middle of the night.

When we sit in front of our scraggly little tree, Whitney says, "We didn't exactly talk about this. I couldn't spend a lot of money, so—"

I take her hand, cutting her off. "Hey, that's not what it's about. Not for me, anyway."

"Well, that's good," she says, relief coloring her voice. "Um, so, here are yours."

She pushes two boxes toward me, one large and one tiny. I reach behind me and hand her pretty much the same thing, making her laugh. "Great minds think alike."

"Hopefully not too alike."

"Big one first?" she asks.

"Same time?" I ask.

Nodding together, we lift the lids off of the larger boxes. When I see what's inside, I really do laugh. "Oh, my god. Did you… ?"

"Buy one of the sweaters that teamster was knitting?" Her grin is huge. "Guilty as charged."

We hold up the matching sweaters. Hers is a lot smaller, of course, but the design is exactly the same. Chunky, dark gray crew necks.

"We'll be twins," she says with a cackle.

"They are perfect for work," I say. "With the dark color, and they seemed like they'd be warm."

"Perfect for nights," she agrees.

She looks at me sideways. "Now I'm wondering about the small box."

I shake my head. "I don't think they can be the same."

With a nod, we open the next gift in unison. Her gasp tells me she's at least surprised, but when I see what's tucked inside the tissue paper in my box, I can barely breathe.

"This is beautiful, Ford." She holds the necklace up and the morning light glints on the tiny bottle.

Swallowing past the swell of emotion, I tell her about the artist and the sand inside before helping her put it on. She presses a hand over it, so that it touches her breastbone, and then leans over to kiss me. "It's perfect."

I haven't taken my gift from the box, and she asks, "Do you like it?"

"I have been missing the old one," I say, removing the friendship bracelet, an exact replica of the one she made me years ago, the one I'd given to her that night in the hospital, the one she's been wearing ever since.

When I slide it over my wrist, my thumb finds the cowrie shell and I realize that I really have missed having it there. That I'd used it as a sort of worry bead.

Arms out, I invite her to crawl into my lap, and then I hold her for a long time, hoping that this is enough for her, that I'm enough for her, because what we have here is plenty for me.

```
Subj: New Year's Eve
Date: 12/29/1999 9:21:40 AM
From: VioletCastingCarolina
To: makeupchick1200, Ford_soundguy, Sully-
Callaway999, DanielleGoodwin856
```

If y'all don't have plans for New Year's Eve--heck, even if you do--we really, really want you to come here and celebrate with us. I'll do my best to stay up till midnight! I just can't imagine NOT spending the changeover from one millennium to another with anyone else.

WHITNEY

THE HOLIDAYS PASS in a whirl of walks on the beach, visits to the new baby, and slow lovemaking. I could get used to spending every break between jobs this way. I just wish I could believe in Ford's idea of a future the two of us could share.

Every time I try to imagine it, something gets in the way.

After the emergency appointment my lawyer arranged with the therapist, I've had a couple more sessions. The brush with Hardy motivated me to make them, but each time I emerge more confused, and less confident of myself instead of more.

Worse, I can't quite let go of the feeling that I'm going to get in trouble with my parents. Just the fact that Ford knows I'm seeing a therapist, even though he doesn't ask what we talk about, feels dangerous.

On top of that, I worry that I'm ruining his holiday with my moodiness. I feel bad for not appreciating this window of time with him. But every time he's sweet and attentive, all I can think is that I don't deserve it. That I'm using him.

The dumbest thing of all is that I hate going to therapy. It's like the worst-tasting medicine, or more accurately, like cod liver oil. Not only is it nasty going in but you know it'll make things worse on the other side. Until, supposedly, you're all better.

Every time I settle on the couch in Laura's office, I politely thank her for fitting me in, even though I'd rather be anywhere else.

She's saying something about it working out because so many of her regular clients are on vacation, so I just nod and smile.

"Whitney?"

"Yes, ma'am?"

Her lips press together. She has a northern accent of some kind, so she doesn't want me to call her ma'am, even though she's older than my mother. "I said, I'm wondering if you've thought about what we talked about last time. If you're having residual feelings of loss, even grief, from the miscarriage and hysterectomy."

"If I didn't want to be pregnant in the first place, why would I be sad about losing the baby?" I mean, I have had those feelings, but they're stupid. I didn't want that baby so

I'm glad I lost it. But saying that out loud feels kind of monstrous.

"Hormones are powerful agents. You may have contradictory feelings about the loss, like grieving the loss even though you didn't plan the pregnancy. Either way, it can be useful to work through them."

"Could hormones make me get pregnant even if I didn't want to? Like my biological clock ticking so damn loud it overrides the birth control pill?"

She smiles, like I'm joking. "That would be a pretty powerful clock. From what I understand, getting pregnant while you're on the pill usually happens because you skip several pills. Is that possible for you?"

"Taking the pill was the only thing in my life that I never forgot. Since I was sixteen years old."

An unwelcome memory, as all those involving Hardy are, flashes in my mind.

I swear, girl, you'd forget your head if it wasn't attached, he says, his smile almost tender. *I watched you take it just a few minutes ago. Before you went to the bathroom.*

How many times did that happen?

My hand goes to my mouth but not in time to stifle my gasp of horror.

"Whitney? What's going on? Can you tell me?"

Laura's voice is filled with kindness. She's promised she won't—can't—tell anyone anything we talk about here. But it's so scary. What if my parents find out that I'm here?

The couch sinks next to me, and Laura takes my hand. "It's okay. You don't have to talk about it. We can just sit here."

"In the months before I got pregnant," I begin, even as I suspect she's using reverse psychology on me to get me to talk. "I'd go to take the pill some mornings, and it would be gone."

"The packet would be gone?"

"No, like, that day's pill. I had no memory of taking it, but my husband always had a story about how he'd watched me take it just a half hour or a few minutes earlier." I seek Laura's gaze, needing something from her. Something I can't name, but whatever it is, I find it in her eyes. "How stupid am I that I believed him?"

She takes both my hands in hers, and her expression shifts to pure steel. "Convincing a partner that a lie is the truth is called gaslighting, and it's a highlight of psychological abuse. You could be a card-carrying Mensa member and still fall prey to it. What makes it possible is a combination of strong motivation on his end and an emotional vacuum that makes you vulnerable on yours."

She hands me a tissue, and I fumble to wipe away tears I hadn't noticed were there.

"This is not your fault, Whitney. But we may have more work to do to get you to a place where you'll believe me."

AFTER A LIFETIME OF TRAINING, I'M PRETTY GOOD AT KEEPING UP a sunny front, but it's getting harder and harder. Or maybe it's that I don't want to anymore.

Christmas was one thing. Everyone but me had family to spend it with. Ford tried to get me to join him at his parents' house for the holiday, but I didn't think I could handle it. I told him I wanted to spend it alone, which was true. Despite protesting that I'd be fine, he didn't stay away long. I didn't exactly complain when he returned either, indulging in the sensual pleasure of being skin to skin with Ford in the little bubble we've created at the beach.

I can't say no to a New Year's Eve celebration with our friends, however. It's a pretty momentous one, this turning over to a new century, and really, I can't imagine spending it with anyone else.

We gather at Violet and Nate's house, so they don't have to leave the baby. Vi even takes a nap so she can stay up till midnight. Luke and Sully—our best chefs—split the dinner responsibilities. We devour a huge meal of local oysters, shrimp and grits, and a gorgeous salad, with a giant chocolate cake for dessert. Even though Vi sticks with sparkling cider while the rest of us drink champagne, she gets as loopy as the rest of us as the evening goes on. Probably from lack of sleep.

By ten o'clock, I'm laughing so hard my belly hurts. After playing Fishbowl—which Luke insists is called Celebrities— we tell embarrassing stories from our childhood.

Vi reminds us about Dani's terrible haircut in tenth grade. "You mean the one that made me look like that guy from *Family Ties*?" Dani asks.

"Is that why everybody wrote 'MJ Fox' under your yearbook picture?" Sully asks.

"Remember when Sully farted doing the pull-up test in gym class?"

Sully groans. "Even the teacher was laughing."

"I swear it echoed through the entire gymnasium," Dani says. "I was clear down the other end and heard it."

Ford bumps fists with Sully. "Legendary, man."

"Oh, I've got one," Ford says. "Remember that time Vi had a crush on that dude and wrote him a love letter?"

Vi groans. "The one I stuck a lock of hair in because I'd read it in a book?"

"What's wrong with that?" Nate asks. "It sounds romantic, babe."

"Apparently not to the guy," Ford says. "He finds it in his locker, opens it right there and then goes, super loud, 'Eww! There's hair in here!'"

"Oh no, I remember that." I cover my mouth, trying hard not to laugh at my poor friend. "You'd cut the hair from the front, so everyone knew it was you."

Luke turns to me. "Didn't Ford do anything embarrassing?"

He asks the question like Ford and I are a unit. Just like the other three couples sprawled around the living room. And for a moment, I wish I could go back in time and change everything.

"You mean besides asking Whitney to go out with me?" Ford asks.

"I thought we were talking about high school," Dani says.

"I am talking about high school," he says, eyes on me. "Well, junior high."

"I invited her to the ninth-grade dance." Ford's face gives nothing away, but mine is suddenly on fire as he continues to describe an incident I'd completely forgotten until this moment. "She was with a bunch of the popular girls and told me she wasn't allowed to date. But when I walked away, one of the other girls said, really loudly, 'You mean you're not allowed to date losers like him,' and they all laughed."

The room is quiet as a church as I whisper, "I'm sorry, Ford. I should've stood up to them. But I didn't know how."

"It's okay," he says, his tone sounding not at all okay. "I should've known better than to ask."

The baby's wail over the monitor breaks the tension in the air. Nate and Violet exit to check on Kennedy and the other four jump up to clear dessert dishes and refill champagne glasses.

"I really am sorry, Ford," I whisper.

"Make it up to me now?" he asks.

"What do you mean?"

"Say yes, this time. In front of everyone."

FORD

For a long moment, I'm afraid I've done it yet again. Asked the wrong way at the wrong time. But then Whitney takes my hand and pulls me to sit on the couch next to her. She continues to hold it even after everyone returns to the room, Nate with a bundle of baby over his shoulder, and the rest with full glasses of beer and champagne.

One after another, I watch my friends notice the seating change and our joined hands, but no one says anything about it. In fact, no one says a word. The room is quiet except for the cooing of the baby.

Until Whitney clears her throat. "I have an announcement to make."

Brows raise and spines stiffen, but no one speaks.

"Ford and I have been together for about a month. We've kept it a secret since I'm still legally married"—she catches my eye and I do my best to send her the biggest smile I can muster—"but I want you all to know. I'm not sure I deserve him, but he seems to be willing to put up with me."

For another long moment, it feels like everyone is holding their breath.

"That's it," Whitney says, before giving me a sweet kiss on the mouth.

Then everyone's talking at once, each one saying something along the line of "Oh my god!" and "Finally!" and "About time!" and "I knew it!"

It's exactly what I thought I wanted, but as Whitney literally shrinks next to me, I'm not sure it's what we need. Still, I vow to show her how much this means to me the minute we get back to our shared bed.

THIRTY-THREE

```
Saturday, 1/1/2000 7:29 AM
VioletCastingCarolina: Finally!
I'm so happy for you and Whit,
Ford.

DanielleGoodwin856: Me too. I
think you two will make the
long-distance thing work.

SullyCallaway999: Good way to
start the millennium, for sure.
```

WHITNEY

WHEN FORD FORCED my hand last night, I felt like I'd stripped down to my skivvies in the middle of the mall. But our friends surprised me. They didn't seem concerned that we won't likely see each other much for the next few months. Less concerned than I am, anyway.

No one questioned our sanity or impulsiveness or whether we're really right for each other. In fact, after the initial excitement, they treated us like we'd always been a couple. And when we got back to the beach house, Ford showed me exactly how much he appreciated my confession. Multiple times.

Still, on this first morning of the year two thousand, I will not take my good luck for granted. Black-eyed peas and collard greens aren't my favorites, but this is not the year to mess with Lady Luck, so I get some Hoppin' John started right away.

I'm not much of a cook, but this recipe's pretty simple. Once the fatback and onions have cooked down and I've added the stock and beans and spices, I remember the whole Y2K scare, so I put the pot on simmer and go to see if the computer still works. When it does, I decide to see if the world wide web is operational too. Worrying that the obnoxiously loud sounds will wake Ford, I take my laptop to an upstairs bedroom to check email.

AOL opens right up like usual, but something is different. The screen doesn't look like mine usually does. Thinking that maybe the internet did break, I click on the top buddy message. When it loads, I let out a sigh, recognizing Violet's username. But as I read through the chat, that relief evaporates.

Somehow, there's a buddy chat between my closest friends that doesn't include me. Dread is heavy in my belly as I read, but it quickly morphs into something else entirely.

Shame. Fear. Outrage.

"What are you doing?"

Ford's voice scares the living daylights out of me, but the minute my heart returns to my body, I whirl on him.

"What the hell is this?" I ask, pointing to the computer. "Y'all have been talking about me behind my back? For months? What the fuck, Ford?"

He leans over my shoulder to see what I've been reading. "Why are you looking at my computer?"

"Your computer?" My attention whips back to the laptop. Closing it, I sweep my hand over the right edge. The nick isn't there. From a month ago, when I dropped a curling iron on it. "I-I thought it was mine."

Before he can tell me I shouldn't have been snooping, I shove the chair back and turn to face him again. "It doesn't matter whose computer it is. Those messages are still wrong."

"Whitney, they weren't meant for you to—"

"They are all about me, though. The four of you gossiping about me like a bunch of old ladies. I can't believe I just told everyone we were together."

Pushing past him, my pulse racing, I rush down the hall to the bedroom. Grabbing my suitcase, I tear my clothes off of hangers and shove them inside.

"Whitney, wait. What are you—are you leaving? Can't we talk about this?"

"What, so you can report back to the others? Tell them how you've handled crazy Whitney? Poor little rich girl Whitney? The girl whose parents sold her to the highest bidder?"

I'm not sure if it's rage or mortification that has me seeing red, but it doesn't matter.

"That's not what we—I mean, I'm sorry if it seems like that, but—"

I hold up a hand to stop his words. "I can't trust a thing coming out of your mouth right now. I don't know if I'll ever be able to believe a word you say again."

I turn, open the dresser drawer I've been using, and sweep everything inside into my suitcase before zipping it closed. My brain has flipped to static to keep Ford's words at bay. The same way I always did with Momma and Hardy. I shoulder past him to the bathroom and shove all my products into my other bag.

I continue to tune him out as I call a taxi. The only time I let myself look at him again is the moment before I walk out the door.

"Don't try to contact me. I don't want to talk to you. Maybe never again."

Sunday, 1/8/2000 10:34 AM
VioletCastingCarolina: I'm starting a new buddy list and this time I'm including Whitney, like I should have from the start. Whit, please don't put all of this on Ford. We pushed him into keeping tabs on you. If you're going to be mad at anyone, it should be me. I could blame it on hormones, but I think it's just me. In my head, I thought we were doing the best we could by you. From everything I heard, it was pretty fucking scary at the hospital, Whit. I'm so glad we didn't lose you then and I'm so, so sorry if, in trying to protect you, we've lost you now.

DanielleGoodwin856: We all piled on, Vi. It wasn't just you. We were all frightened by what happened at the wedding and at the hospital afterwards. At first, I couldn't figure out why you wouldn't want us to call Hardy or your parents. But when we saw how they behaved when they showed up, it made more sense.

SullyCallaway999: I don't know if you were aware Whit, but we saw and heard Hardy screaming at the doctors and nurses. You were dying, and all he could say was, they didn't have his permission to take your womb.

VioletCastingCarolina: We were confused and scared. Didn't want you all by yourself on a job and hurting. And probably way too nosy.

SullyCallaway999: If you can forgive us, Whitney, we're here for you. We love you. And I truly hope you'll give Ford another chance.

Ford_soundguy: I could've said no. I could've told you we were worried about you and left it at that. I'm so sorry that I didn't put a stop to it. But we're all really worried about you. Can you just let us know you're safe?

Makeupchick1200: I need some
time before I'm ready to talk.
I'm staying with a friend from
the movie this fall until I go
to Nashville, so please don't
worry about me.

February 9, 2000

Dear Whitney,

Like I said in the new buddy chat, I take full responsibility for keeping the old one from you. I hope you can forgive us, someday.

I miss you. I know you'll be starting your new job soon, that we'd likely be saying goodbye, or would have already said goodbye, but I hate not knowing when I'll see you again. If I'll see you again.

You have a hold of my heart, Whitney Moore. I wish I'd done things differently, but I don't regret a minute we spent together over the past couple of months. I only wish we'd had more.

I promised to write you love letters, flower petals and all, so I'm going to do that unless you tell me to stop.

I love you,
Ford

Saturday 4/1/2000 9:18 AM

Ford_soundguy: Maybe it's wrong to do this here, and this sure as hell isn't an April Fool's joke, but I feel like I need to say this in front of everybody. Whitney, I don't know how you can ever forgive me, but if you can, and if you ever want to try again, I'll be waiting. You are it for me. I will do my very best to protect you going forward.

Makeupchick1200: I don't need protecting. I need to stand on my own two feet.

Ford_soundguy: I get it. I just feel horrible.

VioletCastingCarolina: If anyone has ever been lovesick, it's Ford.

SullyCallaway999: It's actually getting kind of annoying.

DanielleGoodwin856: Plus we miss you too, Whit. Can you come home so we can talk this out in person?

Makeupchick1200: I'm not ready.

Subj: The Truth
Date: 5/15/2000 8:05:12 AM
From: makeupchick1200
To: Ford_soundguy, VioletCastingCarolina, SullyCallaway999, DanielleGoodwin856

Hello friends,

My therapist says I need to trust you, my
only real friends, with the truth. It is
not easy. Just the thought of sharing the
reality of my childhood and marriage fills
me with shame and fear. I'm learning that
my parents created these reactions to keep
me in their gilded cage, that I have
nothing to be embarrassed about, but the
emotions feel real just the same.

I never thought of myself as a badass. I
never thought I was strong like Dani and
Violet.

But I am not fragile. I am not a doll. I am
not an object of your pity.

I know I need to earn your respect. But you
have to give me the chance to. Like I need
a do-over. A fresh start. A clean slate.

I know that half the time growing up, I
acted like I didn't have two brain cells to
rub together. I know I was a flirt and
flighty and did a lot of stupid shit. I'm
starting to understand why I behaved the
way I did, and I do want to take responsibility for my actions, but I also need you
to accept that the girl that you thought
you knew all those years wasn't the
real me.

That was a girl shaped by parents that wanted her to be a certain way so badly, they lied to her. They made her believe she was the crazy one, that she imagined being yelled at and belittled. That she was only lovable if she did exactly as they demanded. All this groomed her to accept a husband who did the same.

Y'all are the only reason the real Whit exists at all. The only reason I could get myself out. To even understand that the way they treated me wasn't okay. I was so lost for so long, believing my parents, even though I had evidence right in front of me that I wasn't stupid and worthless. That other people don't treat their children like possessions.

I was afraid to break from them completely because I didn't think I could survive on my own. I didn't think I had the strength to live the way y'all do. But I can. And I'm not going back.

I may make mistakes. I will make mistakes. There are deeply ingrained habits in this skull. And y'all should call me out when I do. I just ask that you check your assumptions.

I hope I'll be strong enough to come back to Wallington. I want to be strong enough, but I'm not sure when it'll be. In the meantime, I miss you all.

Love,
Whitney

June 6, 2000

Dear Whitney,

I still avoid karaoke, but I've been spending a lot of time on my guitar. Last weekend, I set up a little recording booth in my hotel room (it was almost like the fort I made, because I used blankets and bed covers to muffle the sound) and I recorded these songs onto my computer and burned them onto the enclosed CD:

"You've Got a Friend" - James Taylor
"Till I Hear it From You" - Gin Blossoms
"Only Wanna Be With You" - Hootie & the Blowfish
"I Will Remember You" - Sarah McLachlan
"There She Goes" - Sixpence None the Richer
"I'll Stand by You" - The Pretenders

I wouldn't have had the gonads to do this without your encouragement (and I hope they're not too awful!)

Love,
Ford

July 1st, 2000

Dear Mother and Father,

Enclosed please find a check for $40,064, as repayment for you covering my credit card debt, plus two years of interest at 8%.

Although I'm sure you'd consider your monetary investment in creating Whitney Moore to be far greater, I now consider my debt to you both cleared. Paid in full. Never to be revisited.

Perhaps someday, if you care to, we can find our way to a healthy relationship. For the time being, know that I am working my way toward financial and emotional independence. To do that, I need to be free of my ties to you.

Your daughter in name only,
Whitney

July 18, 2000

Dear Ford,

I'm writing because I need you to understand something. Even though I know in my head that I shouldn't be ashamed of this, even though I'm not going to be punished for sharing it with you, my whole body thinks otherwise.

In fact, my handwriting might get messy because I'm literally shaking.

I always wanted to choose you, Ford.

I pushed you away to protect you.

Early on, I don't think it was a conscious choice, but I hid my love for all of my real friends from my parents. They said they didn't approve of you (or Sully or Violet or Dani), but I believe they actually saw you as a threat to the status quo. The unconditional love I got from y'all undermined the way my parents used conditional love to keep me in line.

There's more.

That night after college graduation, when I let Sully kiss me? I did it because I knew he didn't really love me, and I didn't love him like that.

But you? If I'd said yes to _you_, I wouldn't have been able to stop at just a kiss. If my parents found out how I felt about you, they would've squashed you like a bug, and I couldn't let them hurt you like that.

Of course, I didn't really understand all that, so by the time Beverly blew through, I'd convinced myself that I was the problem. I'd fucked up with money, true, but I also felt like a ticking time bomb. If I ran away to LA with you, I would've blown any love you thought you had for me to pieces. When I said I couldn't choose that night, I meant that I *couldn't choose <u>you</u>. Because I thought you'd be collateral damage.*

I'm so sorry that I hurt you so many times, but I want—need—you to know that I did it because I love you.

Yours,
Whit

WHITNEY

BEFORE THIS YEAR, I'd never been away from Wallington for more than a few months. Leaving with no plan to return seemed like my only option back in January.

But now, I find I want to go back.

And not just to sign my divorce papers.

I've been on quite the emotional trip the first nine months of this century. A journey I wished I'd taken back in the nineteen hundreds, rather than waste my twenties trying to please parents who would never be satisfied, to fit into a mold everyone else laid out for me.

Thank goodness for therapy, is all I can say.

And for divorce lawyers. I didn't want any money from my ex, but when Rebecca pushed for it, I was glad to have the funds to pay my parents back, so I'd never feel beholden to them again.

The first time my lawyer used the words emotional abuse, they sounded like something out of an *ABC After School Special*. But as I've unraveled my childhood, self-image, and habits of thought through bi-weekly therapy appointments, it's become clear that I was raised by a pair of abusers. My mother was the primary culprit, but my father was the enabler.

And I was the victim they handed off to another just like them.

Every time I use that word, I have to remind myself that it's nothing to be ashamed of. It's not easy, but I need to face the truth of my childhood so I can grow beyond it. I still have a long way to go. I still make impulsive choices that are not the healthiest.

Like leaving the one man who loved me and the friends who, unknowingly, kept me at least halfway sane over the years.

It may have been rash, but I do think I needed to leave. To start over from scratch. To live and work, even for just a few months, in a new place. With people who do not know the old me.

Without others' expectations shaping me, I can be a whole new person.

Not vapid.

Not stupid.

Not broken.

Anyway, if I hadn't left, I wouldn't be able to come back.

I just hope it's not too late.

THIRTY-FIVE

> To: My Best Friends
> From: Whitney
> What: A Celebration of My Divorce
> Where: Wrightsboro Beach at the L-Shaped Lot entrance
> When: Monday, September 25, 2000 at 4:00 p.m.
> Join me for light snacks and beverages as I celebrate my freedom and independence. Bring a chair or blanket but I'll cover the rest.

WHITNEY

VIOLET WILL NEVER BELIEVE that I'm here early. I've changed all sorts of habits over the past nine months, but getting places on time is one I'm especially proud of. Maybe it's because people notice, or that it feels especially mature. It was also one of the first things we focused on in therapy. Laura probably thought it'd be easier to work on something mundane.

Of course, she didn't know how stubborn I could be.

Now that I'm changing the habit, it's clear that she was right. Arriving when I say I'm going to shows respect for others' time, and even more important, for mine.

I couldn't have asked for a better divorce attorney than Rebecca Edelman. She's patiently held my hand every step of this journey, even as I've witnessed the results of her bulldog approach with Hardy and his lawyer.

She's so good at her job, he thinks *he's* won. I didn't want to be tied to him in any way, so instead of alimony, she got him to give me an up-front payment of fifty-thousand dollars, which was enough to pay my parents' back and create a rainy-day fund for myself. That was a suggestion from Cyn, who has seen her share of bust and boom in this fickle industry.

One year and a day after Hardy and I separated, I am allowed to file for divorce, and I am not waiting a second longer than I have to. Rebecca tends to be early too, so we're first in line when the county clerk's office opens, and before I know it, the papers are filed, and we've arranged to have Hardy served by the Sheriff. All I can do now is wait until he signs them.

"That was rather anticlimactic."

Rebecca gives me a hug. "Believe me. I'd rather have that than the climactic version. No need to fight any more than you have to."

And then she's off to wage another battle, and I'm left in the courthouse parking lot, with an entire open day ahead of me.

I'm better about listening to myself these days, so I decide to take the time to revisit my old haunts. After all, if I can't walk around town without worrying about running into people from the life I left behind, I'll never be able to have a relationship with Ford. If he's still interested, I need to be sure I can spend the time between jobs in Wallington worry-free.

The coffee at my hotel is terrible, so I start with my favorite coffee shop. While placing my order at Deluxe, I notice two women from my parents' and Hardy's social circle sitting at a table. My first instinct is to hide, but I remind myself that I have nothing to be ashamed of, so I take my latte and muffin and sit just one table over from Carolyn Wright and Jeannette Hall.

They don't seem to recognize me, so I scan the newspaper the table's previous occupant left behind. I've just begun an article about the differences between presidential candidates Bush and Gore's views on Medicare when my neighbors' conversation grabs my attention.

"Oooh! Guess who I saw at the club yesterday?" Carolyn was the Queen Bee in high school and is still hanging on to her crown with perfectly manicured claws. Naturally, she doesn't wait for her second-in-command to answer. "Hardy McRae. On a date."

"With who?" Jeannette asks, her voice breathy with what sounds like manufactured excitement.

Hard to believe they can't hear the pounding of my heart, but they continue on as if I'm beneath their notice.

"Rachel Lewis." She delivers the name with bated breath, as well she should. Rachel's much older husband died just over a year ago. Leaving her a wealthy widow.

"Well, good for them," Jeannette says after a beat. "They deserve to be happy."

"I can't believe he married Whitney Moore in the first place. She was always loose, hanging around with that arty crowd."

"I heard Rachel's hardly left her house since her husband died. She deserves a little fun."

These two are mean enough to go on like this whether they know I'm sitting right next to them or not. If my divorce was final, I'd tell them exactly what Hardy did to me, but my lawyer warned me against mouthing off about my marriage before he signs the papers. It'd be just like him to contest the deal just to punish me. But the thought of a girl as sweet as Rachel caught in Hardy's web has me wiping the muffin crumbs from my lips and then clearing my throat.

"Excuse me."

When their two heads swing my way, Jeannette's dropped jaw tells me she had no idea I was here, but the feline delight on Carolyn's face makes it clear the show was all for me.

Thing is, this is no longer about me, so I don't bat an eye as I stare them down, one after the other.

"Hey, Jeannette. Hey, Carolyn. I couldn't help but over-hear your conversation and I just wanted to make a little, oh, I don't know…" I pause, scrambling to articulate this in a way that they'll understand, without naming Hardy. "Public service announcement."

Carolyn rolls her eyes, but Jeannette says, "Uh, okay?"

"I happened to learn recently that domestic abuse doesn't necessarily include physical violence. There's also financial and emotional abuse, both of which can be quite damaging in their own way. I just wanted y'all to know in case a friend, or even an acquaintance, tells you that her husband or boyfriend doesn't want her to hang out with you anymore, or see her own family anymore? That's a classic first step."

Carolyn frowns. "What are you talking about, Whitney?"

I smile sweetly. "Just as an example, say that you invite Rachel Lewis to lunch and she tells you that she's much too busy with her new boyfriend to make time for it, you might want to keep checking in on her. Make sure she isn't being brainwashed to believe things that aren't true. Because some people—no one I'm talking about *specifically* at this moment, mind you—but some people take their control to a point that can be life-threatening."

"That's all." After draining my coffee, I lift my chin and

meet each one's gaze. Jeannette's: concerned. Carolyn's: full of doubt.

"Y'all have a nice day, now."

As I stand, my knees feel like they might give way, so I point myself at the door, and just keep putting one foot in front of the other until I've reached the used Honda I bought this spring. After I crank her engine, I crank up the volume on the CD player.

And then I sing along with Tori Amos until my voice is hoarse.

AFTER A DAY SPENT RECLAIMING WALLINGTON, I'M ALSO EARLY to the little party I've arranged at the beach. Once I've set everything up, I check my watch, a little nervously. It's after four, and I suddenly realize that I didn't give my guests any way to RSVP.

Maybe no one's coming.

Maybe they gave up on me.

But that's just nerves talking, I tell myself. *And that's okay. You know you've made big changes, but you can't expect people who've known you practically your whole life to instantly change how they see you.*

Just as I'm about to crack open a wine cooler, I see a familiar hat bobbing down the walkway toward the beach. I should probably play it cool, but I can't help myself. I sprint up the beach towards Violet and the baby I haven't seen since she was no bigger than a breadbasket.

"Oh my god, Vi! She's huge!" I clap a hand over my mouth and check my friend's expression. "I mean, she's beautiful too. I just can't believe how much she's grown."

"She's also very smart." Vi grins before letting her tongue loll out dramatically. "She weighs a ton, though."

I hold out my hands. "Will she let me…?"

Vi doesn't even have time to answer, because little Kennedy reaches for me. As soon as I settle her on my hip, she slaps my cheeks and laughs. "Hmm, I wonder where you got this cheeky personality, little girl?"

"Wasn't from me," Nate says before nodding towards the blanket and cooler and chair I've laid out. "Is this your setup?"

"Sure is. Come on and take a load off."

"Don't mind if I do."

The man is a damn sherpa, loaded down with chairs and bags and I don't even know what. He drops it all next to my stuff and arranges it under Violet's direction while I make faces at the baby.

Sully and Helen arrive next, followed by Dani and Luke. Just like old times, we set the chairs in a circle. Then I set Kennedy on the blanket in the middle and take drink orders, while people help themselves to snacks.

It really is good to see my friends, but my heart can't help but throb with disappointment that Ford's not here. Still, I can't make myself ask about him.

I mean, I wouldn't blame him for giving up on me. He sent me a letter or an email at least once a week, and I hardly ever wrote him back, even though I've played the CD he sent so many times that I've got every lyric memorized. I sing along, pretending that he's in the car with me.

I just haven't been ready to face him. Nor have I known what to say to him.

Dr. Robinson says that the shame may be the hardest to let go of, and I'm sure she's right. But it doesn't feel like a habit to be ashamed of how quickly I gave up on Ford. It feels real.

I'm trying not to check my watch every five minutes, but by four-thirty, I decide to let go. I'm here to celebrate independence, after all.

After I make sure everyone has a cup or a can to raise, I lift my own for a toast. "Thank you for coming today. I can't tell you how much it means that you're here. I know I haven't been the easiest friend to get along with, but you've always stuck by me. I'm especially happy to have you here as I celebrate the official end of the marriage that never should've been."

"To freedom!" Dani yells.

"To independence!" Sully says.

"To never having to look at that jerk's face again," Violet says solemnly.

Before we can all take a drink, a voice calls across the sand, "To Whitney!"

I turn around so fast liquid sloshes out of the plastic cup in my hand. "You came!"

I don't even think; I drop my drink and sprint for the man walking across the sand with a giant grin on his face. When I get close enough, I launch myself at him.

True to form, he catches me.

I LOVE SEEING MY FRIENDS AGAIN, BUT THEY MUST SENSE THAT Ford and I need to talk. The minute baby Kennedy squawks, they're all making excuses and bustling around. Next thing I know, Ford and I are the only two humans left on the beach.

It was a warm day for late September, but as the sun begins to set, the temperature drops too. I blame that for the chill that runs through me and grab a sweatshirt, even as I muster the strength to face the ugliness of the last time we were together.

We've been near each other for the past hour and a half, but now, I plop down on the blanket and sit facing him. Close, but not too close.

"Ford, I'm sorry I—"

He shakes his head, interrupting me. "No, Whit. I'm the one who needs to apologize."

"But you did, in all those letters."

"I need to do it in person, okay?"

There's so much pain in his eyes, I'd do anything to make it go away. "Okay."

His jaw ticks with tension, and he swallows, like he's got a bad taste in his mouth. "Even if you hadn't been put through hell by your ex, talking about you behind your back was not okay. We had good intentions, but I knew it was wrong from the get go. We were trying to shield you from pain, but we just hurt you more. I'm sorry I did that, and I'm going to do my best to never keep secrets from you again."

I take in a couple of deep breaths before responding, like I've been practicing. And it helps, because instead of pretending it was all fine, I say, "Thank you. It did hurt me, a lot. I understand that y'all were trying to protect me, but I need you to hear this loud and clear. It's not your job."

He winces. "It's going to be hard for me to stop trying to protect you."

"Because you see me as weak and helpless? Because that's what it feels like."

He takes my hand, shaking his head as he runs a thumb over my palm. "Because I love you."

He looks up, and the yearning in his eyes is everything. "I love you too, Ford. And because I do, every time you try to save me, I'm going to remind you that I'm not helpless."

His smile is playful as he flops onto his back, hands over his head. "I think I need a reminder right now."

That's all the invitation I need. After a quick scan of the beach to make sure we're still alone, I crawl on top of him. "I do have one more secret to share."

"What's that?" he asks, running his hands down my spine.

"I've never made love on the beach."

"Huh. Me neither." Brows up, he reaches for the other blanket, and flips it over my back.

I nestle into him, hungry to feel all the hard planes of man under me. "How about we take care of that right here, right now?"

"Don't mind if I do," he whispers, before taking care of *me* in all the best ways.

EPILOGUE

Friday, 11/10/2000 11:34 PM
makeupchick1200: Just got back
from work. Can't wait to see you
tomorrow!

Ford_soundguy: We wrapped an
hour ago and I'll get on the
road as early as I can. Aiming
to get to your hotel by 10 AM.

FORD

"Can I open my eyes now?"

"Not yet." Whitney giggles. "Let me just—hang on, no peeking!"

She leaves me standing on the threshold of her hotel room. I've gotten better about missing her when we're apart. My guys say I'm still grumpy, but less so. But when we only have a weekend together, I don't want to be separated from her for a second of it.

She's back in the mountains this autumn for another movie-of-the-week, while I'm working in Wallington on a new TV show through the spring of next year. We both have a long weekend for Veteran's Day, so I told her I'd make the drive to visit even though she'll be back in Wallington for Thanksgiving in less than two weeks.

When I knocked on her door a few moments ago, she came out into the hall to greet me. I was so eager to feel her in my arms, we kissed until a passerby coughed out a "Get a room." Then Whitney got all weird and made me close my eyes before opening her door.

And now I'm standing here with my eyes closed, waiting to be let inside.

"What are you doing?" I ask when something crashes.

"It's a surprise," she whispers, even though there's no one else here.

At least I don't think there is. Until I hear a strange whimpering sound.

"Are you okay?"

"Yep! Everything's fine. Just. One. More. Second."

Her arms go around my waist, startling me, and my eyes pop open. it takes a moment to adjust to the dim light but… "Did you make me a fort?"

She claps and bobs on her toes. "I did! But there's more. Come on."

Her voice is hushed, and she holds a finger to her lips as she leads me by the hand over to the blanket-draped chairs she's set up. Which is really more of an enclosure than a fort.

And the whimpering is coming from inside.

Stepping closer, I peer over the edge and gasp. "Did you get—"

"A puppy!" she whisper-shouts.

It's the tiniest puppy I've ever seen. Really, just a fluff ball. "How old is it?"

"She's twelve weeks."

Whitney steps into the little play area, and gently picks up a sleepy puppy from a little box inside, cooing, "Hello my sweet girl."

"Where'd she come from?"

"Well, that's a story."

She tells me the tale of how one of the stand-ins had a dog with an accidental litter and couldn't keep the puppies, and how the entire hair and makeup departments adopted them. "I got the runt, because… well, that's me, kind of."

"You're not a—"

"I just mean that I'm the smallest person on the crew. Not in a bad way."

I hold out my hands and she nestles the puppy into my palms.

"She likes to be held close to your heart."

"Like me," I say as I snuggle the tiny fluff ball.

Whitney snorts. "Uh-huh. Exactly like you."

Her face glows as she explains how they're keeping the puppies in the corner of the makeup and hair trailer, and how she's so excited to have a little buddy to take on the road with her. I'm a little jealous, if I'm honest, but it's also good to see her so elated.

"Do you think we could find a rental that allows dogs over the holidays?" she asks, and my heart thumps so loudly the puppy whines.

"Sorry, little girl," I say to the dog before setting her back in the box and turning to Whitney. "About that."

"You don't want to get a rental?" Whit asks. "I thought that was the plan. Kind of like last year."

"Something came up."

"Oh. Well, that's fine. If you have to go out of town or, whatever, I can—"

Taking her hand, I say, "Whit. I'm not going anywhere. I have an opportunity to buy a place and I think I'm going to do it."

A whole parade of emotions crosses her face before she speaks. "Wow. That's great. I'm so… proud of you."

"Thanks. I'm pretty excited about it. Nothing's final till the ink's dry, but I made an offer yesterday and they accepted it. It should be mine before Christmas."

She eases her hand out of mine to stop the dog from chewing on the blanket. "Well, I'm sure I can find a rental that'll work."

I pick up the puppy again. "Whit. Look at me."

She does, eyes blinking fast. "I thought we weren't keeping secrets anymore."

I blow out a breath. "I'm sorry if it feels like that. It happened pretty quick, and I didn't want to say anything until I knew it was for sure, and then I wanted to tell you in person..." I trail off, realizing that I've done it again. Kept her out of the loop.

"Let me start over, okay?" She lets me take her hand, and I meet her gaze. "I was hoping you'd stay with me in this house. Whenever you're in town. As long as you can or want to." I hold up the dog. "And... what's her name?"

Whitney's eyes soften, and she sits back to take in me and the puppy. "I don't know yet. I was hoping you'd help me name her."

I don't know why this makes me so happy, but it does. "Well then, puppy TBD is welcome too."

"In that case, we'd love to stay with you. Me and TBD. As long as you'll have us."

I lean over to whisper in her ear, "That'd be forever."

And then I kiss her. Softly—trying not to squish the dog— but with enough passion to show her exactly how much I want to share that forever with her. Just as I'm getting lost in the taste and feel of her, she breaks the kiss.

Leaning back, I search her face for clues, but before I can ask what's up, she takes TBD and settles her in the little crate and drapes a cloth over it. "Night, night little girl," she coos. "Time for your momma to get some attention."

The minute her fanny hits the bed, I launch myself at her.

True to form, she catches me.

That's a wrap for Whitney and Ford, y'all, but you can get a peek at the future for them and the gang now with a bonus epilogue after you sign up to be a Karen Grey VIP at followkarengrey.com. (If you're already a subscriber, don't worry, you won't be subscribed again.)

As a subscriber, you can also read the prequel novella, *I'll Stand By You* for free.

Need even more of the Carolina Classics crew? In *You Get What You Give*, you'll get Vi and Nate's rivals-to-lovers, one-night-stand love story. *Hold On To Me*, is Sully and Helen's boss-assistant romance. And in *I Want It That Way*, you can read about Dani's fake relationship with ex-child TV star Luke.

If you loved this book, leaving a review is the absolute best way to support an author. You can leave one wherever you downloaded the book, or on Goodreads or Bookbub.

What I'm Looking For: *The course of true love never did run smooth*, but in this smart and sexy retro rom-com with a finance-nerd heroine and a drama-geek hero, returns on love can't be measured on the S&P 500.

Forget About Me: An underwear model, a best friend's little sister, and a dog who steals the show make for an unforgettable mix in this bittersweet romantic comedy.

You Spin Me: If two lonely people fall in love over late-night phone calls, will meeting face-to-face make them, or break them? In this heartfelt, slow-burn retro romcom, it may be the end of a decade, but it's the beginning of a love story.

Child of Mine: A single mom gets a job offer she can't refuse but has to work side-by-side with the one-night stand that doesn't know he's a father. Of her daughter.

You Get What You Give: When a fiery redhead and the guy she thought was a one night stand turn out to be rivals, his family feud causes shockwaves bigger than the surf stirred up by the latest hurricane.

Hold On To Me: In this slow-burn, boss-assistant, entertainment biz romance, a bad cop movie production chief takes on a sexy assistant who challenges her every assumption.

I Want It That Way: She's a driver to the stars who just wants to get her tubes tied. He's a former child actor who needs to get back behind the wheel. A fake relationship seems like the perfect solution.

For Fork's Sake: Grumpy, nerdy soil scientist Sam finds passionate, idealist Diane interviewing his grandma for her YouTube channel. Feathers fly between these farm business rivals!

The Single Dad's Guide to Recreation: He's the new-in-town single dad tasked with cutting costs at Climax Parks & Rec. She's the program director with classes on the chopping block. It should be easier for them to keep their hands off each other.

ACKNOWLEDGMENTS

Thanks to you, dear reader, for taking this trip back in time with me. Especially those of you who have been waiting for Whitney's story. I appreciate you being patient and sticking with me until I found it.

Thank you to all the Karen Grey VIPs who brainstormed 90's songs for the book's title. I love the one we chose!

Thanks to coach Cathy Yardley for steering me away from women's fiction and back into the romance lane, and for invaluable feedback from critique partners Liz Alden, Sara Whitney, and Michelle McCraw. If you like my books, you'll love theirs, so please check out their sexy and hilarious romcoms. Beta readers extraordinaire Anni Reynolds and Elizabeth Taylor: thank you for your insightful comments and questions. Thanks also to copy editor Becky from Bookcase and Coffee for catching as many errors as she could.

All my titles require research. Veteran makeup artist Donna Premick played a starring role this time around, sharing stories from the makeup and hair trailer. Top billing goes to my dear sound mixer hubby for answering all my stupid questions about production sound and for putting his cart in the flow of traffic when I visited the set, so I could see more of what was going on. (Instead of hiding in a corner like he usually does.)

All mistakes are my own.

ABOUT THE AUTHOR

KAREN GREY is a *USA Today* bestselling and award-winning author of vintage romantic comedies with smart heroines and hunky heroes. Drawing on a long career as a performer, her retro 80's and 90's romances are populated with characters working both on- and off-stage in theater, TV and film. When not reading or writing, she's lounging at the beach or hiking in the mountains. Or dreaming about both with an IPA in hand and a dog or a cat nearby.

(Author photo: Celestial Studios)

For the latest news and bonus materials, join her free VIP club at: followkarengrey.com

facebook.com/karengreyauthor

instagram.com/karengreyauthor

goodreads.com/karen_grey

bookbub.com/profile/karen-grey

tiktok.com/@karengreyauthor

www.ingramcontent.com/pod-product-compliance
Lightning Source LLC
Chambersburg PA
CBHW071412300726
48976CB00006B/2077